KISSING ON THE CORNER

THE BACHELOR NEXT DOOR - BOOK FIVE

PAMELA FORD

AINE PRESS

BOOKS BY PAMELA FORD

CONTINENTAL BREAKFAST CLUB SERIES

Over Easy

Fresh Brewed

Honey Glazed

BACHELOR NEXT DOOR SERIES

Love on the Lane

Dancing on the Drive

Breathless on the Boulevard

Romance on the Road

Kissing on the Corner

OUT OF IRELAND SERIES

To Ride a White Horse

A Rush of White Wings

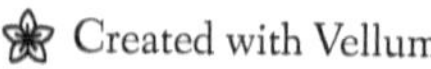 Created with Vellum

To Denise, Vicki, Donna, Mary, Kathy Z., and Laura for great camaraderie, critique, and chocolate. And to Kathy J. who brought us together and set us on the right path.

1

————

Nick hadn't seen Annie since the week after their wedding—six years ago last month.

She'd married him, just as they'd agreed. Had left him a week later, just as they'd agreed. And he'd filed for divorce, just as they'd agreed.

He cleared his throat and tapped his fingers on the steering wheel as he practiced aloud a new version of the speech he had been working on for days now. "Annie, our divorce was never finalized. I left the country and never followed up with the lawyer to make sure everything got done."

She was a practical sort, Annie was. She'd probably offer him a cold lemonade, and they'd have a laugh over how irresponsible he once had been. Then she'd sign the new set of papers he'd brought with him, and he'd kiss her on the cheek when he left. And they'd go back to life the way it had been for the past six years.

Unless, of course, she'd remarried.

He pulled his Range Rover to a stop in front of a big

pale-yellow Victorian house, and lifted his sunglasses to squint at the sign in front.

Unless of course, he'd made her a bigamist.

Bailey House Bed & Breakfast. He drew a breath. This was the place, exactly where the old woman at the gas station on the edge of town said he would find it. Small-town Wisconsin at its finest.

He shoved open the car door and stepped out into the late afternoon summer sun. A crumbled fast-food bag and a toothbrush dropped out onto the pavement. He scooped them up and tossed them onto the passenger seat.

Why was he nervous? Annie would still be Annie. Whether she'd married or not, all she had to do was sign the papers and they'd slip back into their lives—no one the wiser. Well, no one but her *other* husband ... and the judge who would have to remarry them ... and a couple of witnesses—

He buried those thoughts and headed across the walk and up the stairs to the wide front porch, noting the paint just beginning to peel on the old wood. There were layers of old buildup underneath, layers that would make this place a nightmare to scrape and paint. Thank God he wasn't the owner.

He jabbed the doorbell and put a pleasant expression on his face. After a long minute without a response, he pushed the bell again. Maybe he should have called instead.

No, it was bad enough they were still married. It would have been far worse to tell her that over the phone.

Suddenly the door swung inward, and Annie stood before him in cutoffs and a T-shirt. Barefoot. Radiant. Deep blue eyes shining. Tawny blond hair pulled back into a ponytail, a grin on her face as though she were ready to take on the world.

Annie.

He couldn't remember the Annie he knew, the waitress in the all-night coffee shop, looking so gorgeous.

"Hey, Annie," he said.

Her eyes widened. Her grin disappeared.

An older woman's voice floated down the hallway from somewhere behind her. "Tell Vivian I'll be right out."

"Get out of here," Annie said in low voice. "Now."

What? He took a step toward her. "I know this is a surprise, but I need to talk to you."

The older woman spoke again, her voice closer, louder, with each word. "Annie, dear, I'll be back in time to help you flip the mattresses."

Panic stole over Annie's face—panic that was instantly replaced by an expression of fierce determination. In one nearly seamless movement, she launched herself out of the doorway and into his arms and began to kiss him like he was the long-lost love of her life.

She pressed herself against him as if willing him to put his arms around her, and for a brief stunned moment, he pulled her close and returned the kiss. Then his brain kicked into gear and he took her by the arms and pushed back a bit.

"What—" he choked out.

"Good heavens!" the older woman screeched as she came through the doorway and spotted Annie in his arms. "He's here!"

Behind her, a gold poodle mix dog bounded out onto the porch and began to bounce around them, barking incessantly.

Nick tore his gaze from Annie and focused on the diminutive gray-haired old woman; every line in her soft face angled upward from her joyous smile. Almost dancing with excitement, she reached up to tug his head down and kiss his cheek.

And the dog just kept barking as if he'd spotted the bone of his dreams.

"Chester! Quiet! Chester!" Annie shouted.

"I'm Luella!" the old woman cried over the chaos.

"Be quiet!" Annie grabbed hold of the dog's collar and dragged him toward the door.

"So happy to finally meet you. You look just like your picture," Luella said in a voice still loud and high. "I've been the inn's housekeeper for twenty years. I keep your Annie from overworking herself, what with that little bun in the oven."

Bun? His heart seemed to slow. *Pregnant? Husband?*

He shifted his gaze to Annie just as she snatched up the squirming dog and spun around, the desperate expression on her face now a mixture of horror and hope.

Bigamist?

Her eyes locked with his.

"I, ah—" he stammered.

Behind him a car horn blared and he jumped, startled. He turned as the driver slammed on the brakes of her silver Lincoln and skidded to a halt just inches behind his SUV.

"Oh! Vivian's here!" Annie almost screamed in panicked glee. "You don't want to be late for Women's Club." She shoved the dog into the house and pulled the door shut before he could escape.

Luella shook her head. "That old lady. Always has to make a grand entrance."

The blue-haired woman at the wheel laid on the horn once more, and then a third time.

"Oh! She's in fine form today." Luella patted him on the

arm. "I'll just have to find out everything later. Just wait until Vivian hears the news."

She headed down the steps. "I believe this calls for a glass of wine with our supper, don't you think?"

"Have two," Annie called. "Take your time."

Luella glanced back at Nick and grinned. "Oh yes, dear. I see what you mean. We'll make it a long meal." She'd hardly gotten into the car and closed the door before it sped off, leaving the faint smell of burning rubber in its wake.

"Good God," Annie muttered. "This is going to be all over town in half an hour."

"What the hell is going on?"

She sighed and shook her head. "You might as well come in. Want a lemonade?"

At least he'd been right about one thing. "Sure."

As Annie pushed open the front door, the dog leapt toward them, whining excitedly, wiggling side to side as it nuzzled Nick's legs in greeting.

"Just ignore him, he'll calm down." She led the way to a big, bright kitchen filled with the sugary, buttery-rich scent of chocolate chip cookies baking.

"I always have homemade cookies for the guests. I want them to think of Bailey House as *home* while they're here." Annie took a pitcher of lemonade from the refrigerator and a couple of tall glasses from a cupboard. "Bake up a fresh batch every couple of days so the cookie jar is always full."

She handed him a glass of lemonade, slice of lemon floating on the top, and he took a seat at the old oak table in the center of the room. The tall windows facing south opened to the kind of view most people only dreamed of having—a long expanse of lawn sloping gently toward a sandy beach on a lake that looked to be surrounded by pristine forest.

A moment later, Annie set a plate of warm cookies on the table and slid into the chair opposite him. The dog collapsed on the floor beside her, apparently exhausted from expending so much energy in five minutes.

"I guess I owe you an explanation," she said.

He waited.

She looked down at her hands, clasped together on the table. "Two years ago I bought this B & B with the money you gave me. Well, first I went to college so I could learn how to run a business. Then I found this place." Her voice quivered and she reached down to rub the dog's head. "It's a great little town ..."

Enough with the color commentary. What about the bun in the oven? "Annie—are you pregnant?"

Her expression shifted as though the question caught her completely off guard. She looked like she was about to say something and stopped herself, then drew a slow breath and exhaled. Avoiding his eyes, she stared at the ceiling for a long moment before finally bringing her gaze back to rest on him. She bit her lower lip and made a futile gesture with one hand, as though the motion might give him an answer.

He raised an eyebrow.

She nodded.

Shit. "Married?"

"No."

He let out a breath. At least he hadn't made her a bigamist. He picked up a cookie. "So where's the father?"

She locked eyes with him, and he waited. A charged silence seemed to fill the room.

"I'm looking at him," she finally said.

He jerked his head back to look over his shoulder but no one else was in the room. What was she saying? *"What?"*

"Everyone thinks I'm married to you—"

"Wait a minute, wait a minute, wait a minute—" He tried to force his brain to catch up with the conversation.

The words poured out of her. "I didn't plan for it to happen—I didn't. It just ... happened. I've been meaning to put an end to it, really I have, but—oh, now that you're here, they're going to know I'm a fraud. They're going to know you're not the father. They're going to think I lied on purpose." She let out a groan. "Actually I did lie on purpose, but I didn't intend it to go this far. It just ... got out of hand."

She heaved a sigh and flopped back into her chair. "Everyone in town is going to think I'm just another fake taking advantage of their trust—"

"Hold it! You're not making any sense. How did *I* get into this story? What about the real father? Isn't he interested at all?"

"Interested?" She shook her head. "He doesn't even know."

"That's your first mistake! With all due respect, don't you think it might help if you told him?"

"Sperm donor."

"Huh?"

"Artificial insemination."

"Oh." *Ohh.* He found his brain empty again. How was he supposed to respond to an announcement like that? *Good for you, I see it worked? Shit, I'm relieved that some guy wasn't sleeping with you and left you hanging like this? What the hell, why would you get yourself artificially inseminated, anyway?*

"So you did this on purpose." A bit witless, but at least he said something.

"No."

His eyes widened.

She snorted. "Well, of course I got pregnant on purpose. How else do you think one gets artificially inseminated?"

"No need to get testy. I'm not the one who lied about who the father was."

"I didn't lie about the father."

He frowned. Why did it feel like he was just seconds away from being sucked into a whirlpool?

"I lied about being married. So, naturally, everyone just assumed who the father was."

"Oh, well then it's all okay," he said sarcastically.

"I didn't mean for it to happen like this. I was researching Bed & Breakfasts so I would know how to run one when I finally bought a place. I came here to visit because it was called Bailey House, and it was in *Bedford*." She gave a sheepish grin. "You know, kind of like the movie, *It's a Wonderful Life*. While I was here, there was this college kid who was doing yard work for the summer who kept asking me out. It was just easier to say I was married. Besides, I thought I'd be gone after a week."

The timer sounded and she jumped up to slide a tray of cookies from the oven. "But then I got to talking with the owner. She and her husband wanted to retire. *They wanted to sell*. They hadn't put up a For Sale sign because they were being really picky about who they'd sell to."

"You're losing me."

Annie turned to face him. "They raised their family here. They loved this place and wanted to pass it on to someone who would love it as much as they did. Someone who would raise a family here. *Someone who was married*."

She scooped hot cookies off the baking sheet with a spatula, her words coming faster. "And there I was, enamored of the place, and *married*—or so everyone thought because I'd said I was. And then, somehow, suddenly, I was buying the place from them and staying on. I figured I would eventually say you and I had gotten divorced, but I couldn't do it too soon or everyone would be suspicious."

She looked him straight in the eye. "You know what I mean?"

"Not really." He took a large swallow of lemonade and had the fleeting thought that by the end of this story he was going to wish he had something stronger to drink.

"Didn't anyone ever wonder where your husband was?" Nick couldn't keep the incredulity out of his voice. "And—how did you explain the pregnancy?"

Annie shook her head. "You're a top-secret military guy. The only way we ever got to see each other was if I met you at military bases around the world. So every now and then I took a trip. That's when I got pregnant." She put both hands on the counter. "I didn't see any hope for love, or marriage, in my life. So I decided to quit hanging my hopes on some guy I hadn't even met and go for it alone."

"Annie! This is no little white lie—you've created a whole other world. Didn't your parents teach you not to lie?"

"I don't need a lecture, thank you, Mr. Not-So-Pure-Yourself."

She picked up what looked like a miniature ice cream scoop and began to attack the bowl of cookie dough, scooping and dropping neatly rounded balls of dough onto the baking sheet. After sliding the tray into the oven, she took the chair opposite him again.

"It was never supposed to go this far." She gave him a pointed look. "And you were never supposed to show up. What are you doing here, anyway? Don't tell me you just decided to drop by so we could rehash old times, because I might kill you."

"We're still married."

"In the eyes of everyone in town, yes."

"No, Annie, I mean we're still married. The attorney never filed the divorce papers."

2

SHE GAPED AT HIM, EYES WIDE. "ARE YOU KIDDING me?"

Nick shook his head. "Sorry, no."

"How could this have happened? When I left California, you said everything was taken care of."

"I thought it was. I took off right after you did—left the country thinking it was all settled. I thought the lawyer would do his job."

She let out a snort. "Why wouldn't you follow-up to make sure?"

"Because I paid him a lot of money. Because I trusted him. Because I was out of the country and didn't go back to California for more than five years."

"I should have known I couldn't count on you to follow through." She slapped a hand on the table. "I upheld my part of the bargain. I married you and left you. You got your trust fund seven years before you were supposed to. The only thing you had to do—the only thing—was make sure the divorce went through."

"And pay you $250,000. I did that, remember?"

"Fine." She shook her head. "If only Luella hadn't seen you. I've made a life in this little town. For the first time, I belong. I'm part of a community. Now, with you showing up, I'll lose it all."

Guilt slipped through him. He remembered what she'd told him of her childhood. How she'd grown up an Army brat and hated always being the new kid in school. That just before her father retired from the Army, her parents died in a car accident, and the kids were split up among the relatives. How she'd been on her own since graduating from high school.

He started to reach across the table toward her but stopped himself. "I'm sorry."

"Sorry? Sorry won't fix this." She gave a rueful laugh. "How am I supposed to support myself when I'm run out of town? Alimony?"

She leaned sideways to grab a short stack of envelopes from the counter and wave them in the air. "As the husband in this family, you should know the bills are due. The lawn needs mowing, the storm windows need to be washed before fall comes, and oh, in case you hadn't noticed, the exterior could use a coat of paint."

"I noticed. Look, Annie, I know this is a bit of a shock."

"That may be the understatement of the year."

"But this is all easily fixed—we just need to get divorced for real. I've got the papers in the car. You just sign them and I'll get out of here."

"Great. And what reason do I give for why my *husband* only stayed one afternoon?"

"Whatever you want. How about a top secret military emergency?" He grinned.

Annie pursed her lips but didn't answer.

"What are you thinking?" he asked.

I'm thinking you don't know that you can't file for divorce if the woman is pregnant."

His blood seemed to slow. "What?"

"Not in Wisconsin, anyway. Business law 101."

"You learned about divorce in business law?"

"We got off on a tangent." She gave a cynical laugh.

"Some tangent. Look, that just doesn't sound right to me—"

"It doesn't matter how it sounds. What matters is that it's true. I'm pregnant—you can't divorce me. The law was written to protect the unborn child. It's probably the same for every state." She tilted her head. "I can double check with my cousin, Delaney—she's married to a lawyer over in Birch Harbor."

Disbelief quickly gave way to irritation and then panic. He was supposed to marry Melissa Morgan in six months— the date was set. Everyone agreed Missy was the perfect woman for him—gorgeous, fun, *and* she liked the outdoors. Plus, he loved her. Not in a head-over-heels, gasping, stomach-flopping kind of way, but in a more sedate, comfortable, *mature* sort of way. They were good together— which was better than a lot of people ever got.

Everything had been going along great. But then, two weeks ago he learned his divorce had never gone through. His new attorney had assured him a divorce could be finalized in time for the wedding, as long as he found Annie and got her to sign the papers right away. Who would have guessed she'd be pregnant?

He raked a hand through his hair. "Wait a minute. What about those quickie divorces people talk about. You know, in Mexico, or Las Vegas, or someplace like that?"

Annie just looked at him.

He plunged onward. "We could get one of those. We'll

just fly out—like tomorrow—get the divorce, and then go our separate ways."

"That's rich. My husband arrives on a military leave to announce he's taking me on an exotic vacation—to divorce me while I'm carrying his first child."

Nick tried to grin but the expression on Annie's face told him she didn't find his comment funny. "Okay, so it sounds bad," he said without missing a beat. "How about if you don't tell anyone we're getting a divorce right now—just say we're taking a trip. Once I've gone ... back to the military ... you can pretend you're married for the whole pregnancy if you want. No one has to know we're not. Then six months from now—or whenever—just say we've gotten divorced."

He paused, weighing whether or not he should tell her about Melissa. Well, why not? She was a female, she'd understand how upset Melissa might be about all this. Besides, it wasn't as if he and Annie were ever *really* married. "Look, Annie, the thing is, I need to be single ... soon. So I can—" suddenly the words felt awkward "—get—married—again."

A sharp laugh burst out of her. "I can't believe this is happening. It's like a bad daytime soap opera. Nick, the problem is that Luella and Vivian will already have spread it all over town that you're back. No one's going to believe we'd leave on vacation right away— especially when this is your first trip home." Her voice turned pleading. "Couldn't you just stay a while and pretend you're on leave?"

He was sure he could make her see reason. "Annie, I've got a fiancé. A life. I can't just hang around here and playact. You can just continue to tell the same story you've always told. No one will know the difference. But you and me—we need to get divorced. Now."

She fixed an unreadable look on him and he waited for her to acquiesce. A minute passed and then another without a word spoken. Her expression grew thoughtful. "Hmmm," she finally said. "You need a divorce. And I need a husband. Seems to me we can work this out."

He squinted at her and nodded. This was totally unlike the Annie he remembered. Just what was she up to?

"I might be open to flying off to God-knows-where for a quickie divorce..." She smiled and he felt like a noose had dropped around his neck.

"Yes?"

"If my *husband* were to stick around for a while."

He exhaled. "Annie—"

"Come on, Nick, if it wasn't for me, you wouldn't have gotten your trust fund early like you did."

"You were paid handsomely."

"I helped you out in your time of need. Now it's my time of need. All I ask—"

He crossed his arms over his chest. "Do you have any idea how much this will screw up my life?"

"About as much as it already has mine?"

Touché. "What exactly do you want?"

"Nine days—"

"Nine days? Are you out of your—"

"A mere nine days pretending we're happily married, and I promise I'll go wherever we have to go, do whatever you need me to do, to finalize our divorce."

"Three days at the most. *Three.*" What had happened to easy-to-influence Annie?

"Not long enough. Look, you were granted a leave to come home to see your pregnant wife. You wouldn't stay just three days."

She leaned toward him, eyes glistening with excitement.

"Besides, it'll be easy. You won't have to answer any questions about what you do—it's top secret, remember?"

"I'm engaged to someone else."

"I didn't say you had to fulfill the connubial duties—"

"That hadn't even crossed my mind. How do I explain to Melissa that I'm staying here another nine days? She doesn't even know I've come to see you. She thinks I've been divorced for years."

"Do you even work?"

What did that have to do with anything?

"I mean, you have that trust fund ..."

He sat up straighter. "Yeah, I work. I'm an adventure writer. One of those guys who gets to travel all over the world, kayak down rivers, climb mountains, eat fried bugs in exotic countries, and then write articles about it—sometimes books." He leaned back in his chair and crossed his arms over his chest. "In fact, right now I have a proposal in with my agent for a television-book deal that just might make me a household name. I want to track down the Almasti in Mongolia. They're kind of like Big Foot—some people think they're actually Neanderthals who survived. You ever hear of them?"

A slow appreciative grin filled Annie's eyes with warmth. "You did it. You actually did what you wanted to do with your trust fund money?"

He nodded.

"I have to admit, I thought you'd blow the whole fund on the L.A. party scene."

She knew him better than he would have guessed; he might have done just that had he stayed in Los Angeles. "Two weeks after you left, I took off for Nepal. Sold my first story from there and didn't go back to California for years."

No need to tell her that L.A. reminded him of a night-shift waitress he used to tell his dreams to in a dive restaurant at two in the morning, a waitress he'd once married—and had never really forgotten.

"Perfect." She jumped to her feet and paced the room, her voice all business now. "Then you don't have to ask anyone for time off from work. Just tell your fiancé you're doing another story. Right here in Wisconsin."

"Oh, she'll buy that. There's *lots* of adventure to write about in this little town."

"Snobbery is not attractive," she said. "Make it up. She's not going to know—after all, you're not actually writing an article. How can you? You're a top secret military kind of guy—not a writer."

He stared at her.

"You owe me," she said. "Think of it as repayment."

Repayment? More like *extortion*. "One week. I'm pretty sure the military only gives its really important guys leave in very short increments." The noose around his neck seemed to tighten. "Nine days. I spent an entire childhood moving from base to base—the military gives leaves in any amount of time they damn well please."

He threw his hands up in frustration.

"Nine days?" Her face glowed with hope, and at that moment he might have agreed to anything just so he wouldn't be the reason she'd lose that hope.

"This is bordering on the absurd," he said, stalling.

"We can do it."

"We hardly know each other."

"Nick, we faked it well enough to fool everyone about our marriage six years ago."

She was right about that—to this day no one had a clue the marriage had been a sham. The day after the wedding, Nick's parents had flown back to Chicago. As far as they had ever known, Annie hadn't walked out on their son until six months later, ostensibly because they had married too quickly and soon learned they were completely incompatible.

"My parents never quite got over why you left me," he said. "I think they couldn't believe that *anyone* would leave a Fleming."

Annie laughed. "If we can fool your family, we can fool people who don't know you at all. Come on, Nick."

"A week. I'll give you a week. What difference does it make, seven days or nine, as long as I play my role right?"

She sighed. "It has to be nine. There's a ribbon-cutting at the new general store museum, and I'm on the board and chaired the fund-raising committee ..." She grimaced. "We've, ah, made a donation—"

"We?" General store museum?

"Well, I couldn't very well ignore the fact that I was married when I made the donation, could I?"

"Is my name on your checking account, too?"

She bent to peer into the oven. "Looks like the cookies are done."

"Annie! You took this all the way, didn't you?"

"One thing just seemed to lead to another," she said slowly as she pulled the cookie sheet from the oven. "It was kind of like a snowball rolling downhill."

"I think the snowball just smashed into a tree."

"Not if you stay for nine days."

"I don't remember you being so ..."

She spun to face him and grinned. "Stunningly beautiful?"

"Pushy," he said.

"I do remember you being irresponsible."

The truth of her words stung.

"Not anymore."

"Prove it."

He met her gaze and held it, saw the challenge in her eyes, and knew he wanted to stay, wanted to help her. With her looking at him like that—strong, competent, vulnerable all at once—what he wanted to do right now was—

He gave his head a shake. What he wanted to do was make things right.

He exhaled. "Nine days? Eight nights? And then we fly off to get a quickie divorce and everyone thinks I've gone back to the military?"

She nodded.

"Promise?" What was he thinking? Nine days? Melissa would never buy it. She thought he was writing an article about a road trip from California to Chicago—which he was. What she didn't know was that he had made a little detour into Wisconsin to find Annie.

"Promise."

"Today is day one?"

She nodded.

"*Okay.*" He had lost his mind.

She beamed at him, her relief palpable. "Thank you."

Oh, what the hell—might as well roll with it. He raised a wicked eyebrow at her. "So tell me, what do we do now ... *sweetheart?*"

3

Annie frowned. "What am I thinking? This isn't going to work—no way you'd come home for nine days and only have enough clothes for a weekend." She tapped her lower lip with her finger. "I suppose we could say the airlines lost your luggage. That would be a good excuse for why you're buying a bunch of new stuff. Yeah, that might work for—"

"I didn't fly—I drove."

"From L.A.?"

"I'm doing a story about a road trip, cross country to Chicago. I've got a duffel in the trunk. With a job like mine, you have to be prepared."

A grin spread across her face. "You *have* changed! What are we waiting for? Let's get you moved in."

He held up a hand. "No, no. I'll get it."

He started across the kitchen, but Annie was on her feet and pushing through the old-fashioned screen door ahead of him. "I'll help you carry something," she said over her shoulder.

The door banged shut behind her.

He shrugged. She was about to see just how much he *hadn't* changed. He followed her down the driveway to his dark green SUV and popped open the tailgate, stifling a laugh when he heard Annie gasp at the sight inside.

Okay, so it looked even worse than he remembered. Sure, his tent and sleeping bag were rolled up nice and neat. And there was a duffel just like he'd said there would be. Admittedly, it was nearly empty, but at least he had one. Everything that had been packed neatly inside it when he'd set off from L.A. was now strewn across the back end in a sea of assorted newspapers, magazines, empty water bottles, and crumpled snack bags.

He grabbed the dirty jeans that were draped over the back seat and shoved them into the duffel. Wrinkled T-shirts came next, and socks and—uh, those silky boxers Melissa had given him the night before he left.

"I see organization is not one of your strengths," Annie said, eyes riveted on the mess.

He scooped up the boxers in an armful of clothing. "Too much order stifles creativity."

Suddenly she smacked him hard on the shoulder. "Drop that stuff! Get out of the way!"

He dropped everything and jumped back just as she slammed the tailgate shut.

"What the ...? You almost broke my fingers!" Was the woman crazy?

Smiling, she looked past him and waved at a heavyset, middle-aged man in gray, loose-fitting exercise pants and a t-shirt power-walking toward them down the sidewalk. "Hello, Father."

Father? He slanted a sideways glance at Annie. But her dad wasn't alive—

"Priest," she whispered out of the corner of her mouth.

"Father, I want you to finally meet my husband, Nick. He's home on leave. Nick, this is Father Thespesius. I've mentioned him in some of my letters."

The priest pumped Nick's extended hand. "Welcome to Bedford! It's so good to finally meet you. How goes the secret service?" He waved a hand back and forth between them. "No, don't tell me. I don't want to jeopardize our national security."

He started to walk around them in a circle, arms swinging. "Have to keep moving. If I stop too long my heart rate drops and I don't get the full cardio benefit. You're a lucky man to have a gal like Annie. And a baby on the way. Twice blessed." He strode off down the sidewalk and called over his shoulder, "See you in church."

Nick looked at Annie. *Church?* He hadn't been to church in years. "You go to church?"

"Everybody goes to church in a small town."

"Everybody? Annie, don't you think we should keep a low profile for the next week? Can't we pretend we just want to spend all our time alone together?"

"You'd rather the whole town be talking about *why* we're not in church and what we're doing instead on Sunday morning?"

"Oh, come on. No one will even miss us."

She laughed knowingly. "Not only will they miss us, but the next time they see us, half the town will probably comment on why we weren't there—and the other half will be snickering. Welcome to Bedford, population 7,500."

What had he gotten into? And what had happened to Annie? She was taking charge here like a general with a mission. He contemplated this change in her and realized he didn't find it unattractive. The old Annie, the one he used to know in L.A. could have used a dose of self-confidence.

She motioned at the driveway that led to a big garage behind the house. "Why don't you pull your car up so you can repack your duffel in private. The washer's in the basement, detergent's on the shelf next to it. Maybe you'd like to do some *wash*." She smiled sweetly and headed up the front steps.

"Maybe you'd like to do some wash," he muttered under his breath as he slid into the driver's seat.

Snapping up his phone, he called Melissa and was relieved when she didn't answer. He left a quick message—a lie—saying he'd received a sudden assignment that would keep him in the Midwest for another week or so, and promised to call her later.

Then he pulled his SUV up to the garage and dialed his attorney, this time disappointed that no one picked up the phone. He left a detailed message—the truth—about Annie and the situation in Bedford, and asked the man to look into what Wisconsin law had to say about divorcing a pregnant wife. He winced. Any way you looked at it, it just sounded bad.

He threw a load of dirty clothes in the washer, then went up to the living room—parlor, he supposed they called it in an old house like this. Annie sat on the sofa, one elbow on the armrest, chin cupped in her hand, an apprehensive look on her face. He set his duffle on the floor in the doorway. "What's wrong?"

"It just hit me—where are you going to sleep?" she asked.

"Don't you have an open room?"

"Sure. But it's not that simple. Luella would know we were in different rooms—hell, my guests would know.

Married people sleep in the same room. Especially married people who hardly ever get to see each other."

The thought of sharing a room, *a bed*, with Annie slowed his brain. He walked over to the hearth and forced his thoughts to organize. "We can do that," he said finally.

"I suppose you could sleep on the floor."

Floor? "Hardwood?"

"Uh-huh."

"A couple of little throw rugs, I bet."

She tilted her head. "Your point exactly?"

"I'm not sleeping on a wood floor for the next eight nights. Surely you've got enough room in your bed."

"Surely you jest."

"Surely not. I stay nine days—eight nights—I sleep in a bed."

"But I saw a sleeping bag and one of those ground pads in the back of your car."

He narrowed his eyes at her. "You're welcome to them. But I'm sleeping in a bed. Those are *my* terms."

She blinked at him.

As he rested a forearm against the mantel and waited for her to respond, a framed picture caught his eye, a wedding photo set next to an antique oil lamp. He leaned toward it for a better look, and a rush of tangled emotions tumbled through him. It was them—him and Annie—on their wedding day six years ago, smiling at the camera with all the enthusiasm of young lovers. A week later, Annie had left.

A long-forgotten ache zig-zagged through his gut. Once he'd lost his late-night confidant, all he wanted to do was get out of L.A. Without Annie as a counterbalance, the city seemed all the more superficial—and off-putting. In retrospect, it had been her leaving that jump-started him into his dream of becoming an adventure writer.

He shoved aside the memory and the feeling of loss. "Nice prop." He nodded at the photo. "I was wondering how Luella recognized me."

Annie shrugged sheepishly. "How could I be married and not have a picture of us out?"

He sat beside her on the sofa and patted the top of her knee. "Annie, you were safe with me that week after our wedding. You don't have to start worrying that I'll take advantage of you now."

"I know, I know. And I can't very well move another bed in the room. That would be as bad as separate rooms." She sighed. "Okay, so we share a bed. That's the easy part, anyway. The hard part is going to be not making any mistakes in public. So tell me some things about you I should know, as your wife."

"Like what? I grew up outside Chicago. My dad's a retired banker from a long line of successful—and rich— bankers. I have a sister—"

"I know that stuff already."

"My mom died last year."

Annie's eyes softened and she reached out to cover his hand with her own. "Oh, Nick. I'm so sorry. How's your dad taking it?"

"It's hard for him to be alone—they were married forty years. I was going to stop by and surprise him after I left here. Guess that'll have to wait nine days." He gave a small smile.

"And your sister?"

"Still in Chicago, too. Working for the family bank, which is good for dad in a lot of ways. Not the least of which is that she's seriously dating some guy who's also in banking—

"Ah, kind of like the number-cruncher son he never had."

"Something like that. He doesn't bug me to join the bank anymore. I think my mom's death made him realize life is too short to be disappointed that your kid isn't a financial wizard."

A long pause hung in the air between them, but he had no desire to jump in and fill it.

Finally Annie spoke. "So, do you still drink your coffee black?"

"I hate coffee."

"Really? Then why were you always stopping in the restaurant in the middle of the night for coffee?"

He cocked his head and stared at her a moment. "You were the only person who ever took my dreams seriously, the only one who seemed to believe I might actually make them come true." It was more than that, though. She'd had this openness about her, an honest realness that was really hard to find in L.A. He gave a casual shrug. "As for coffee, I still drink it—black—when I need a jolt. You?"

"Pregnancy's put an end to my coffee-drinking. Now it's decaf, with cream. What else?"

"I don't know. I eat red meat, though not as much as I used to. Does that help?"

"Yeah ..."

"I run. Seven or eight miles every day."

"What else?"

"You tell me. You're the one who's created a profile for me. What do I do exactly?"

She flashed him a grin. "Something for the military, so top secret even I don't know what it is."

"Well, that makes job questions easy. Have we been married for six years?"

"That would be correct."

"When's the baby due?"

"Six months."

"You're three months along? You don't even look pregnant."

"Oh, I do. You should see me without clothes on."

He raised an eyebrow, and two spots of pink appeared on her cheeks. "Forget I said that."

"So where'd you get your degree?" he asked. "What's it in again?"

"Hotel and restaurant management. University of Wisconsin-Stout—"

"Hence the bed-and-breakfast." He gestured toward the doorway. "Why don't you show me around while we have this conversation so I can really get up to speed?"

"Good idea. This is the parlor. You've already seen the kitchen and basement." She smiled like a proud parent and headed across the hall. Nick grabbed his duffel and followed her into a second sitting room and the dining room, both decorated with antiques in a style reminiscent of the late nineteenth century.

"On the second floor, I—*we*—have five guest rooms." She mounted the stairs and glanced at the dog bounding ahead of her. "Oh, something else you probably should know—everyone thinks Chester is yours."

He gave the mutt a long look. "I hate little dogs. And I don't like big ones much better."

She screwed up her face as they continued up the stairs. "He's fifteen pounds. And how can you be a man and not like dogs?"

He shrugged. "Never had one, never saw the need to have one."

"Well, since everyone thinks this dog is yours, you'd better put on a good show."

"Would a man pick out a mutt that looks like that?"

Chester wagged his tail as though he knew they were talking about him, and he wanted to make a good impression.

"You did."

"A poodle?" Nick raised his eyebrows.

Ahead on the landing, Chester excitedly pranced, tongue hanging out of his happy grin.

"We're acquaintances," Nick said to the dog. "Not friends. Remember that." He turned his attention back to Annie. "Is there anything else I should know about myself? Like, I sing opera or paint my toenails or ...?"

She rolled her eyes and headed down the second-floor corridor. "Offhand, I can't think of anything, but who knows? I've been embellishing you for quite a while."

"I guess I should feel flattered, but for some reason ... I don't."

A laugh slipped out of Annie. "All good things. After all, why would I invent a bad husband?"

She pushed open the doors to a couple of unoccupied guest rooms. Each had similar decorating—lace curtains at the windows, antique furniture, a patchwork quilt, rag throw rugs. The look was warm, the feel welcoming. By the time they reached the third floor, Nick was beginning to think this might not be the worst situation he'd ever gotten himself into.

Annie opened the first door they came to. "This is my—our—room."

Nick stepped over the threshold. "A double bed? Couldn't you at least have a queen?"

"*Queen* isn't historically correct."

"Ha! But it *is* a lot more comfortable for two people."

'Two people hasn't been a concern of mine since I bought the place," she said with a sniff.

"Never?"

"I'm married, remember?"

How could he have forgotten?

4

———

Nick dropped his duffel on the floor next to her dresser.

Annie stared at it for a long moment, as though the reality of sharing a room with Nick was finally sinking in. Then she smiled. "I'll empty some drawers for—"

"Yoo-hoo, anybody here?" An elderly female voice came up the stairs from the front hall. "Annie!"

Panicked, Annie spun toward the door and clasped his forearm. "Oh, my God! Luella's back already! You need to know—she's a wonderful person but she can be a little ... nosy. So, when in doubt, keep your mouth shut."

Annie hurried into the hall. Chester pushed past her, running ahead, his tail beating the air in frenzied excitement.

Nick paused in the doorway to take a last look at the cozy room. Old-fashioned and feminine with its flowered wallpaper and white chenille bedspread, the room was a picture of an era gone by. He envisioned stolen romantic moments between a young man and young woman in the upstairs room while her father sat in the backyard smoking his pipe and talking politics with the other men. His lips quirked, and he wondered whether such thoughts ever crossed Annie's mind living in this big, old house.

Unbidden, he heard her words again—*you should see me without clothes on*—and an image slipped into his head, one of Annie lying across the bed in a general state of undress. The thought took him aback. This was his friend, Annie. They were just helping each other out. And he was engaged to someone else. What the hell was the matter with him?

He swallowed hard and hurried down the hall after her. *Maybe this bed-sharing thing wasn't such a good idea after all.* He almost ran her down in his haste to catch up, stopping behind her to stare over the balustrade at the gathering of women below them in the foyer—one, two, four, six, eight. *Holy shit.*

Eight faces, all crowned with silver hair smiled up at them—and said nothing. And then the sound of heels clipping briskly upon the hardwood floor of the corridor was followed by Luella's face, and her gasp. "Oh, my dears, I thought I gave you enough time. I had no idea you might still be upstairs."

Annie's face flamed. "Inquisition," she muttered. "There's going to be an inquisition. And I'm going to be hung."

Nick took her by the elbow and gently guided her down the stairs. "Not if I can help it," he murmured in her ear.

"Ladies, you'll have to excuse our surprise," he said when they reached the bottom step. "It's been some time since my wife and I have seen each other."

The small group let out a collective embarrassed laugh,

and suddenly the women were chattering around them, introductions flying as each shook Nick's hand. Luella spoke over the clamor. "As soon as the ladies heard Nick was here, they insisted we cut supper short and come right over. I tried to discourage them, said you two needed time alone, but it was to no avail as you can see."

Annie looked shell-shocked.

"Oh, it's all right, isn't it, *sweetheart?*" Nick gave Annie a loving smile.

The endearment seemed to loosen her up. "No problem at all, *darling.*"

"I'm just glad to finally be able to put faces to the names Annie has mentioned in her letters," Nick said. "I've heard so much about all of you I feel like I know you already."

Annie gave a slight nod of approval for his quick adlib. This wasn't so hard. All he had to do was charm, charm, charm. "Ladies, I think we'd all be a bit more comfortable in the parlor. Would anyone like a lemonade?"

"Oh, what a dear," someone said.

Annie smiled and put her arm through his.

"You go on and sit down." Luella bustled toward the kitchen door. "I'll get the lemonade. But don't you talk about anything important until I'm back."

Nick brought in a couple of chairs from the dining table so there would be enough seats for everyone, then settled in next to Annie on the loveseat. The ladies pulled their chairs close, as though Nick were a movie star come to visit from Hollywood. He draped a casual arm around Annie's shoulders and pulled her close, letting his fingers play with the soft strands of hair that had pulled loose from her ponytail, purposely wanting to present the picture of the long-absent husband unable to keep his hands off his wife.

Annie tried to subtly shift away, but he held her firm.

"It really is wonderful to finally meet Annie's husband," one woman said.

"No talking, no talking!" Luella's voice rang out from the hall. A minute later, she appeared around the corner with a wooden tray covered with glasses of lemonade. She made her way around the room passing out the drinks. "All right. Now we can talk. Who's going first?"

The women tittered and said nothing, suddenly tongue-tied. Finally one asked, "Are you back for good?"

Nick put on a disappointed expression. "Just nine days, I'm afraid. Then it's back to business as usual."

The room filled with sighs of disappointment and clucks of the tongue.

"Poor Annie," someone murmured.

"Annie says you work for the military. What exactly do you do?"

Nick pursed his lips in studied contemplation. The ladies straightened, hanging on his every word.

He smiled apologetically. "I—well ... it's classified. Top secret. I could tell you what I do ..." He bent toward the woman who had asked the question, holding in a laugh as everyone leaned forward in expectation.

"But then I'd have to kill you," he said in a stage whisper.

With a collective gasp, the women sat back in their chairs. He grinned and let out a sharp laugh.

"Nick!" Annie slapped him on the arm.

He chuckled. "Just kidding. Truthfully, though, I'm really not at liberty to talk about it. National security and all that."

A few of the women laughed nervously.

"You must be thrilled about the baby."

"You have no idea what an effect that baby is having on me," he said with a smile.

"Oh, Annie, he'll be such a good father."

The woman directly across from them waggled a flamboyant hand. "Some of us were beginning to wonder whether you weren't a figment of Annie's imagination."

Annie's smile faltered a bit. "Nick, this is Vivian. We sit together on the board of the new museum."

"The general store." Nick nodded as though he knew everything about it. "I'm so proud of Annie's involvement here in Bedford." He pressed a kiss to the side of her brow and ran his fingers over the soft skin at the back of her neck.

"We're actually so very pleased you're here, Nick, because we have another reason for stopping by," Vivian said. She focused her attention on Annie. "Who better than Nick to help judge the Women's Club flower arrangement contest?"

Right. Who better than the man with the black thumb?

He felt Annie tense. She shook her head and said, "I thought you had the judges all lined up."

Vivian smiled at Nick, as though she was imparting some secret. "The Fletchers just cancelled—their daughter had her baby a month early and they've gone to help out. But it leaves us in a bind because the contest is in two days!"

"Wouldn't you prefer someone who has more experience with flowers?" Nick asked.

"Annie tells us you're a gardening whiz."

He slanted a look at Annie. *Gardening whiz? He couldn't even keep a cactus alive.*

Her eyes widened slightly and she nodded.

Maybe he was going to learn he painted his toenails after all. He gave Annie's shoulder a gentle squeeze as he smiled humbly at Vivian. 'That wife of mine. She loves me so much, she sometimes exaggerates my abilities. What else has she told you about me?"

The ladies laughed again.

"Oh, lots of things. How you love dogs ..."

As if on cue, Chester came over and sat at his feet, tail whipping from side to side. Forced into the moment, Nick reached down to give the dog a pat and was rewarded with a series of quick licks. *Nice touch.*

He wiped his hand on his pant leg. "That's me. Never met a dog I didn't like."

Luella smiled. "You can see how much Chester loves you. Dogs always stay devoted to their masters no matter how long it's been since they were together."

"So, will you do the flower judging?" Vivian asked. "It's a worthy cause—part of our annual Flower Festival. All the arrangements are auctioned off and the money will be used to fulfill our pledge to the new museum."

"Well, I, ah—"

"Ple-e-ease."

He looked to Annie for help and she gave an almost imperceptible shrug, one that seemed to say, *Sorry, you're on your own.* Oh, she was going to pay for this.

After a silence that bordered on being too long, he finally said, "Okay." And then because he thought that sounded sort of lame, he added, "It'll be fun." *It'll be fun? Yeah, right.* A flower arrangement contest? Somehow in the course of an afternoon, he'd acquired a pregnant wife, a love of dogs, an in-depth knowledge of gardening, and a seat on the judging table of a flower arrangement contest. This had the potential to go bad very quickly. He had to get out of here before, someone, he agreed to anything else.

Taking Annie's hand, he stood and pulled her to her

feet. "Ladies, I really hate to be a party pooper, but my wife promised to show me the lake—and of course, some of the gardens." Clasping Annie's hand tightly in his, he towed her toward the doorway. "It was very nice to meet all of you. I'm sure we'll be seeing each other around town."

"Only if Annie will let you out of her sight," Luella shouted with glee.

He waited until he and Annie were in the kitchen before he pulled her close enough so she could hear his irritated whisper. "A gardening whiz?"

"I didn't think you'd ever actually be here. You should have called first."

"And a dog lover? You're so far from the truth, this gig will be over before it gets started." He glanced toward the parlor and discovered several of the ladies craning their necks to see down the hall. The last thing these busybodies needed was juicy gossip about a spat between Annie and her just-returned husband. He had no choice but to make it good—fast.

Without warning, he drew Annie against him and pressed his mouth to hers. She didn't exactly melt in his arms, but her response wasn't too bad for spur of the moment. Definitely more stiff than she'd been on the porch, but then, it sounded like she hadn't had much practice in the past few years.

He grinned as they pulled apart, and he went over to open the door. "Want to show me the lake, my love?"

"That's enough!" she said under her breath as she stepped out to the back porch. Her cheeks glowed pink.

He followed her out and let the screen door slam shut behind them. "The ladies were watching."

"That's no reason."

"Oh, but it was reason enough for you to kiss *me* when I arrived at the front door."

"That was different." She glanced away.

"Was it?"

"Yes, you're over the top. All that touchy, lovey-dovey stuff in the parlor. All those honeys and sweethearts. And then a kiss in the kitchen?"

"You're my wife. *I've missed you.* I'm just acting the way any red-blooded American man would act if he hadn't seen his wife in months."

He put an arm around her as they headed across the wide back lawn toward the lakeshore.

"Nick—" Her voice was full of warning.

"Don't look now, but the ladies are lined up in the kitchen windows."

She jerked her head around. "Oh! And you're egging their curiosity on with all this romantic stuff."

"I'm just doing what you told me—make them believe we're married. Now, put your arm around me. If you want them to believe we're in love, you're going to have to act like it."

She rolled her eyes but complied. "Lots of married couples save these public displays of affection for private moments. We could be one of those types."

He let his arm slide down her back until his hand rested on her derriere. "Nope, I don't think so. Not after how the ladies saw me acting in there. I have to be consistent."

"Get your hand off my butt or I'll deck you."

He laughed and gave her rear end a pat before letting go of her. "Don't tell me we have trouble in paradise already?"

He sauntered onto the pier and dropped casually onto the bench across the end of the dock like he owned the place.

———

Annie stopped to watch him for a moment, to drink in all that was Nick. His black hair was longer at the neck than current styles dictated, his T-shirt worn and faded as if he'd had it in his closet for years. His jeans, obviously old favorites, hugged his hips and fell straight to his ankles, creasing just a bit at the top of his running shoes. Lean and muscular, he still walked as if he owned the world.

It was amazing that after all these years he still had an effect on her—and he still had no clue about it. She knew she was overreacting to the affection he was showing as her make-believe, long-absent husband, but every time he touched her she found herself fighting feelings she thought she'd gotten over a long time ago.

Though they'd never been anything more than friends, she'd always thought that, given half a chance, she could have fallen head over heels for him. She, an army brat. He, the son of a wealthy banker.

Nothing would ever have been less likely.

Not that it mattered anyway. The man was engaged and it was just as well. The last thing she needed was some casual fling with an irresponsible charmer who was about to marry someone else.

Although, to be honest, it would sure fit her pattern. She'd always chosen the wrong kind of guys to get involved with—and it had taken months in therapy for her to finally realize it. She wasn't going down that path again. No way. Nick Fleming had *bad choice and broken heart* written all over him. Besides, she had a baby to think of now, and somehow she didn't think Nick Fleming would ever be the fatherly type.

Problem was, the way Nick was acting, the way he was touching her ... was bringing back every old feeling she'd ever had for him. Which meant, she was going to have to be diligent about keeping those feelings in check while he was here. She sighed inwardly. As if she needed one more thing to stay on top of.

She walked out on the pier and joined him on the bench. "Thanks for being so nice to the ladies. And for agreeing to judge the flowers."

"Just doing my job as your beloved husband. If I'm going to be here for nine days, I might as well have something to do."

"Well, thanks for being so gracious anyway."

He shrugged dismissively. "This is an amazingly beautiful place."

He gestured at the lake shimmering under the late afternoon sun, the opposite shore thick with towering pines and white-trunked birch trees. A few houses down, almost out of earshot, a group of kids were throwing themselves off the dock doing cannonballs, trying to outdo one another with the volume of their splashes. In the distance, a couple of sailboats slipped slowly across the nearly flat water. "I almost feel like I'm on a movie set," he said. "It's so peaceful, it can't be real."

She understood exactly. "This lake was half the reason I bought the place. Most of the land is state forest so it can't ever be developed. The view will stay like this forever."

"And you'll be able live here happily ever after, as long as we pull off this charade."

"I hope so." She sat in silence for several minutes. "I've got about eighty acres over there. There's a stream that runs through it." She nodded toward a heavily wooded area that bordered her lawn. "The thing is, if the B & B doesn't start making more money, I'm going to need to sell that land just to stay afloat. I've been contacted by a couple of developers. The question is, what will they want to put up? A resort? Condos? All I picture is lots of powerboats and Illinois license plates."

"Hey, watch it. I'm from Illinois—a long time ago, anyway."

She gave a wry laugh. "Sorry. I'm feeling a little protective. Could be lots of Wisconsin license plates, too. Either way it changes everything around here."

"Annie, you're not thinking like a business person. More tourists would mean more business for you, too."

"Yeah, I know. It's just ... the wrong kind of development would wreck the whole charm of this place."

She pointed across the bay. "Try to picture it. A big aluminum-sided complex of condos along the water's edge, just like every other development you see in every other lake community. A perfectly manicured lawn that no one ever walks on, let alone plays on. Or just as bad, maybe a massive four-story brick hotel with hundreds of rooms—and an outdoor swimming pool right next to the lake because, you know, lakes have fish in them and leaves and stuff. Just not my idea of paradise."

She stood, suddenly wanting to get away from the pictures in her mind. "Let's walk. I'll show you all the flower beds I'm sure you'll be itching to dig your gardening fingers into. That is, of course, after you walk your beloved dog!" She grinned wickedly.

Nick jumped off the bench and came after her, and she took off running, laughing with glee.

He caught her by the arm and spun her around. "I should be really mad about all this."

Annie could see the twinkle in his eyes. "But you're not."

He brushed his lips across hers, a gentle, spontaneous kiss. Her heart took a wild leap, and her brain chastised her for allowing herself to respond to his touch.

"But I'm not," he said. "Now, show me the flowers."

5

———

Nick slid into the driver's seat of his SUV and turned on his cell phone. He'd just spent an hour looking at more flowers than he'd ever wanted to see in his life. Not that it would help him during the flower judging, but at least he now knew the difference between delphinium and phlox ... or was it flax?

He wiped the back of his hand across his mouth and brushed away the crumbs from the chicken salad sandwiches Luella had brought out to them. She'd practically dragged him and Annie out of the flower beds and onto the porch to make sure they ate something for dinner. Then she'd sat across from them the whole time, beaming. The woman was definitely happy that Annie's husband was back.

Giving a groan, he punched in the code to retrieve his messages.

"Hi, Nick." Melissa's sultry voice came on the line. "I can't believe you got an assignment out there. I'm leaving, too. Tomorrow. Just got a photo shoot in Paris—an emergency. The girl they hired broke her leg and they need me there the day after tomorrow. I'm missing you already. And now we won't see each other for three weeks." Her voice rose a notch. "Leonard called. There's a party tonight at Marlene's. I wish you were here to go with me. Call me later and I'll pass the phone around so you can say hi to everyone. I miss you. I love you. Talk to you tonight. Ciao."

If he wasn't so tired, he might be envious. Los Angeles was rocking and he was stuck here. The whole town of Bedford probably closed down at ten o'clock.

A second message began to play, from his lawyer. "Nick, she's right—you can't divorce her in Wisconsin if she's pregnant. We could pull it off out here, but you don't meet California residency requirements anymore. Give me a few days do some checking. Call you back when I know something. Hey, bummer about the baby."

Bummer big time.

His attorney had nine days to figure it out, and the man better have an answer for him soon. Nick let his head drop forward until it rested against the steering wheel. What was that old saying? Marry in haste, repent at leisure? It was beginning to sound very profound. He let his eyes close for a moment and felt himself immediately slide toward sleep. Yesterday had been a long day on the road; he'd really pushed it, driving almost all night, stopping just once to sleep in the car for a couple of hours at a truck stop before putting in another seven hours to get here. He looked at his watch. Seven o'clock. Even though the sun was only now beginning to drop on the horizon, it would still be early to bed for him tonight.

He grabbed his laptop case, climbed out of the car, and pushed the button on his fob to lock the doors. Then he stopped. Did people even lock their car doors in small towns? Their house doors? When he was kid, his grandmother never locked her doors, but the world had changed a lot since then.

The sound of a car interrupted his musings, and he looked up to see a black Volkswagen bug pull into the driveway. The driver door flew open, and a woman dressed entirely in black stepped out and strode toward him. Black thick-rimmed glasses framed her eyes, and fuchsia hair hung stick straight to her shoulders. A tattoo wrapped its way up her left arm. She looked as though she belonged in L.A., not small town Wisconsin.

"Nick Fleming? Francis Troutline." She reached out to vigorously shake his hand. "You can call me Minnow."

He raised an eyebrow. "Girl Scout camp?"

"What?"

"Your name? Camp nickname?"

"Oh, no. Never went to camp. Everyone calls my dad Trout. I was the baby of the family. Get it? Minnow. It just stuck."

He nodded.

"When I heard you were here I couldn't wait to meet you," Minnow said. "I cut Annie's hair—other people's hair, too—so if you need a trim ..." She narrowed her eyes, inspecting him. "You're looking a little shaggy around the collar."

Excuse me? "I like it this way. If you don't mind, Minnow ... I was just going inside."

"Oh yeah, me, too." She strode past him up the stairs and let herself in the back door.

He stared after her for a moment, then gave his head a shake and followed her into the house. He paused in the doorway. Minnow had Annie in a big hug and was babbling something about how she couldn't believe Nick was here and Annie hadn't told her he was coming. *This woman wasn't really a friend of Annie's, was she?*

Minnow spotted him in the doorway. "Hey! Shut that door! The mosquitoes around here are so big we fry 'em for dinner." He stepped into the kitchen and the door smacked against the jamb with a bang. Someone really should fix that.

"Uh, sorry," he said.

"Just kidding. A little up-north humor."

The diameter of her neck looked as if it would fit nicely between his two hands. He suppressed a grin at the thought.

She looked at his computer case. "Is that briefcase full of secret military papers?"

He opened his mouth, then shut it, not sure how to answer. "Kind of. It's a computer."

"Have you had the house swept?"

"I'm sure Luella takes care of that," he said with effort.

Minnow snorted. "For bugs. You know, listening devices?"

Was she nuts? "I don't think we'll need to worry about that."

Minnow looked incredulous. "Considering your line of work, I'd think you could never be too careful."

He looked at Annie for help, and she burst out laughing.

Fine. So Annie was nuts, too. "I'm going to put this stuff upstairs."

"She knows," Annie whispered.

"Knows what?"

"About us."

He looked from one woman to the other. Minnow was nodding at him and smiling.

Careful, careful, he didn't want to blow anything here. "Knows ...?"

"About our marriage, our divorce." Annie's voice rose a notch. "She knows—"

"Everything!" Minnow chimed in.

Luella came through the doorway carrying a vase of wilting flowers. Petals dropped to the floor as she crossed the room. "Who knows everything?"

The three of them froze. When neither Annie nor Minnow replied, Nick finally jumped in with, "Minnow. She knows everything about ..." He faltered. What was he supposed to say? He didn't even know the woman. "Oh, just everything, I guess."

Annie nodded vehemently. "Right. You know, she's always learning, always reading—"

Luella snorted. "Movie-star magazines and spy thrillers."

"Well, she really knows hairstyles," Annie said weakly.

Looking at Minnow's hair, dyed as it was that odd shade of reddish fuchsia, Nick thought Annie was stretching it a bit. "She does seem to know a lot about ... espionage," he offered. "You know, I think I'd better get this stuff upstairs."

"I'll help you." Annie grabbed the computer bag from his hand and raced from the room.

"Me, too." Minnow chased after her.

Nick shrugged at Luella and followed the girls upstairs. So there was one person in this town who knew all of Annie's secrets. That certainly put a new twist on things.

He walked into the bedroom just in time to hear the end of Annie's explanation of how he had come to be in Bedford. Minnow flopped back into the pillows on the bed. "Wow. Exciting. Nine days, huh? This is a lot like a book I read last year. The hero is in love with this woman, but the

Russians are after him, so to protect her, he ends their relationship, but the Russians kill her anyway and make it look like his own guys did it, and—"

Nick held up a hand. "No Russians, no love story, no murder. How is that anything like this?"

"Well, I think it is," Minnow said, sitting up. "What do you really do, anyway?"

"I'm a writer."

Her back straightened. "For the movies?"

"No. I do manuals on how to run machinery."

Annie let out a laugh. "Just ignore him. He writes stories and books about adventures—you know, whitewater rafting, mountain climbing ..."

"An outdoors guy, huh?" Minnow asked. "Are you ever on TV?"

Before he could answer, Annie brought her hands together with a clap. "First things first. The most important thing, Nick, is if you're ever in town and get into some sort of trouble with the story—"

"Your *cover,*" Minnow said.

"Right, your *cover.* Then Minnow might be able to help."

"I'll bet," he muttered.

"Consider me one of your operatives," she said. "I own a hairdressing shop in town—Whoop de Do."

"Do? As in hairdo?"

"That's right." Minnow pulled a business card from her back pocket and handed it to him. "Like I said ... when you're ready to take care of that shaggy stuff on your neck, give me a call."

"And like I said, I like it that way."

"Never let it be said that I failed to warn you your haircut is woefully out of date." She pointed a finger at him.

"All that aside, what this operation needs right now is a name and a plan."

Great, she was going to stay a while. Nick dropped into an overstuffed chair in the comer, pulled off his shoes, and stuck his feet up on the ottoman. "A plan for what?"

"Where you'll go each day, what you and Annie will do, code words for if there's been a breach in security—"

"Minnow. This is a no-brainer," he said, holding back a scowl. "I've already got the garden club ladies convinced. The rest of the town will follow suit. Believe me, this *operation* doesn't need a plan."

"Let's think about this," Annie said. "On the one hand, we'll be spending most of our time here at the house, so how many people will Nick actually see? On the other hand, we can't keep him captive here for nine days or people will begin to talk." She crossed the room, then turned back to face them. "Still, will a plan help us or complicate things unnecessarily? Life is not—"

"Annie! We don't need a plan. Don't overanalyze this." Nick couldn't keep the exasperation out of his voice.

"I think he's probably right, Minnow. Sorry."

Minnow looked from Annie to Nick and back again. "Get real, you two. Don't tell me you're just going to wing it for nine days."

They nodded, and she heaved a long-suffering sigh in response. "At least we should have a code word in case there's a security breach."

Silence stretched out between them for what seemed like minutes. The hell if he was going to agree to this ridiculousness.

And then Annie caved. She sat on the edge of the bed and cast a hopeful look at him, her blue eyes entreating. "I suppose a code word might be helpful in an emergency."

He snorted. "How about Deep Throat?"

"That's a code *name*—not a code word," Minnow said. "But now that you mention it maybe we should have code names, too. I could be ... Barracuda."

Oh, shit. "I think a code word will be plenty."

"Really? Okay." Minnow tapped a finger on the side of her head as she concentrated. "We just need to make sure it's a good code word. Like what? How about, ah ..." She sat up straight and threw her hands in the air. "Hold it! I've got it! We're worried about a breach in security. Babies can be in breech position. Annie is pregnant." She paused and looked into each of their faces as though the answer was obvious. "Our code word will be *baby!* It's perfect. If any of us says *baby* to one another, it means something's gone seriously wrong."

Nick mentally groaned. "And what happens if Annie mentions that the *baby* just kicked? Are we supposed to panic then?"

"Oh. Yeah." Minnow's grin collapsed. "We just need a modification. So, the code word will be ... let's see ... how about ... *oh baby. Oh baby!* How often would you use those two words together?"

Nick could think of a few times he'd used that combination, but decided he'd be smart to keep his mouth shut about it.

"*Oh baby*," Annie said. "It has a ring to it. Nick, what do you think?"

What he thought was that it was smarter to humor Minnow rather than prolong this conversation. "Fine."

Annie seemed relieved. "*Oh baby*, it is then."

"We should also have a rendezvous point," Minnow said. "How about if any of us uses the code word, we meet at the fountain?"

Nick restrained the urge to roll his eyes. "Sounds great."

"Do you know where the fountain is?" Minnow asked pointedly.

Caught. "No."

"It's in the city park. Do you know where the park is?"

"I'll show him tomorrow." Annie rubbed her eyes.

Nick stifled a huge yawn. "Ladies, I hate to break up this mission-planning session. I know it's not very late. But I've been driving for days, and I need to get some sleep."

Minnow scooted off the bed. "We should all get a good night's rest so we're sharp tomorrow. Oh! Phone numbers! We need to be able to get in touch."

She pulled out her phone. "Text me your number," she said as she rattled off her own number.

Nick dug his phone from his laptop case and did as she instructed. Two seconds later, Minnow's phone dinged to let her know a text had arrived.

She grinned at him. "Awesome! See you guys later. Don't forget—*oh baby!*" She strolled out the door humming the theme song to *Goldfinger*.

Nick turned to Annie ready to make a smart-ass comment, but she beat him to the punch.

"Don't say a word. I know she's a little eccentric. But she's about as true a friend as anyone could find. And at this moment in my life, I can use every friend I've got."

"I wasn't going to say anything," he lied. "Except that I really need to get some sleep."

Annie headed for the dresser. "I'll empty out a couple of drawers for you."

"Don't bother. I'll live out of my duffel. It's no different than how I live whenever I'm on assignment."

"You're sure?" At his nod, she gave him a lopsided smile. "Okay. Then I'm going back downstairs. I have to get some things ready for breakfast tomorrow, lock the back door, put out the dog—"

"Post a guard, patrol the perimeter ..."

A laugh bubbled out of her. "Bathroom's through that door, towels are in the closet. If you need a toothbrush or anything, let me know. I keep a supply of new toiletries for guests who forget something." She took a step toward the doorway and stopped. "I—are you sure—"

"Go. It'll be fine. I'll probably be asleep before you get back."

"Right. Okay, good night." She slipped out of the room.

He clicked off the switch on the standing lamp beside the chair and cast the room into hazy gray stillness. The only illumination came from the soft glow of the streetlamps filtering through the white lace curtains at the windows. A sense of peace washed over him, a remembered feeling from childhood, of sleeping overnight in the front bedroom of his grandparents' house. He closed his eyes and let his mind drift.

Minnow was making this more complicated than it needed to be. The poor woman must be so desperate for excitement she wanted to turn this charade into her own personal spy thriller. Still, she was Annie's friend. And she'd kept Annie's secrets. And that was no small favor.

He forced open his eyes and pushed himself out of the chair. What he wanted first, before climbing into bed, was a hot shower to wash away the dust of traveling. He pulled the shades, then peeled off his clothes and let them drop to the floor in the darkness.

6

———

ANNIE OPENED THE DOOR TO LET CHESTER OUTSIDE and spotted Minnow's car idling in the driveway. Music blared from the open window, while Minnow, illuminated by the dome light, tapped a message out on her phone. Annie hurried down the steps, eager to have a few minutes to talk without Nick around.

"Can you believe this is happening?" she asked.

Minnow looked up with a start. "No. But at least he's cute."

"Oh, yeah. He always was."

"You still like him?"

She shrugged and scrunched up her face. "No. Anyway, he's engaged."

"Liar. If I had a husband who looked like that, I'd be fighting him every step of the way to the lawyer. You ought to think about keeping him on."

Annie let out a burst of laughter. Minnow's words were exactly the warning she needed to keep a firm lock on her attraction to Nick. "Like I have anything to say about it. Get out of here."

Minnow threw her a knowing smile. "I'll talk to you tomorrow," she said as she put the car into reverse.

Annie watched her drive away, then dropped her head back and stared up into the endless black sky, only a few stars visible through the clouds that had blown in tonight. Her mind was a jumbled mess of conflicting thoughts about this grand deception she and Nick had put together. She hoped she wasn't making a big mistake. Still, what choice did she have? The only way she could hold on to the life she'd built in Bedford was if she and Nick played these roles to perfection.

Thank goodness, things were a bit slow—only two rooms rented tonight. She didn't think she could handle having a full house to deal with right now. As it was, with Luella around most of the time, this would be a tough charade to pull off. They'd have to be on stage almost every minute of the day.

As she walked toward the house, Chester ran out of the darkness to join her. She looked down at him disapprovingly. "Couldn't you have taken your time tonight? I'm not in a real hurry to go to bed. If you get my meaning."

The dog wagged his tail.

"Yeah, I know. Blah, blah, blah. Come on."

They went into the house together, and Annie locked the door; she wished it were as easy to lock away her attraction to Nick. The problem was, he was still so much the same as he'd been six years ago—still handsome in a rugged sort of way, still charming, still used to getting what he wanted, *still able to make her heart pound.*

At least now she knew better than to go there. When she married him, there'd been this part of her that had dreamed of a Cinderella story—that Nick would tell her he actually loved her, that he didn't want them to divorce. Sure, there was no denying she wanted the money he'd offered her to marry him.

But she would have married him even if there had been no money involved at all.

Because she'd been a dreamer then. A hopeless romantic. She shook her head, remembering. She'd followed a boyfriend out to the West Coast, certain he was *the one.* Within a month of her move, he'd dumped her for some beautiful aspiring actress. And there she'd been stuck. No money. No friends. And a crummy job as a waitress in an all-night diner.

Nick had been a two a.m. regular at the diner. On slow nights they would talk, and somewhere along the way he told her about the trust fund his grandmother had left him, how he couldn't get it until he turned thirty-five—or married —so all he had to do was find someone to marry him.

He had a quick, easy grin and a devil-may-care attitude, and when he asked if she would marry him in exchange for $250,000, she'd agreed, rationalizing it as a means of getting herself back on her feet. But once they'd actually wed, it had broken her heart to leave him. The thought of never seeing him again nearly did her in.

After leaving L. A., it had taken several years, a couple of other short-lived relationships, and a stint in therapy before she finally realized that while she was spending her time romanticizing, the men she was dating were walking all over her. She'd finally learned her lesson—never again would she throw her own life to the wayside because of some guy.

As long as she remembered that, she'd be fine this next week. Absolutely fine.

Problem was, she had to share a bed with the man.

Minnow would say this was an opportunity, not a problem.

Maybe. Maybe if the guy weren't already engaged. Maybe if Nick Fleming was the kind of guy she wanted. Maybe if she were the kind of woman Nick Fleming found attractive. She gave her head a shake. This train of thought was a complete waste of brain waves.

She sighed. The muffins were mixed and ready for baking in the morning, the table set. Luella had long since gone to bed. Annie moved around the dining room table, straightening a knife here, a fork there. She filled the salt and pepper shakers and checked the sugar bowl. She swept the floor and washed the windows in the cabinet doors. She made a list of chores for the next day and tried to stifle the yawns that just kept coming. There must be something else she had to get done. She yawned again. Ever since she got pregnant, she couldn't stay up late.

"Come on, Chester, either we gather our courage and go upstairs, or I collapse here and now." She flipped off the last light switch.

Slowly, she made her way to the third floor, gave her bedroom door a little push and peered inside. Darkness stretched across the room. Good. Nick was asleep. She grabbed her nightgown from the hook behind the door and tiptoed to the bathroom to change. Maybe this room-sharing arrangement wouldn't be so hard after all.

She tugged open the bathroom door. Light flooded out at her and she blinked a couple of times to adjust her eyes to the sudden brightness.

Nick.

In a towel.

A little towel.

Various, disjointed thoughts flooded her brain: what

great shoulders ... look at those arm muscles ... he must lift weights ... why isn't he in bed? ... perfectly flat abs ... stop staring at him, say something quick. Oh. My. God. Say. Something.

She opened her mouth but only a squeak came out. He probably thought she was insane.

"Thought I'd shower. Hope you don't mind."

"No—no absolutely not. I'll wait—" She took a couple of steps back and grasped the door to push it closed, but Chester bounded past her into the small room, leaping with joy as though he'd just discovered someone new in the house who needed to be welcomed. He jumped up at Nick, his nails catching on the terrycloth. The towel dropped.

Good God! She slammed the door shut, heart pounding at the sudden sight of Nick in all his Roman statuesque glory. She drew a breath and tried to still the racing of her pulse.

The door opened six inches and the dog slid out of the bathroom on the end of Nick's foot. Chester barked at her and wagged his tail excitedly.

"Oh, be quiet. Sometimes you're more trouble than you're worth," she muttered.

A minute later the door opened again and Nick stepped into the room wearing running shorts and a T-shirt. Annie let out a quiet sigh of relief. One part of her brain had been afraid he might sleep in the buff.

Avoiding his eyes, she slipped past him into the bathroom and took her time getting ready for bed. When she was certain he had to be asleep, she took several quick steps across the room, slid under the covers, and tried to forget that a mere one foot away, a man was sleeping in her bed.

Not just any man—*Nick Fleming.*

Her heart thumped. So much for being exhausted. At this rate it might be hours before she fell asleep. She could hear Nick's breathing, slow and deep. Well, at least one of them would wake refreshed tomorrow.

Chester leapt onto the bed and climbed over her to find the perfect spot. She could feel him go through his nightly routine, digging at the bed with his front paws, then turning several circles before finally settling down with a big exhale. For Chester, all was certainly right with the world.

If only her own life were so simple.

She closed her eyes, turned onto her side, and hugged the edge of the bed. One day done. This really wasn't so bad. Tomorrow morning they'd get up, rejuvenated, and work out a plan for the day. Before they even knew it, another day would be past, and then another and another, until finally it would be time for Nick to leave Bedford. And time for her to go back to life as she knew it.

She closed her eyes and let the sound of Nick's rhythmic breathing lull her toward sleep. *One day down, only eight to go,* her mind whispered as she slid into unconsciousness.

———

Wild piano music jarred her awake. Heart pounding, Annie pushed up on her elbows just as Nick shot from the bed and fumbled through his computer bag in the dark until he found his phone and swiped across the screen.

"Hello?" he murmured in a voice heavy with sleep. "Hi, sweetheart." He yawned and rubbed his eyes. "I went to bed early. What time is it?"

Without thinking, Annie glanced at the clock and said, "One o'clock."

Nick slashed the air with his free hand, warning her to be quiet.

"Sorry," she whispered.

He climbed back into bed and shoved a couple of pillows behind his back so he could sit up against the headboard. "It's not a big deal, really," he said into the phone. "Just a story about all the things there are to do in Wisconsin. I figured as long as I was already out here—"

He paused.

"Yeah, I miss you, too, but I'll be home before you know it," he said. "When you're back from Paris, we'll go away for a couple of days— What? No. I'm really beat—it's two hours later here— No Missy, I don't want to talk to anybody else— Melissa, hey— Oh, hi, Chelsea. Yeah, good to talk with you, too. Having fun?"

There was a long break, as though Chelsea was filling him in on every detail. Annie grimaced.

"Sounds great. Really. Hey, give me back to Melissa, will you?" After a pause, Nick said, "Hey, Miss— Oh, Bill, thought you were Melissa. Give her the phone, will you?"

Annie grinned at the growing exasperation in his voice. "Missy, I'll talk to you later, I'm really tired. I was already asleep— Of course not. No, I'm not mad at you. Talk to you tomorrow. I love you, too."

He ended the call and dropped back into the pillows. "Sorry. She's at a party."

"It's okay." Annie rolled onto her side and closed her eyes.

"She misses me."

"Umm." She was nearly asleep when Nick's voice dragged her back to consciousness again.

"She's pretty young."

"Sounds pretty ditzy, too," Annie muttered under her breath.

"What?"

"Nothing." She turned to look at him, just a shadow in the dark room. He seemed restless suddenly. "Is everything okay?"

He didn't answer for a long time. "Remember when I'd come into the coffee shop and we'd talk about all the things we were going to do with our lives?"

"Uh-huh."

"I don't remember ever—did I ever—do you remember ..."

"Spit it out."

"Was I going to get married?"

She laughed, and her heart warmed. "Only to me. What's the matter? You getting cold feet?"

He shrugged. "Sometimes it doesn't feel exactly like I thought it would. This being engaged—getting married—thing."

"Can't help you out there. I only did it once and that was fake." *Even though she wished it hadn't been.* "Nick, as long as you love her, it's going to be okay."

"Yeah. And I do. Love her. Whatever love is." He drew in a long breath and exhaled. "Well, good night."

"Good night." She wanted to reach out and run her hand over his hair, down his cheek. Wanted to somehow make him feel that it would be all right. This was the Nick she remembered. The one who was trying to find his place in the world, trying to figure out who he was. Despite all the places he'd been, all the adventures he'd had, he was still searching.

Her heart twisted in empathy, and she mentally recoiled from the feeling. She couldn't care for him—not again. He was here for nine days and after that he would be gone, off to marry the woman he'd chosen.

Her thoughts settled, her pulse calmed. But it was a long time before she finally fell asleep.

———

"Dammit!"

Annie's eyes flew open just as she heard the thud of Chester's feet hitting the floor. She could see Nick sitting up in the darkness.

She tried to force her sleep-muddled mind to waken, her eyes to focus on the bedside clock. The red numbers glowed three-thirty. God help her if Nick was one of those light sleepers who woke all night long.

No, God help him.

"What's the matter?" she mumbled.

"Your dog was sleeping on my pillow."

"So?"

"Dog breath. Not exactly minty fresh. And he sure stretches out—we're like sardines in here with the three of us."

"He sleeps on that side every night. He probably thinks you're stealing *his* pillow." A big yawn escaped her.

"Get him a basket. He can sleep downstairs while I'm here."

Annie sat up. "He's supposed to be *your* dog. How will it look if the day you come home you oust him from the bedroom?"

"Like I'm taking my rightful place?"

"He's been sleeping on the bed since I got him. He won't understand if he's suddenly banished to the floor."

"We're only talking eight nights here. All I want is a

decent night's sleep. Problem is, your dog is gluing himself to me."

Annie swallowed a laugh. She knew how tenacious Chester could be.

"I push him away, and an hour later he's back, sleeping between my legs, across my chest, on my pillow. He needs his own bed."

Annie set her shoulders, prepared to give Nick a lecture about compromise. Then reality broke through. If Nick was miserable, he might decide not to stay the whole nine days. And if that happened, the jig was up. She'd have to deal with all sorts of questions about her marriage and why Nick was leaving after just a day or two at home. Her whole lie—her whole life—could collapse under the scrutiny.

Put that way, it seemed reasonable that Chester could sleep somewhere else for a few nights—it would be his sacrifice for the cause. "I'll get him a basket tomorrow," she said.

7

Nick dropped down onto the bottom stair and laced up his Nikes. A nice long run was just what he needed, a chance to clear his head and try to forget that he'd agreed to pull the wool over the eyes of everyone in town. Not to mention he now was a father-to-be. Sort of.

Annie had left the house before he'd even gotten up. "She's off running errands," Luella said. She'd frowned at him as she set a plate of strawberry-filled crepes in front of him at the table.

Then her frown had turned into a scowl and she'd sweetly but pointedly said, "Seems to me you two would want to be spending the morning together."

He'd gulped down his food and escaped the kitchen before she could press the issue.

Shoes laced, he leaned against the wall and began to stretch his calves in anticipation of the miles to come. After so many days in the car, he couldn't wait to get some exercise.

"Here's the leash."

He turned to find Luella holding out the dog's leash and

some plastic sandwich bags. Chester danced around her legs, biting and tugging at the end of the leash. "Annie said you wanted to take the dog running with you while you were home."

She did? He forced the comers of his lips to curve upward. "Yeah. I do."

He took the leash, one of those fancy types with a molded plastic handle and retractable cord, and snapped it to Chester's collar.

Luella shoved the bags at him. "For poop."

"Right. Thanks." He shoved the baggies into his pocket, stepped out into the sunny morning, and headed down the narrow road that wrapped around the lake. Chester ran alongside him, roaming out the full fifteen feet the leash allowed, stopping to investigate just about everything he spotted or smelled on the side of the road. A quick tug at the leash and the dog would race to catch up and bound past him.

Nick cast his gaze at the canopy of trees arching overhead and the thick woods that bordered the road. A cool breeze slid over his skin and he inhaled deeply, savoring the freshness and reveling in the deep scent of pine. He had to admit the smog in L.A. left something to be desired.

A sense of peace settled over him. Chester ran ahead, turning back every now and then, a wide canine grin on his face. "Don't get too used to it, mutt," he said. "I'm out of here in eight days. Then Annie can walk you."

His feet hit the blacktop in a steady rhythm, and he broke a faint sweat. He glanced at his watch. Perfect—on track for a six-minute mile. Now, if only Chester would mellow a bit. The dog was outpacing him, straining against the fully extended leash as if the effort would enable him to get even farther ahead. Nick gave the leash a slight tug and moved to shift it to his other hand. Suddenly, Chester began barking explosively and tore into the tall grass at the side of the road, ripping the leash from Nick's fingers and disappearing into the woods.

"Shit!" Nick said on a sharp exhale. "Chester!" he shouted. "Chester! Come!"

He listened for a moment, then shouted again. And again. When the dog didn't appear, he slapped a hand on his thigh in disgust and set off into the woods. "That's right, you'd better keep hiding. Because, mutt, your days are numbered."

That stupid dog probably ran home. Actually, with his luck Chester was deep in the woods with the handle of the leash caught in a bush. Was there some reason why Annie couldn't have a normal leash? The kind with a loop at the end for your hand so a dog couldn't pull it away from you and escape like this?

He shouted for Chester again and turned in a frustrated circle to scan the area. The dog could be a mile away by now. He began to trudge deeper into the woods, shoving branches out of the way, swearing as brambles in the underbrush scratched his legs. Swatting at the mosquitoes that were feasting on his sweaty skin, he let loose a string of curses.

After a few minutes, he reached the bottom of a steep esker. He started up the side, slipping once on the damp soil to land on his knees in mud. *And Annie wondered why he'd never wanted a dog?* If he couldn't spot the mutt once he reached the top, he was abandoning the search. Only a lunatic would expect to find a dog in the middle of a woods.

Reaching the top of the ridge, he looked down the other side, hoping beyond all rational thought that he would suddenly come upon Chester and be able to put an end to this little adventure. A river wound through the ravine below him, raced along its path through the unspoiled forest. The sight drove all anger from his mind.

"Damn, Annie," he said in awe. "Is this the *stream* you were talking about?"

His gaze swept the nearby area—pine trees, hardwoods, scrubby bushes, wild-flowers. He inhaled slowly and started down to the river for a better look. From the bushes behind him came the sound of frenzied rustling, and he scooped a thick stick off the ground as he pivoted to face whatever was coming after him. A staccato of barks preceded Chester shooting out of the underbrush like a cannonball.

Nick swore. He grabbed the leash and gripped the handle tightly. "Mutt. You're not getting away from me again." Chester dipped his head, and Nick took some satisfaction in the fact that Chester had the decency to look a little chagrined ... even though his tail was still wagging furiously.

Nick threw a last look at the river before turning to retrace his steps. He couldn't believe Annie owned this property. She was so worried about finances, and here she was sitting on a gold mine. Cross-country skiing, hiking, rafting, tubing ... all she had to do to fill her rooms was offer her guests a little adventure.

———

Annie hefted the wicker dog bed into her arms, pushed the door of the hardware store open with her hip, and headed down the sidewalk for home. She loved days like this— warm, sunny, dry. Made you appreciate being alive. Even if half your life *was* a big fat lie.

She shifted her hold on the basket as if to shift her thoughts, and focused her mind on the idea that Chester, her loyal companion for the past four years, was about to be relegated to the corner. She exhaled. Maybe he wouldn't mind.

Yeah, right.

She only hoped he didn't whine all night long. Then again, maybe that would be poetic justice—poor Nick still wouldn't be able to get a decent night's sleep. Eyes down, she kept her stride brisk so she looked purposeful, like she was on a mission with no time to chat. Avoidance was her key word today; she didn't want anyone to stop her and ask questions about Nick.

The smell of fresh-cooked bacon wafted through the air and she hurried past Tommy's Diner without looking up. Maybe tomorrow or the next day she'd feel differently, but right now she just didn't want to engage with anyone. She needed a little time to work into this whole charade, more space to—

"Annie!"

She jerked her head up and turned to see Carol, a middle-aged waitress from the diner chasing her down. Busted.

"You stop right there!" Carol called.

"You almost gave me a heart attack!"

"No way you're walking right past us and not stopping in."

She forced an apologetic smile and gave a shrug. "I'm in kind of a hurry."

Carol grabbed her by the arm and steered her back to the open door of the diner. "Honey, that handsome hunk of a husband can wait a few minutes longer. We've been dying to talk to you since we heard the news."

She took the dog bed from Annie and set it on a chair, then went back behind the counter.

Annie sighed. It was probably better to get this over with right in the beginning. Maybe then everyone would leave them alone for the rest of Nick's stay. She dropped onto a red vinyl padded stool at the counter and looked up into Carol's grinning face. Behind her, a balding head peered over the high pass through into the kitchen. Yeah, even the owner didn't want to miss out on the latest news in town.

"Hey, Tommy," she said. "You'll be able to hear better if you come out here."

Carol set a brown ceramic mug on the counter and filled it with decaf. "On the house. In celebration of Nick's first visit home."

"Thanks." Annie peeled open a creamer and poured it into her cup, swallowing a smile as Tommy nonchalantly wandered out of the kitchen.

Carol leaned her elbows on the counter and rested her chin in her hands. "Well? Talk, girlfriend. Tell us everything."

———

Nick rounded the corner on the highway at a moderate jog —and let out a curse. No town in sight. He'd left the country lane behind a while ago and, now, all he could see was acres of farm fields and the two-lane road he was running on. He usually had an incredible sense of direction —how could he have gotten lost?

He looked down at Chester, loping along beside him on the gravel shoulder. The dog looked back, tongue lolling out dripping saliva onto the warm ground. "I know just how you feel," Nick muttered.

He glanced at his watch; sweat dripped off his face onto his arm. His shirt, wringing wet, stuck to him. It had to be into the eighties by now. He wouldn't be surprised if steam was rising off his back. He squinted at the sky, flawless blue, perfectly clear, not even one cloud to provide some respite from the heat. The best he could tell, he'd probably gone eight or nine miles already, but it was hard to know for sure since he'd had that pleasant little dog-chasing break in the middle. He should have checked out the route online or driven it beforehand so he'd known where he was going.

Or maybe he shouldn't have headed north at that intersection way back. The road had gradually veered due west, forcing him to go in the wrong direction. Then he'd had no choice but to follow it until he came to a crossroad so he could work his way back to where he thought Bedford was.

Bedford. Since the moment he'd arrived here, nothing had gone according to plan. Not that plans were that important to him; he'd always flown by the seat of his pants. But the events of the last day had been so unexpected, even for him.

Annie had always been the planner, insecure, wanting to force her life into a starry-eyed mold, searching for a permanence she'd never had. Obviously, she'd found it here. And he was glad for her. She'd changed. Had a confidence he'd never seen in her in L.A. *A confidence that allowed her to fly by the seat of her pants and come up with a harebrained idea about pretending to be married.* Who would have ever thought Annie McCarthy—

His arm jerked backward from abrupt resistance on the

leash. He stopped and turned to find Chester stretched out on his belly on the gravel shoulder, exhausted.

Nick let out a groan. "Oh, no. Come on, Chester." He tugged at the leash. "It can't be far now."

The dog didn't even lift his head from between his front paws, just looked up with big brown eyes and wagged his tail back and forth very, very slowly. Nick gave another, more assertive pull on the leash. "Move it! Chester! Come!"

When the dog still didn't move, Nick felt the stirring of sympathy. He dropped down onto the road next to the dog and rubbed him between the ears. "Had enough, boy?"

His only answer was the thumping of Chester's tail.

"Yeah, I hear ya."

He sat there, forearms resting on his bent knees, waiting until he cooled down a little, until his breathing evened out. Then he picked up the dog and began to walk with him in his arms. "Don't read anything into this. I'm just carrying you a while," he said. "Because it's either that or sit here for an hour. We're still not friends."

Fifteen minutes later, the front of his shirt drenched with a new layer of sweat from carrying the dog, he reached the gas station where he'd asked directions yesterday. He set the dog on the ground. "Let's go, Chester, we're in the home stretch."

When they passed the *Welcome to Bedford* sign, he felt a grudging sense of satisfaction. Not too far to Annie's place now, just through the downtown, and then another half mile up the road. He began to salivate at the thought of a tall, cold glass of water.

Ahead, a sprinkler rotated across a front lawn, spraying out a steady sheet of water that glistened in the sun before falling to the earth in silver droplets. Nick stopped and looked at the dog. Chester perked up, tail whipping back and forth.

"You thinking what I'm thinking?" Nick glanced in either direction to make sure no one was around, then ran across the yard and into the spray, pulling the dog with him. The shock of ice-cold water on his overheated skin made him laugh out loud. Invigorated by the spray, Chester began jumping and barking and biting at the falling droplets. Nick laughed again as the coolness covered them both, soothing away the heat.

Eyes shut, he stuck his face close to the sprinkler head and let the water gently pummel his face while he opened his mouth to drink from the icy stream. He cupped his hands together and held them under the spray, then stepped away to let the dog lap up the water his hands had captured.

Chester shook himself from head to tail; droplets of water flew out in every direction. Nick pushed back his wet hair and shook his head in much the same manner. "My sentiments, exactly. Come on, dog. Let's go home."

Dripping, they headed down Main Street toward the road leading to Annie's bed-and-breakfast. Nick glanced at each building they passed, checking out the town that would be his home for the next week and then some.

Tavern on the corner.

Bakery. He drew in a long, slow breath. Was there anything as mouthwatering as the scent of fresh-baked bread?

Insurance agency. Antiques store. Beauty parlor— must be Minnow's place. He made a point of facing straight ahead as he passed, hoping she wouldn't notice him going by and rush out to tell him he needed a haircut.

Tavern. Laundromat. Two laughing kids ran out the door and he dodged left and then right to avoid them.

Coffee shop ... with a *Free Wi-fi* sign in the window. Three people were inside working on laptops. Amazing; Bedford had an Internet café. He looked at another sign in the window: shipping/printing/photocopies. Hell, what a good idea—a coffee shop that doubled as a virtual office. Maybe Bedford wasn't as behind the times as he'd thought.

He walked on. Hardware store. Tavern. Flower shop. *Diner.* High in the window, an old-fashioned root beer sign caught his attention and, suddenly, an ice cold mug of frosty root beer was all he could think of. He stared through the window into the diner and considered asking whether they'd let him ran a tab.

8

RELIEF ROLLED THROUGH ANNIE, AND SHE SMILED AT the diner staff. She'd gotten through her whole story about Nick and no one questioned a thing.

"That's really about it," she said, swiveling back and forth on her stool, suddenly confident beyond words. "Nick's got eight days to spend in Bedford before he has to report back to Secret Ops."

As she spun to the left, she caught sight of a strange man staring in the front window—looked like an escapee from an institution—his hair slicked back and sticking out in places, his clothing dripping wet and clinging. Beside him, a wet, scraggly dog had its paws up on the window sill, and his tongue was hanging out, dripping saliva onto the glass. She stared back, all words trapped in her throat.

He smiled at her.

No, it couldn't be ... She closed her eyes, counted to five, and opened them again.

He waved. *He wouldn't dare come in—*

She watched as he tied Chester to a sign pole, pulled

open the door, and sauntered over to her. "Fancy meeting you here," he said.

"Fancy." Her heart went crazy, alternately pounding in horror and leaping in ardor. "Carol, Tom, this is ... my husband ... Nick."

Nick tried to wipe off his wet hand on his wet shirt, then reached out to shake hands all around. "Sorry. I was out for a run and ended up cooling off in someone's sprinkler."

Annie gave a weak smile, completely at a loss for words. Her *husband* looked like a lunatic—and admitting he was running through someone's sprinkle just reinforced the image. At least he didn't stink.

Nick leaned over to kiss the top of her head. "Boy, am I glad you're here, honey. I was dying for a root beer. And *my dog*," he said as he hitched his thumb toward the outside, "could use a bowl of water."

"You came to the right place," Carol said, clearly unable to control her smile.

Please. The woman was almost giddy.

Tommy's head nodded up and down like a Bobblehead statue, and Annie had the sudden urge to run screaming from the diner and ram a *For Sale* sign in the front lawn of her house.

"Glad to meet you," Tommy said. "Root beer's on the house. Are you hungry?"

Annie shook her head. There was no way she was going to let Nick be in this diner any longer than she had to. God only knew what people might ask him, *what he might say.* Anyway, it wasn't even eleven-thirty yet. "No, thanks, we're having lunch at—"

Nick dropped onto the stool next to her. "Famished,

actually. How about a burger and fries with the works? Fried onions—not raw. Onion rings."

"You got it." Tommy headed back to the kitchen. "Annie, anything for you?"

She wobbled her head and forced her voice to remain light. "I guess I am a little hungry after all. Pregnancy does that to you. I'll have the same."

She leaned toward Nick and whispered between clenched teeth, "Stay quiet and let me handle any questions."

Carol set a glass of foam-topped root beer in front of Nick and plopped a fat red straw into its center. After handing Annie a bowl of water for the dog, she focused her full attention on Nick.

"I swear there were times I started to wonder if Annie had made you up," she said. "The way this girl talked about you, I thought no way there's one package with all those ay-tributes—an exciting job, handsome, muscles, brains, and—

Annie's heart stilled. She waved a hand in the air in a desperate attempt to cut Carol off. "I'll take one of those root beers, too!"

"Hot-blooded to boot," Carol finished.

Annie could feel her face burning. Though she refused to face Nick, she could tell he had swiveled his stool so he could look directly at her.

"I'll give the dog his water." She jumped to her feet.

Carol just kept talking. "But now that I got a good look at you, she weren't exaggeratin' none. *I* could go for a little *hot-blooded."* The woman leaned her elbows on the counter so she was eye-to-eye with Nick. "You got any older brothers?" she asked in a conspiratorial tone.

A laugh burst out of Nick. "Nope."

"Shoot." Carol straightened. "If Annie ever throws you

over, I get first dibs. Another root beer coming up." She sashayed down to the other end of the counter and tossed a grin over her shoulder at Nick.

Annie fled outside with the bowl of water and waited for Chester to drink his fill. What could Carol be thinking, saying this stuff to Nick? The man was going to think Annie spent all her time talking about him. Okay, so maybe she had when she first moved here, but it had been a long time since she'd been so forthcoming with information about her mysterious husband.

Maybe she should just escape this madhouse and go home, not even go back into the diner.

She huffed out a breath. If she left Nick unattended, there was no telling what kind of troublesome conversations he could get into. He could blow their whole operation. She glanced into the window and watched him chatting away with Carol. Oh my God, what was she thinking? He could blow their whole operation *while she was out here on the sidewalk.*

Snatching up the bowl, she forced down her rising panic, put a pleasant expression on her face, and went inside. She slid onto the stool beside Nick, determined to regain control of the situation.

"Nick, maybe we should—" she began, but then he put his arm around her and pulled her close. Beneath his damp shirt she could feel the hard muscles of his chest—what were those called? Pectorals—yeah, pecs— His lips touched her ear and a jolt raced through her.

At this rate, she'd be lucky to control her drooling, let alone the situation.

"Hot-blooded?" he murmured. His warm breath tickled the side of her neck, and her stomach flopped.

"So I got a little carried away." She could hear the

defensiveness in her voice and forced herself to lighten up. "After all, you didn't really exist. If I had to create a husband, I figured he might as well be perfect."

"Are you implying I'm not already perfect?"

Hardly.

Carol arrived with their food, and Annie realized she had never been so happy to see a burger in her life. At least they'd have something else to talk about.

"Enjoy, folks." Carol lay the check next to Annie's plate and went off to wait on a group of teenagers at a nearby table.

As the clock ticked closer to noon, the number of customers coming into the diner became a steady stream. Time and again, Annie introduced Nick. And time and again, the response was the same—they'd heard he was in town, and how was the military, and would he be staying long, and, congratulations about the baby, and didn't he want to quit his job and settle down here for good?

The only thing that saved them from people asking even nosier questions was that she and Nick were in the middle of eating. Which no doubt meant the grillings would come in a day or two.

Maybe she shouldn't have insisted he stay nine days. Maybe he would have to become an introvert and stay at home the rest of the time. She sighed. That would be like trying to push the genie back into the bottle.

She wondered what Minnow, the resident espionage expert, would have to say about how visible Nick had suddenly become. It couldn't possibly be a good development for their covert operation.

As if on cue, the door opened again and Minnow breezed inside, dressed all in black, and grinning from ear to ear. She slid onto the stool next to Annie.

"Hey, Annie. How's married life treating you? Hey, Nick. Saw you slink by the shop earlier. Thought you might be stopping in to get that stuff trimmed on your neck."

He threw her a wan smile, tossed his napkin on the counter, and stood. "Sorry we can't stay to chat, Minnow, but we were just leaving." He motioned with his head to Annie and started for the door without waiting for a reply.

"Yessir." She restrained the urge to give a crisp salute. Pulling a few bills from her wallet, she threw them on the counter and pushed herself off her stool.

Minnow took hold of her arm. "Have you shown him the rendezvous spot? The fountain?" she whispered.

"No, but I will. Call you later." Annie grabbed the dog basket and went outside to catch up with Nick where he was untying Chester's leash from the parking meter.

"You didn't have to be so obvious."

He looked up, all innocence, his fingers working the knot in the leash.

"I can tell you don't like Minnow and she probably knows it, too."

At the flash of irritation on his face, she walked away quickly so he couldn't answer without shouting. He and Chester were beside her in seconds.

"Doesn't the woman have any boundaries?" he asked. "She's obsessed with my hair."

Annie looked at the dark, thick hair curling at the back of his neck, just begging for someone's fingers to play in it. No, not just someone's fingers—hers. *Yeah, well, Minnow wasn't the only one obsessed with his hair.*

"Annie?"

She jerked her eyes to his face as heat rose up her cheeks for the second time in half an hour. "Uh, Minnow is kind of a free spirit. She can't help the way she is. Her parents were into peace and love and telling it like it is. That laid-back stuff."

"It's all coming together for me now."

"So, go easy on her. She means well."

Nick's noncommittal grunt made Annie a little apprehensive about mentioning the rendezvous spot. She wasn't in the mood to have Nick go off about Minnow's obsession with all things related to espionage. One part of her agreed that the idea of having a rendezvous spot seemed ridiculous, but her other side figured, better safe than sorry.

After hesitating another minute, she took a breath and dove in. "Hey, before we go home, I need to show you the fountain ... remember? In the park."

"Really?"

"I know it seems silly but, just in case, let's make sure our bases are covered. Humor me. Please?"

He handed her the leash. "Lead on. You take the mutt, I'll carry the basket."

"It's pretty easy to find." She led him down a side street and into a large, central park. "Sidewalks from the four corners of the park each lead to the center. Find a sidewalk and you'll find the way to the fountain."

A few minutes later they were standing in front of a hulking, circular sculpture with water shooting out of several openings and cascading down a multitude of uneven faces.

Nick stared, an expression of incredulous disbelief stamped on his face. He walked all the way around the fountain without saying a word. "Chester, maybe *we* should get into the fountain-designing business. We couldn't do any worse than this."

The smile that had been tugging at Annie's lips burst

into a full grin, and she laughed. "I thought the same thing the first time I saw this ... work of art."

"What is it? Don't tell me they paid someone to make this."

"Second question first. It was designed and donated by Minnow's parents—"

"Why doesn't that surprise me?"

"—after they moved here from New York, because they wanted to get back to nature. It's an abstract stone sculpture."

He looked at the fountain through narrowed eyes. "Abstract I get, but come on, this abstract stuff always symbolizes something—so what is it? You know, a mother and child ... or the world at war, or ..." His voice trailed off as he walked around to the other side, stopping every few steps to look at the monstrosity from a new angle.

"I really don't think it's anything but a bunch of shapes," Annie said. "You know, that ultra-modern look."

Nick set the basket on the ground and crouched down to tie his shoe. He glanced up at the fountain. "Maybe," he said, not sounding like he believed it.

"And, maybe not." He straightened slowly, never taking his eyes off the piece. He started to chuckle. "Annie, don't tell me you don't know what this sculpture is."

"What?" She moved to stand beside him.

"Come here." He threw an arm around her shoulders and pulled her up against him.

Twice in one day, body to body with Nick. She prayed her knees didn't give out.

"Do you see it?"

"See what?" Her eyes were unable to focus with him this close to her.

"Bend over a little. Now tilt your head—to the left." He

put a hand on her head and gently forced her to bend farther. "It's not real obvious. Just let yourself feel it."

Oh, she could feel it, all right. From the tips of her toes to the top of her head. *Lust.* "Give me a hint."

"Okay, it's a couple."

"A couple of what?"

He exhaled in exasperation.

"Ohh. You mean, like a man and woman." She frowned in concentration. "I don't see it."

"They're, ah ... kissing."

"What? You're crazy. Show me again!"

He pulled her directly in front of him and reached over her shoulders to put a hand on each side of her face and turn her head. The touch of his fingers almost sent her stomach into spasms. *And she thought it was hard to concentrate before.*

He pointed. "See how he's bent over her—"

"No."

"How his hand is behind her head—"

"No."

"Come on. Look, she's got one hand around the back of his neck, her other hand is on his shoulder ..."

Her forehead furrowed as she tried to concentrate on something other than Nick. She pointed. "Is that her leg?"

He snorted out a laugh. "No, that's nothing—just an abstract shape." He moved her head down and to the left, then rested his hands on her shoulders.

Weak. She was getting weak with all this nearness. Nick was going to have to carry her home.

And then, suddenly, she saw them, the couple, *nude,* arms around each other, engaged in a kiss—and moment—of unmistakable passion.

She gasped. "Oh my God. I see it. You're right. They're

— Oh. My. God. They're ... kissing, all right. I almost feel like a Peeping Tom." She twisted round to look Nick in the face.

His eyes met hers and something flared there. *Heat.* He was going to kiss her. Her heart began to hammer. And she was going to let him.

Her dream was about to come true.

"Hey Annie," he said softly. "I've got something to tell you."

He'd never forgotten her, either? "Yes?" She moistened her lips and raised her chin a bit in anticipation.

"When I was out running this morning ..." He took a step back and picked up the wicker dog basket.

Huh? The thudding of her heart skidded to a stop.

"The dog ran off and I had to chase him into the woods. How much of that land is yours?"

"What?"

"The land in there is incredible. I wouldn't doubt if there are eagles nesting."

"Yeah—"

"There's a river—is that your property?"

She nodded. "I told you there was a river." *What the hell happened to the kiss?*

"You called it a stream. That's a *river*. Forget selling to the developer. Put in some landings and you can offer tubing, rafting, canoeing. Cut some trails through that forest for hiking and in the winter use them for cross-country skiing. That's how you can bring more bookings into the B & B."

She felt as if she'd just *fallen* into the river. *Nick the dreamer.* She remembered this guy from six years ago. "Yeah. I'll do that in my spare time." *With a baby on my hip.*

"Annie, think of how this would help your business."

She let out a sharp breath. "Nick. Everything I'd make, I'd have to spend to keep the trails groomed and the rafting going. Close, but no cigar."

He hadn't changed a bit. Lots of big ideas, most of them not grounded in reality. "Let's go home. I've got to change for a museum-board meeting this afternoon."

She didn't want him to kiss her, anyway.

"Okay, but I'm telling you. The answer to all your problems lies in the woods next door."

9

ANNIE RESTED HER CHIN IN HER HAND AND STUDIED the spreadsheet detailing the amount of funding that would be needed to run the museum once they opened the doors. They hadn't yet hit their fundraising goal, but then again, they hadn't yet heard back from some of the foundations to which they had applied for grants.

At the head of the long oval conference table, Vivian was droning on about the need to set yearly fundraising goals in order to ensure the museum stayed viable. The other members of the committee were bobbing their heads in agreement. Annie nodded along, her thoughts leaping from the museum's financial situation to her own.

Too bad she couldn't do some fundraising of her own in order to keep the B & B viable. Nick might think her answer lay in the woods, but his ideas weren't exactly the kind of thing a single woman with no experience in outdoor adventures took on alone. Especially one with a baby on the way. No matter which way she looked at his solution, she kept coming to the same conclusion—the only thing his idea would bring her was more headaches.

She rubbed her forehead with the palm of her hand. Her life had been going along just fine until Nick showed up. Well, okay, so she'd hit a little rough water here and there, and financially it wouldn't hurt to get a few more bookings every week, but by and large, she was doing pretty well.

Who did he think he was, anyway, coming up with ideas for her business when she hadn't even asked him for help? She didn't need Nick to save her. She'd been running her own life for so long now, she didn't need a man to validate what she was doing or to come up with more work for her to do as he was walking out the door and—

"Annie? Is that all right with you?"

She started and looked up to see the other eight members of the board staring at her.

"Ah ... could you repeat that, please? I drifted off a moment there. Late night. Sorry."

Vivian smiled knowingly. "No need to apologize. We all understand your mind might be on other things now that Nick is home."

Annie forced a smile.

Vivian continued, "We were thinking that since you helped write the original grant proposals, you might follow up with the foundations about their possible donations. It has been quite a long time since we filed the paperwork. Maybe they need a little reminder that we haven't heard *anything* from them yet."

Ohhh, she hated doing that kind of stuff. It felt too much like begging. "Sure, I'd be happy to."

"Perfect. All right, then, we have seven days until the grand opening and plenty left to do. You all know your assignments. Let's get to it. We are adjourned." Vivian tapped her pencil on the conference table as if it were a gavel.

Annie pushed back her chair just as Nick stuck his head through the conference-room doorway. She mentally groaned. Couldn't the man stay home? The more he showed up around town, the more likely he would be cornered by nosy community members intent on interrogation.

Vivian put on her *welcome to my parlor, said the spider to the fly* smile. "Nick! What a surprise. How nice to see you again."

Annie jumped to her feet, hoping to hustle him out of the building before Vivian could ask any questions. "Honey, hi!" she said. "We're just breaking up here."

Before she could begin to move him back out the door, others in the room stepped forward to introduce themselves and engage him in that oh-so-familiar small talk about the military, his marriage, the upcoming baby, and how long would he be staying in town?

"I've heard so much about the new museum, thought I might be able to get a preview tour." Nick flashed her a smile, and she refused to let herself be affected by the warmth in his expression.

"Oh, I don't really have time right now," she said. "How about another—"

"I'll show him around." Bill Baken, one of the town old-timers, reached out to shake Nick's hand.

She was half-tempted to kick Bill in the shin.

"Once the museum opens, I'll be one of the volunteer guides," Bill was saying. "Might as well get some practice."

The two set off down the hallway that led to the museum. Annie watched them for a long moment, then charged after them in frustration. Someone had to make sure Nick kept his story straight. And someone had to know when to interrupt long-winded Bill or the tour could take all afternoon.

She reached the men just as they halted in front of a wall of photographs. Century-old black-and-white photos of Bedford juxtaposed with modern-day color shots of the same locations. It was a stunning contrast between then and now, and everyone associated with the museum expected the display to be a hit with visitors.

Annie waved a hand. "Bill, I can take over—you don't have to stay. I actually have a little more time than I thought."

"I don't mind. It's good practice." Bill launched into a story about the founding fathers and how Bedford began as a farming community. He sailed from that into a description of the stagecoach routes that went through the town. From there he rolled into a telling of how Bedford became a summer destination of Chicagoans who arrived by rail to vacation at resorts on the lake.

As Bill's presentation went on and on, Nick shoved his hands into the pockets of his shorts and turned his head slightly to raise an eyebrow at Annie. She swallowed a grin. Time for a well-placed interruption—just as soon as Bill came up for air.

He pointed to the thick forests on an old aerial map and dove into a history of logging in the area.

Nick straightened and pulled a hand from his pocket to trace a logging road on the map. "Are these roads still there?"

"Yup. Some are pretty grown over by now. But—"

"Where's Annie's—our—house?"

Bill searched a moment, then pointed a finger.

Nick nodded, a thoughtful expression on his face. "So

these are the woods ... and there's the river. Look at this." He grabbed Annie by the arm and pulled her closer to the map. "We've got a logging road on our property, honey."

"You planning to cut down some trees?"

He laughed and threw an arm around her shoulder, pulling her close enough to kiss her temple. She let herself sink against him, then drew a shaky breath. This would be way too easy to get used to.

"No. But I am planning to do some canoeing and tubing. And I need to be able to get the boats in."

"Bet you could do some fine cross-country skiing in that woods," Bill said.

Annie turned to stare at him. She shifted her gaze to Nick and then back to Bill again. "Have you two met before?"

Bill pointed at a section of the map. "Look at the topography. The glaciers left the whole area full of ridges and valleys. I bet you could have a ball skiing in those woods."

Annie opened and closed her mouth several times before finally getting anything out. "You ski?"

"My grandkids do. Out in the fields behind our house. Always pushing me to try it."

Nick nodded. "You know, I had the same idea. I was thinking you could chop some trails through the woods. Hike in summer, ski in winter. Bring people into the B & B. What do you think?"

Annie frowned. "It's a lot of work."

Neither man so much as glanced her way. *What? Had she gone invisible?*

Bill traced a finger along a ridge and tapped a couple of times at one spot. "You could go into the woods right here, follow along the river for a ways, then go up this esker. It'd be awful pretty. Yeah, probably draw folks all year round if they got something like that to do right on site."

"That's just what I was telling Annie."

What was it with these guys? It was *her* property— not theirs. Nick was her nine-day husband and he was acting as if he would be around for the next ninety years. Who cared if Bill thought it was a great idea? Who cared if the whole town thought it was a great idea? In the end, she'd have to be the one to make it go. And the truth was, it was more than she cared to tackle. Nick didn't seem to have a clue about how different her life would be six months from now, once the baby was born.

His lack of appreciation for her situation was just another of Nick's flaws ... one her brain would no doubt do its best to overlook in the coming days. It was a really good thing that Nick was marrying someone else. "Excuse me, boys, think we can speed up this nickel tour?" she asked, aware of an edge in her voice. "I've got some phone calls to make this afternoon."

"Okay, okay." Bill turned away from the map and proceeded to lead them through the museum. Forty-five minutes later they finally stepped outside. Bill put a hand on Nick's shoulder. "Listen, if you want some help cutting trails, I'd be happy to give you a hand. Being retired, I've got time to spare. Could probably get some other fellas to help out, too. Map it out and we'll get it done."

A look akin to awe crossed Nick's face. "You sure? Wow, that'd be great."

"We help each other out around here."

Annie cleared her throat and sent a warning message to Nick with her eyes: *Nice dream—not gonna happen.*

He frowned. "Annie and I have to talk this over some more," he said. 'Tell you what, though, stop over sometime and I'll show you the property. You're not going to believe it."

Bill chuckled. "I grew up here. I'll believe it."

The two men shook hands, and a feeling of melancholy washed through Annie. Once she heard Bill echo Nick's enthusiasm for outdoor adventures on her property, she grudgingly admitted to herself that Nick was probably right —it would be a great idea. But she was a single woman running a bed-and-breakfast. She couldn't do everything associated with running the inn—and also maintain trails and run canoeing and skiing expeditions. No way, no how.

She and Nick walked in silence almost all the way home. Finally, Nick said, "You know, I'm not trying to force you into something you don't want to do."

"You're not?"

"How could I? I'm not even going to be around. I just get carried away at the potential."

Yeah, and I get carried away just looking at you.

"It's just, Annie—"

Oh, no, here it came again.

"You've got the best piece of property around here. Right on the edge of town. Wilderness out your back door, civilization out your front—"

"Nick, I appreciate your interest in trying to help my business, I really do. But it just isn't feasible for a single woman ... *especially a single woman with a baby on the way.*"

If that didn't drill it home for the guy, nothing would. He turned to look at her, his eyes boring into hers for a moment before he looked away. He shoved a hand through his hair and nodded, clearly not pleased with the direction of their conversation. "Okay, yeah. I get it," he finally said.

———

Hours later, with dinner long over and the sky beginning to darken over a perfect summer day, Nick stood in the doorway leading to the broad back porch and took in the scene before him. Annie was kicked back in the porch swing spooning a hot fudge sundae into her mouth, bare feet and legs swinging beneath her like a kid. Luella sat in a nearby rocking chair, her attention focused on her own bowl of unadorned vanilla ice cream. The sweet scent of roses wafted up from the bushes surrounding the porch.

He marveled at the tranquility, so opposite to the life he and Melissa led in Los Angeles. If he was there, they'd have only just begun to make plans for dinner—or rather, choose which restaurant to go to. They sure wouldn't be having dessert, barefoot, on a porch in the falling darkness.

His mind wandered over the extremes of his lifestyle. Most of his adventure trips involved roughing it in the wild —often for months at a time. He'd stayed away from L.A. for years, moving from one assignment to another. The life had suited him well—the only certain thing about it was the uncertainty. It kept him on his toes, fed his adventurous soul, left him wanting for nothing.

Everything had been great until he'd come back to the States for a friend's wedding and gotten the nagging sense that something was missing in his life. Maybe it was because of his age; turning thirty kind of moved you into a new stage. Maybe it was knowing that this was the year he would have inherited his trust fund if Annie hadn't helped him out six years ago. Maybe it was his mother's death last year.

Whatever the reason, he'd gone back to L.A. looking for stability and a home base. And he'd found Melissa. And slid right back into the nonstop lifestyle he'd tried to leave behind.

Interesting. He'd never thought of it that way before.

Annie looked up at him, her shining face radiating peacefulness. There had always been something so appealing about her, even when she'd been a down-on-her-luck waitress. Something ...

He pushed through the door went out to join her on the porch swing.

10

———

"How's the scream?" he asked, playfully pushing a shoulder against Annie's.

"Mmm. You sure you don't want some?" She grinned at him.

He shook his head. "I couldn't eat another bite. Luella, I think that was the best roast beef I've ever had."

The old woman smiled.

"*Everybody* loves Luella's cooking," Annie said around a mouthful of ice cream.

"Then I'd better be careful not to overeat. Don't want to go back to the military overweight—won't be able to fit in my uniforms."

Luella scraped the last bit from her bowl. "Sure has been nice to have you around. I wish you could stay longer."

"Yeah, I know. But I've got a commitment ..."

Luella put a hand on the armrest of the rocker and pushed herself to her feet. "I'm going to head on home. Leave you young people alone. See you in the morning, bright and early."

When she was gone, Nick turned to Annie. "She's not moving real fast tonight."

"Arthritis. Some days it's worse than others."

"And she still keeps working here?"

"Says she likes it. And, I think she feels sorry for me because my husband is gone so much of the time."

"Oh, great. And I'm leaving in a week."

"She'll get over it." Annie smiled.

"Yeah, only I'm divorcing you after I get back to the military. Then she's really going to hate me."

A gentle laugh slid from Annie. "At least you won't be here to face her wrath."

"That's comforting." His stomach gave a wrench. He didn't want Luella not to like him.

He pushed his feet hard against the porch floor and sent them swinging. The gentle coolness of the night air brushed over his bare arms and filled him with a wistfulness that seemed to exacerbate the gnawing sense that his life was missing something. Impulsively he put an arm around Annie's shoulders.

Annie tensed and slanted a sideways look at him.

He grinned. "Don't panic—it's just me."

After a moment of what appeared to be serious consideration, she relaxed and settled into the crook of his arm.

"Tell me about the places you've been," she said. "What you've been doing the last six years."

He hesitated; for the first time since he'd become an adventure writer he didn't feel like telling his stories. Somehow it didn't feel right to spell out to her all the excitement he'd experienced, all the places he'd been—as though he was pointing out how dull this place was in contrast. Somehow, all the things he'd done didn't feel all that impressive anymore.

As the silence stretched, Annie looked up at him, bemused. He shrugged carelessly and proceeded to give her an abbreviated version of the past six years, a quick listing of locations and adventures, starting with that first trip to Nepal and finishing with the cross-country road trip that led him to her.

She twisted beneath his arm and ran a finger along a small scar on his left cheek. "And how did you get this?"

"Denali in Alaska. The highest mountain peak in North America. Stupid of me. A misstep that could have cost me my life. Instead I got this warning, a permanent reminder to be more cautious when I'm challenging nature." He rubbed her shoulder. "You get any scars since we last saw each other?"

She chuckled. "Only on my heart."

"Love still hasn't been kind, huh? I thought you learned your lesson with that idiot you followed to L.A. Maybe I should beat some sense into those jerks for not knowing a good thing when they have it."

"Yeah, well, it's probably good none of them stuck around. I seem to have the perfect ability to choose the wrong type of guys."

"As in?"

"You know, the ones who aren't going to stick around for the long haul. The *you're a great girl, but* ... kind of guys. Problem is, when you're in the middle of infatuation you think, *Oh, this is the guy, he'll be here through thick and thin, through rich and poor, through labor and delivery.*" She laughed. "Haven't found him yet."

Nick wondered whether or not she would consider him the wrong type. Sitting like this, with her in his arms, he sure didn't feel like the wrong type. Then again, he *was* engaged to another woman, so that probably made him the wrong type in spades. The thought didn't sit well.

They rocked back and forth in the swing, quiet in the still night air, and he searched for something to say, some other subject that wouldn't be a painful reminder to Annie that she'd failed at love. Hell, even with marriage to Melissa in his future, sometimes he wasn't so sure he'd succeeded at it himself.

Chester trotted up the steps and dropped a yellow tennis ball at their feet.

Perfect. They could talk about the dog. The mutt clearly adored Annie.

"Doesn't he ever get tired?" Nick scooped the ball off the porch floor and tossed it into the yard. "We must have run ten miles this morning and now he's back for more."

Chester took off after the ball at warp speed.

"One nap and he's as good as new."

"That's what I was afraid of."

He stood and watched the dog retrieve the ball, then turn and tear through the yard and up the steps to bring it back. Nick took the ball from Chester's mouth and fired it into the yard again. With a bark of joy, Chester flew down the steps in hot pursuit.

"Careful, he's going to take a liking to you."

Nick dropped down onto the porch swing. "Enough of that," he said. "This morning's run wore me out."

Seconds later, Chester dropped the ball at Nick's feet and danced excitedly, waiting for the next round of fetch.

Nick let out a groan of exaggerated agony. "I'm done, dog."

Chester barked at him.

Annie laughed. "I warned you. You're trapped now."

The dog jumped up to put his front paws on Nick's knees. He barked again.

"Okay, you're asking for it." Nick picked up the ball and let it fly as hard as he could. A splashing sound told them it had landed in the lake. "Well, that should take care of that," he said.

As Chester raced off to find it, Annie let out a groan. "Bad move."

"Why?"

In the moonlight he could see Chester come to a skidding halt on the beach, right at the water's edge.

"He won't go into the water," Annie said.

"Great. The game's over."

"Not hardly."

As if backing up her reply, Chester began to bark at the ball floating in the lake. And bark. And bark. And bark.

"How long will he keep this up?"

"Until someone gets the ball." Annie stood.

Nick let out a sharp exhale. "I threw it, I'll get it."

He took off for the lake, stopping at the water's edge to search the dark surface. He dug his toes into the soft sand and let it massage his feet. Where the hell was the ball? The dog wiggled with excitement, barking as he ran back and forth across the beach.

"Shut up, you dumb mutt," Nick muttered.

Chester ignored him.

Nick spotted the ball bobbing in a shaft of moonlight some fifteen feet off the shore—and moving farther out every second. He stepped into the lake and began to wade through the water, still warm from the afternoon sun.

"Chester, hush!" Annie said from behind him. The dog quieted instantly.

Nick looked back over his shoulder and pulled his

shorts up higher as he waded into thigh-deep water. "This stay pretty shallow going out here?"

"Yeah ... but be careful, there's a—"

Her words came just as his front foot slid over the edge of a slope and carried him into water up to his chest.

Laughter bubbled out of Annie. "Oh, Nick—"

"Drop-off. Thanks for the warning," he said. He reached for the ball and secured it in his hand, then looked back at Annie, laughing her head off, and decided it was payback time. He tossed the ball onto the grass and jumped to one side in the water, as though trying to get out of the way of something beneath the surface.

"Hey, what was that?" He looked down.

"What?"

"Something big. Brushed past me." He swung his arm as though fending something off. "What do you have in this lake, anyway?"

"Nick?" She took a step toward him.

He jumped to the side. "There it is again! Hey!" He jerked the other direction. "Help! Annie!" He dropped under the water and shot back up through the surface. "It's got me!"

She screamed and dashed into the chest-deep water swinging her arms. Nick dropped below the surface again and came up next to her. "Loch Ness monster!" he shouted before grabbing her by the waist and lifting her up.

She screeched, and he burst out laughing. Then she smacked him on the arm and smacked him again before beginning to laugh along with him. Like village idiots, they stood there in the lake, clutching each other, laughing in the moonlight. Her wet tank top clung to her breasts, and droplets of water sparkled across her face like diamonds. He brushed them off one cheek.

And then he kissed her. He didn't mean to, the impulse just came over him. Later, he knew he was going to ask himself just what the hell he thought he was doing at that moment. But right then, all he knew was that he wanted Annie's lips beneath his.

It was no gentle kiss, either. Not a first-date kind of kiss at all. It was wet and sloppy and passionate and romantic, and he pulled her tight against him, could feel her body against his with only their T-shirts between them. And when they finally drew apart he was shocked at the sensations a simple kiss had invoked in him. This was Annie, after all, his friend Annie, pregnant Annie.

His wife, Annie.

His heart started to pound.

"Hey," he said, looking down at her. He brushed the long, loose hair back from her cheeks. She had a look of abject terror on her face. Probably wondering herself what he was doing.

"Sorry, I got carried away." He let go of her.

"You scared me half to death." She shivered and wrapped her arms across her stomach as she started toward shore. "Water's kind of cold."

He followed her out, mentally kicking himself for what he'd just done. *What had he just done?*

Maybe this kiss was just one of those passionate things people do in the midst of extreme emotions—like when they think they're going to die. Everyone's heard those stories about people making love with a stranger in the middle of a war. Yeah, that had to be it. Annie thought he was about to be eaten by a sea monster, and when that didn't happen, her emotions all came out in that kiss.

So what was his excuse?

The sensual nature of water? The moonlight? The

warm temperature? The fact that she was here? *Love the one you're with?* God, was that what he was doing?

Guilt nagged at him. This was Annie—the woman who'd helped him out six years ago. The woman who'd been hurt too many times by the wrong guys.

And he, Nick, was engaged. He sure fit the mold for *wrong guy.* How could he have forgotten Melissa so easily? Lingering doubts about his upcoming marriage pushed into his mind, and he quickly shoved them back into the dark corner they'd escaped from.

Nothing about this sounded like it would work out well for Annie. Kissing her had been about just the worst thing he could have done. For her sake, he had to keep his distance from her. Starting right now, he had to go back to *Annie and Nick, good friends.* And he had forget all about the kiss. Because the last thing he wanted to do was to lead on his good friend, Annie.

11

———

ANNIE OVERSLEPT THE NEXT MORNING. SHE LEAPT OUT
of bed in semi-panic, a complete list of things she needed to
accomplish running through her head, and half a smile on
her lips over the kiss she'd relived in her dreams all last
night. As she showered, her mental clock ticked off how far
behind she already was. No time for makeup this morning.
She pulled on her shorts and noted how snug the waist had
gotten. These were her largest shorts—she'd have to buy
some maternity clothes soon.

She wiped off the vanity mirror with a towel so she
could see to put her hair up in her usual ponytail. This
roommate thing—especially when he was still in bed—sure
made it difficult to get dressed in the morning. Thank
goodness morning sickness was no longer part of her
morning routine.

She nudged the bathroom door open and spotted Nick
in a chair by the window, the shade half drawn to allow the
pale yellow sunrise into the room. She watched him for a
moment as he alternately inspected and scratched his
ankles.

"Fleas?" She reached down to switch on a table lamp, then strapped her watch around her wrist and checked the time. Good—she'd made up some time already.

"Hmmph. Looks like poison ivy," he said.

"How'd you get that?"

He glared at the dog stretched diagonally across the bed. "Chasing your mutt through the woods yesterday."

Chester thumped his tail.

Annie swallowed a smile. "Should have kept him leashed."

"He pulled the leash out of my hand—remember?"

He bent to scratch his ankles again.

"Let me have a look." She stepped across the room and knelt on the floor beside his chair. An angry red, bumpy rash poked out from between the dark hair on his legs. *A runner's legs—muscled and lean.* Her face begin to warm and she stood abruptly.

"Yep, that's poison ivy." She reached out to pat Chester on the head. The dog rolled onto his back and thumped his tail some more. Annie rubbed his belly.

"I've got to get downstairs." And then because she couldn't resist, she grinned and added, "I see the dog basket is working out nicely."

Nick snorted. "Must have been four times I shoved him off the bed last night. He just jumps back up as soon as I fall asleep."

She glanced at her watch. "What do you expect? He's been sleeping on the bed ever since— Oh, shit!"

She stared at her hands, turning them palm up and then down. If Nick had poison ivy, then the dog— "Chester's probably covered in poison ivy resin!" She raced into the bathroom, shouting over her shoulder, "Strip the bed!"

Flipping on the hot water, she began to scrub her hands

with soap. "This is just what I need. I'm already running late and now the dog needs a bath."

She stuck her head out of the bathroom. "The guests! Did any of them pet him yesterday? If he had poison ivy resin on his fur we could have an epidemic in the house!"

"Annie—take it easy! He got wet in a sprinkler—probably rinsed most of the stuff off him."

"Plain water won't do it. I can't take any chances." She stepped back into the bedroom and threw an oversized bath towel over Chester, who promptly jumped to his feet and began to bark as he tried to shake off the towel.

"What are you doing?"

"He's got to go out and I don't want to touch him."

Nick threw back his head and laughed.

"You may think this is hilarious, but I have a business to run. And I overslept, and the last thing I need is—" She groaned. "If anyone gets poison ivy from Chester—"

"I'll take the dog out."

Relief slid through her. "Oh, thanks. Afterward, just quarantine him in here and I'll give him a bath later." She started for the door. "By the way, breakfast will be served in an hour."

"Crepes again?"

"Would you prefer the hungry man's breakfast? Eggs over easy, hash browns, bacon, sausage—"

He gave her a boyish grin. "My mouth is watering already."

She smiled back at him. "That would be at the diner. A dollar ninety-nine every morning until nine o'clock. Here at Bailey House Bed & Breakfast, we'll be having spinach-and-mushroom omelets, seven-grain nut bread, and fresh squeezed orange juice."

She slipped out into the hall before he could reply, but his groan was audible through the shut door.

———

Nick watched the door close behind Annie, then reached down to run a hand over the little red bumps on his shins and ankles. "Chester, now I know why I never got a dog. You are just one big pain in the ass."

The dog jumped to the floor and pranced over to Nick's chair, wagging his tail as though he'd just been offered a treat.

"How would you like to live at the pound?"

The dog's tail whipped back and forth in gleeful anticipation.

Nick shook his head. "Dumb as a stone. Come on, let's take a run."

Fifty minutes and seven miles later they were back upstairs.

Nick reached behind the shower curtain and turned on the faucet. Hot water sputtered and then burst out of the showerhead above the old claw-footed bathtub. The plastic curtain shivered under the spray.

He stripped off his sweaty running clothes and let them drop to the floor. Chester padded over from the doorway and turned a couple of circles before settling himself on top of them.

"Hey! Get off." Nick gave Chester a shove with his foot. "I don't want poison ivy all over the rest of my body."

He stepped into the shower and let the hot water cascade over his head and shoulders. "This is what it's all about," he said with a groan of contentment. He stuck his head out from behind the shower curtain to grab his shampoo from the vanity countertop and spotted Chester lying contentedly on top of his clothes again.

"Dammit dog! By the time Annie gets around to giving you a bath, everything in this room will be contaminated. Get over here."

Chester lifted his head but didn't move.

Nick let out a sharp exhale. He shoved the shower curtain aside and climbed out of the tub, water running in rivulets from his body to the floor as he stepped across the small bathroom. Chester jumped to his feet and squirm in excitement.

Nick picked up the wiggling dog and held him as far away from his body as possible. "You're getting your bath right now."

Stepping carefully back into the tub, he held Chester in the warm spray until his fur was thoroughly soaked, then set him down in the tub. Instantly, the dog tried to scramble over the side.

"No, you don't." Nick grabbed hold of Chester's collar and began to lather his hair with Annie's shampoo. The sweet smell of berries filled the air. He poured out more shampoo, scrubbing hard until the dog's golden fur was nearly a solid white mass of suds. "If that doesn't get rid of poison ivy, nothing will," he muttered.

"Nick?" Luella's voice carried through the open bathroom door. The dog's ears perked up and he turned his head.

"In here," Nick called, happy that Annie didn't have a clear shower curtain. He stuck his head out. "What do you need?"

"Annie sent up this calamine lotion for your poison ivy."

"Oh, thanks. Just put—"

The shower curtain jerked, and Nick didn't even have

to see what was happening to know that Chester was making a break for it. He lunged for the dog, catching him by the scruff of the neck with one hand. The sudden movement threw him off balance, and his feet began to slip out from under him. Teetering, he grabbed the shower curtain with his other hand, stopped his descent, and mentally congratulated himself on circumventing disaster. And then he heard the distinct sound of the plastic shower curtain tearing under his weight.

He let go of the dog and threw his other hand back, grabbing at air until his fingers connected with the shower hose. As if in a pirouette gone awry, he fell in slow motion over the side of the tub, shower curtain clutched in one hand, shower hose in the other—and the entire maneuver accompanied by the creaking of the metal shower curtain rod as it collapsed, the crack of the showerhead breaking, and the sound of Luella screeching.

Clearly Luella was getting an eyeful. And Chester had escaped, soapsuds and all.

———

Annie had just set breakfast before her guests when she heard Luella's scream followed by a loud crash. "Excuse me," she said to her guests as she backed toward the doorway. *"Bon appétit."*

She took the stairs two at a time and arrived in the bedroom to find Luella sitting on the edge of the bed, with one hand over her heart. Beside her, Chester wiggled and shook himself, sending water and suds in every direction. "Luella! What happened?"

Nick stepped out of the bathroom, a towel wrapped around his hips. "I fell out of the bathtub giving Chester a bath," he said, water dripping from his hair onto his shoulders. He held up an arm to show her his scraped elbow. It was all she could do to drag her eyes off his bare chest and look at the wound.

Luella nodded, her blue eyes wide. "I thought he'd killed himself for certain."

"The bathroom's kind of a mess." Nick winced.

Annie looked past him through the door, and her mouth dropped open. The floor was underwater. The shower curtain was ripped in half. The metal rod that previously circled the tub was twisted into an unrecognizable shape. Even the showerhead was dangling—torn from the hose like a flower from its stem.

"You're certainly thorough," she said.

"It'll be good as new by tonight."

"A handyman, are you?"

"One of the best." His grin shot straight to her heart. "You'll come to wish you could keep me around here forever."

That's the problem, she thought to herself. *I already do.* She looked at the dog, now rolling suds all over the bedspread. "I'll rinse Chester off in the basement laundry tub. Luella, can you take over breakfast?"

Without waiting for an answer, she wrapped the dog in a towel and headed downstairs. Day three. They were only on day three and already too much had gone wrong. Besides the stress of lying about Nick, now she had to contend with their kiss last night and an almost constant attraction to him. What a hopeless case she was turning out to be.

———

Half an hour later, Nick stood alone in the bathroom, pad of paper in hand, making a list of the parts he figured he'd need to fix the shower. If he was repairing a sailboat, this would be a no-brainer. But a shower? Still, how hard could it be?

Hard enough for someone who'd never done it before. What kind of idiot lied about his home-repair abilities to impress a woman? Annie couldn't care less that he climbed mountains—but fix her shower and her eyes practically gleamed with affection.

He stood on one foot and used his toes to scratch his ankle—this poison ivy was driving him crazy. Luella's calamine lotion clearly wasn't doing the job. He wrote *cortisone cream* on the sheet.

Squinting, he surveyed the destroyed rod and showerhead. Maybe he could swing by the library and get one of those fix-it books that gave step-by-step instructions for everything from appliances to home repairs. That would probably make this really simple. Then his only challenge would be getting it up here before Annie spotted it.

He shoved the list into his pocket and bounded down the stairs. Seeing no one in the hall, he sprinted out the door, shouting, "I'm off to the hardware store," before Annie had a chance to say she was coming along.

At the library, he flipped through several home repair books until he found one that described exactly what he needed to do. Then he modified his list of materials to purchase. He considered photocopying the necessary pages instead of checking out the book, but decided against it. Who knew what other projects he might undertake at Annie's in the next week? With this book close at hand, she never had to know he wasn't a handyman extraordinaire.

He checked the book out under Annie's name and

headed down the sidewalk toward the hardware store. In the distance, he spotted a familiar figure striding toward him —Father Thespesius on one of his exercise walks.

"Morning, Father," he called as the man neared.

"Nick! Good to see you! I trust all is going well?"

"Good, good. Just getting ready to do a few repairs." He motioned with the book.

"I imagine you're enjoying Luella's cooking?" The priest closed his eyes. "Be sure to ask her to make her oven-fried chicken while you're here. No offense to anyone above, but you'll think you've died and gone to heaven."

"I'll do that. Maybe tomorrow—I know tonight we're having pork chops."

The priest's eyes flew open and then narrowed. He swallowed, then began to walk a circle around Nick, who turned with him.

"Luella's pork chops, you say? I don't suppose you'd have room for one more at the table?"

"I don't know—"

"Not that I would presume to invite myself—"

"Oh, I didn't think that, it's just—"

"It so happens my housekeeper is gone this week and I've been cooking for myself, alone as I am ..."

Nick nodded. Annie was going to kill him. "Father, we'd love to have you join us." He tightened his grip on the book.

The priest walked another circle around him, arms swinging. "You're sure you'll have enough food?"

"Absolutely. Why don't you come over about six?"

Father Thespesius bobbed his head up and down. "Well, thank you so much! I'll bring the wine." He strode off in perfect power-walk precision.

"Great," Nick muttered. "I'm going to need it."

12

<hr>

An hour later, Nick was back at home, new parts from the hardware store and old tools from the basement laid out in a row on the bathroom counter. Back behind the clothes hamper, where it couldn't be seen from the doorway, the fix-it book lay open on the floor.

He eyed the job at hand, then looked at the diagram in the book again. This was pretty easy stuff. First he'd take down the shower curtain rod. Then he'd deal with the showerhead. He climbed into the tub to get a better angle to work from.

"I hope you don't fall out of there again." Annie stepped through the open doorway.

"Very funny." He glanced at the book behind the hamper and hoped Annie didn't come too far into the room.

She laughed, a sweet lilt that made him remember the first time he kissed her—six years ago. The judge had declared them married and told him to kiss the bride. So he had. And afterward she'd laughed just as she had right now, with a kind of joyful abandon. It had touched him then, shot a jolt of happiness right into his heart, but he hadn't realized just how much—until later, after she was gone.

"Need any help?"

"Nah, I should be able to do it." He unscrewed part of the rod, and she reached out to take it from him.

"How hard is it going to be?"

"Not too bad." *Even for a non-handyman like me.* He cleared his throat. "Ah, by the way, I ran into Father Thespesius in town."

She looked at him expectantly.

"Nice guy. He was raving about Luella's cooking. Her chicken ... and her pork chops."

"You didn't tell him, did you?"

Nick pursed his lips and put the wrench to the pipe again. "I think I might have."

She frowned. "Think?"

"I'm pretty sure I did."

"Oh, no, Nick! He'll be calling any minute now, looking for a dinner invitation."

"I don't think so." He handed her another piece of the shower curtain rod.

"You don't know him well enough yet."

He shook his head. "He doesn't need a dinner invitation because ... he's got one already."

"Oh, Nick!" Annie wailed. "Father Thespesius has always been overly curious about my marriage. How are we supposed to keep this charade going when you invite him to dinner?"

"It was like I didn't have a choice."

Annie glared at him.

The ringing of his phone in the bedroom interrupted their stand-off. Nick exhaled. It didn't matter who it was; he was happy to hear from them right now.

He climbed out of the tub, unobtrusively nudged the hamper over the book, and bolted to the nightstand where his phone was charging. An unfamiliar number showed on caller ID. He dropped into the wing chair and put the phone to his ear. "Hello?"

A woman's sultry voice whispered, "Ohhh baby!"

What the hell. He sat up and threw a questioning look at Annie.

She tilted her head and gave a shrug.

"Oh baby!" The woman said again, this time with an insistent edge.

A laugh welled up inside him and he swallowed it down. "Minnow?"

"You're not supposed to identify me," she said, irritably. "I'm giving you the code word."

Annie leaned up close to him and he caught the scent of berry shampoo. He inhaled. It sure smelled better on her than on Chester. *Oh, baby was right.*

"What's going on?" Annie reached for the phone and he caught her hand with his to prevent her from succeeding. Their fingers interlocked. Their eyes met. His male anatomy started to react. Good God, all because of berry shampoo?

This was Annie. His friend, Annie. And he was engaged. He dropped her hand as if it was covered with poison ivy resin.

Minnow's voice blasted out of the phone. "Hel-lo? What's going on over there? I've got *big* news. Meet me at the fountain."

"Minnow," he said, fighting to keep his patience. "We're both right here—there's no reason to go to the fountain. Just tell us what's happening—"

"You're on a cell phone. There's no privacy—anyone can intercept it."

"Minnow! Just tell us what's going on."

"No. I'll call the Bailey House land line," she said and disconnected the call.

Nick let out a sharp laugh as he let his head fall against the back of the chair. "Your friend is certifiable. She's calling back on the land line so we don't risk the chance that someone might intercept the cell phone signal and hear us."

The phone on the other nightstand rang, and Annie raced around the footboard to snatch it up. She plopped down on the edge of the bed. "Bailey House Bed and Breakfast. Can I help you?" she said breathlessly.

Nick sat beside her, and she turned on the speakerphone.

"Are you ready for this?" Minnow asked.

The scent of berries washed over him again and he forced himself to concentrate on Minnow's voice.

"Yes," they replied in unison, and grinned at each other.

"Am I on speaker? Turn it off. I don't want to anyone to hear this but you two."

Nick rolled his eyes. Annie shut off the speaker, then held the phone between them so they could both hear.

"Speaker is now off," she said briskly.

"Okay, good. Some guy just came in for a trim *and he was pretty curious about both of you.*"

"Who was it?" Annie asked.

"Nobody from around here. He talked kind of formal."

Nick frowned at Annie. "What did he want to know?"

"Well, first I thought he was just a tourist because he was blabbing about how quaint the town is, the old buildings and stuff. And then he started talking about your B & B, and next thing I knew he was asking how long you two have been married. And what do you do in your spare time. And how busy are you with reservations. And whether I thought Annie would ever move out of town to be closer to her husband."

She gave a snort of disgust. "Like I was too dumb to get suspicious. I knew right away he was up to no good. Maybe we ought to meet tonight to work up a plan of action—you know, strategize. Bet you a million, he's going to hang around a while."

Annie sighed. "We can't get together. Father Thespesius is coming to dinner."

"That's the last person you should be having over! Why did you do that?"

"Nick invited him."

"I didn't invite him. He invited himself."

"Be prepared," Minnow said. "He's the nosiest person in town. Come on, you two! You won't have a secret left after tonight."

Annie flashed an I-told-you-so smile at Nick before answering. "There's no getting around it. He'll be here at six."

"Well, then, so will I," Minnow declared. "You're going to need me to keep things in control."

"Oh, is that what you do?" Nick muttered under his breath.

Annie swatted his arm. "Just so you know, we're having *pork chops*."

"What's more important right now? Vegetarianism or helping the two of you? I'll bring along a soy chop. Just make sure you tell Luella so she doesn't give it to Father T."

"Ahhh ..." Annie looked at Nick and raised a questioning brow.

Oh, hell, why not? He shrugged and muttered, "The more the merrier."

"Okay, be here at six," Annie said into the phone. "Your assignment is to keep the conversation off me and Nick and our marriage."

"Righto. And after Father T goes home, we'll have our strategy meeting."

Annie hung up the phone and turned to stare at Nick. "What if someone's on to us?"

"How could they be? I've only been here a couple of days. This guy probably has some other reason for asking questions."

"Like?"

"Your land? Eighty acres right on the lake. He asked if you might move away to be near me. Maybe he's a developer."

She nodded. "Maybe ..."

Nick held out a hand, palm up. "Or, maybe he's a reviewer. He asked how busy the B & B is. Those guys always go incognito so you can't try to influence their review."

She nodded again. "What if he's a private detective sent by your fiancée to find out the real reason you're staying an extra nine days in Wisconsin? What do you think? Is it possible?"

A pit formed in his stomach. *Melissa?* She did have the tendency to pout. And after he'd told her he wouldn't be back for a couple more weeks, she *had* come up with that shoot in France awfully quickly. He exhaled. Jesus. All he needed was Melissa to find out he was in Wisconsin sharing a bedroom with ... his wife. She thought he'd been divorced for years.

He swallowed hard. No, Melissa hadn't hired anyone.

She had her own life, had been totally unfazed by the news that he'd gotten another assignment and was staying out here longer.

"There's no way it's Melissa. Now, don't panic, Annie. There's got to be a reasonable explanation. Whatever it is, we'll deal with it. We'll find out who the guy is and what he's up to—and we'll deal with it ... together."

———

Father Thespesius arrived promptly at six.

"We're so glad you could come." Annie hoped he didn't detect any insincerity in her voice.

Nick gave her shoulder a supportive squeeze, and a shiver raced through her. She met his gaze and smiled, felt herself start to sink into his dark eyes, and jerked herself back. What a sorry case she was. All the guy had to do was touch her and her thoughts turned to lust.

"Didn't want to be a minute late for Luella's pork chops," the priest said with a jovial grin. He handed Annie a bottle of red wine. "I know we should be having white. But in my business, red is always the top choice."

Minnow came up the front steps and followed him through the door.

"I hope you don't mind, Minnow's joining us, too," Annie said.

"Not at all. Not at all." He turned to pump Minnow's hand. "Thought you were a vegetarian."

"Brought my own." She dashed past them into the kitchen holding a brown lunch bag.

Annie handed the bottle of wine to Nick, who eyed the label and whispered something under his breath like, "Bet this is the same stuff they use in church on Sunday morning."

She stepped on his toes.

Fifteen minutes later, they were seated around the dining table, their plates full, the conversation light and flowing easily. Luella beamed as Father Thespesius praised of her cooking, while Minnow chatted on about the hair salon. Despite the fact that everything was going well, Annie was terrified something would go wrong. She took a swallow of her lemonade and wished she could have some wine to help her relax.

Father Thespesius leaned forward. "Nick, have you given any thought to leaving the military and coming home to settle down now that there's a baby on the way?"

Minnow choked on her salad, and Annie leapt up to slap her on the back.

"Don't forget to chew before you swallow, dear," Luella said.

"Well, I ... yes ... not really ... hadn't ... too soon, anyway," Nick said. He tried to cut a bite of meat and dropped his knife with a clatter onto the plate.

Minnow stopped coughing. Annie stared at Nick. Apparently he wasn't a natural at lying. *Not like her.* A sick feeling settled in her stomach. She certainly had gotten adept at it the last couple of years.

"Annie's going to need you around here," the priest said. "Hard for a woman to run this place all by herself, especially with a young child."

Annie returned to her chair and smoothed her napkin across her lap. "Nick's income from the military really helps us stay afloat. I don't know if we could make ends meet here without it." Not a bad adlib; that should put an end to the questioning. She reached for her fork.

Father Thespesius took a bite of pork and talked around it. "All the money in the world won't do you a bit of good if you've lost sight of what's really important—love and family."

"My thoughts exactly," Luella chimed in.

Annie's stomach tightened.

Nick covered her hand with his. "That's one thing we're not worried about—our love." His eyes bored into hers with a deep, albeit faked, affection. And though she knew this was an act, she couldn't hold back the warmth that flowed through her.

Eyes locked with Nick's, she nodded.

"Food's getting cold," Minnow said, shattering the moment.

Nick dropped her hand, and they all dug back into dinner.

"Luella, I know I said this already, but you have truly outdone yourself," Father Thespesius said after several minutes. He cleared his throat and Annie intuitively knew he was about to return to his previous topic—their marriage. "But tell me—"

Minnow leaned forward suddenly. "Did you hear the Carow boy was caught spraying shaving cream all over the teachers' windshields in the high school parking lot?"

Their heads swiveled in unison to look at her.

"No," Annie said, grateful for Minnow's effort.

"Doesn't that just sound like him?" Luella said.

The priest shook his head. "I'm going to have to talk with him again. That boy is always getting into one scrape or another." He settled his gaze on Nick again and gave a nod.

Oh, shit, here it came, whatever it was. Father T looked like he was on a mission. Annie searched her mind for a topic, something—anything—to say that would prevent the priest from being able to ask ... whatever he was planning to ask.

"Tolerably fine weather we're having, isn't it?" she said in what she sensed, too late, was an overly bright voice.

This time, all heads swiveled to look at her, forks half lifted to mouths.

"*Tolerably fine?*" Nick asked.

"Cinderella," Minnow interjected. "The prince says it when he meets Cinderella—in the television movie."

Nick snorted out a laugh. "Well, now we know the *real* reason Cinderella took off at midnight."

"Actually, one of the stepsisters says it to the prince," Annie said. What an inane conversation. Still, anything was better than talking about her marriage to Nick.

"You know the lines from Cinderella?" Father Thespesius asked.

"Well, why wouldn't she?" Luella answered. "It's one of her favorite movies, right up there with—" She broke off and turned to Nick expectantly.

As he blanched, Annie prayed he would get it right.

"Ah ... *It's a Wonderful Life?*"

"A round of applause for Nick Fleming, Husband of the Year." Minnow let out a strained chortle.

Annie stuck a spoonful of applesauce in her mouth even though she was now so stressed she would rather quit eating altogether. The sooner this dinner was over, the sooner Father Thespesius would go home.

"Speaking of husbands ..." the priest began.

"Oh, oh!" Minnow waved her fork. "You know how Bill Butterfield left his wife and all those kids and took up with some woman he met on a business trip? His wife was in today for a cut and color. And she told me that now, just a month after he left, he wants to come back. The best part is, she told him she needs some time to think about it."

"Which leads right into what I was about to say," Father Thespesius said.

Annie's heart sank. He was bound and determined to speak his mind. Of course he was; he'd had plenty to say about their long-distance marriage over the two years she'd already lived here. Whatever gave her the idea that Nick's arrival would make him stop?

She finished off her lemonade and refilled her glass.

"I'm wondering if you've given real, serious thought to what happens once the baby is born." Father Thespesius said. "What it will mean with Nick halfway around the world. A separation like this is just not a good situation under any circumstances. I don't mean to push myself into your lives, but I just feel strongly that a child needs its father."

Annie stared at Nick, pleaded for help with her eyes. He lifted one eyebrow ever so slightly.

"You make a good point, Father," Nick said. "But there are married people in the military the world over. Somehow families survive. It takes a little more work to stay connected, but when you're as committed to making this work as Annie and I are ..." He smiled at Annie. "God willing, my job won't stop us from having the family we want. Maybe two boys and a girl. Or two girls and a boy. Or three the same. Right, sweetie?"

Her heart constricted and she nodded, unable to speak. He made it sound so real.

This whole lie was getting completely out of hand. They were getting in deeper and deeper with no end in sight.

The sound of the front door latch opening filled her

with relief. Any interruption was better than the subject at hand. Chester jumped up with a bark, while Annie leaned back in her chair so she could see down the hall. One of her guests, a stately, middle-aged balding man, stepped into the foyer and was instantly greeting by Chester, his whole body wiggling with excitement.

"Oh, Mr. Lewis!" Annie motioned him into the dining room. "How was the supper club?"

He stopped in the doorway and reached down to pet Chester's head. "Quite good. Thank you for the recommendation."

Minnow twisted out of her chair onto her feet and pushed through the heavy swinging door to the kitchen. "I'll get dessert ready," she tossed over her shoulder. "Baby, baby, baby."

13

Annie frowned after her, then exchanged a look with Nick. What was the rush—dinner wasn't even over yet? Was that the code phrase or was it just Minnow ... being Minnow? She turned her attention back to her guest. "I made a fresh batch of cookies so be sure to help yourself whenever you're hungry."

"Thank you, I will. If you'd care to share that recipe, I'm sure my wife would love to have it," he said in his precise way of speaking. With a nod, he strolled down the hallway toward the kitchen.

Seconds later, Minnow barged back through the swinging door looking a little frazzled.

"Where's the dessert?" Annie asked.

"Dessert? Oh, I decided I should probably wait until everyone was done with supper," she said in an unnaturally high voice. She tilted her head toward the swinging door. "Oh baby, it looks good, though. Oh baby, oh baby!"

Annie threw a questioning look at Minnow and was answered with an almost imperceptible nod. Obviously,

Minnow had something to report. She slid out of her chair and said, "Since I'm done eating, I think I'll get dessert ready after all."

"I'll help." Nick pushed back his chair.

Luella set her napkin on the table. "Now, you just stay here, Nick. Let us women pamper you while you're home. I'll help the girls."

"Oh, no, no, no!" Minnow cried. "You made dinner. We'll get dessert." She slid her arm through Annie's and turned her away from the kitchen door.

Annie choked back a laugh. For a spy buff, Minnow wasn't too smooth at acting normal when subterfuge was called for. Then again, maybe that was because Minnow wasn't too smooth at acting normal even when times were normal.

Mr. Lewis passed the dining room entry, munching on a cookie as he headed toward the stairs. Spotting him, Minnow spun through the door to the kitchen with Annie in tow. "Let's get dessert," she sang out.

As soon as they were in the kitchen, Annie dragged Minnow into the walk-in pantry and closed the door. "What's the matter with you? Are you using the code word?" she asked.

"It's him! The guy from the salon. Mr. Lewis is the one who was asking all the questions about you."

Annie's jaw dropped. "He's staying here."

"No kidding. I didn't want him to see me—to know that we're friends."

Annie's heart thudded into her stomach. There was something more going on here than they realized. She let her head drop back and stared up for a moment at the bare lightbulb hanging from the pantry ceiling. "You think he really knows something? Maybe he's just a developer wanting my property." Her tone brightened. "Or he could be a reviewer and I'll get a four-star rating in the bed-and-breakfast review book."

"Yeah. And maybe he's a P.I. hired by Nick's girlfriend."

Annie slumped. "That's what I said."

They stared morosely at each other.

The pantry door opened, and Nick stepped into the little room. "What's going on? And hey, thanks a lot. You two left me out there with Father Nosy and Mother Curious."

Annie grabbed the apple pie off the pantry counter and pushed past him into the kitchen. "Sorry. Get out the ice cream," she said. "Mr. Lewis is the man Minnow called us about today."

"The one asking all the questions?"

"The same," Minnow said, nodding. She pulled a five-quart pail of vanilla ice cream from the freezer. "Maybe he's from the IRS."

"I never thought of that angle. When did he check in?" Nick paced across the room.

"Couple of days ago. He's supposed to stay a week." Annie began to cut the pie and lift it onto dessert plates.

"By himself?" Nick looked incredulous.

"Uh-huh."

"He said he has a wife," Nick said. "Isn't it kind of odd the guy is taking a vacation alone?"

Annie shrugged. "I don't interrogate guests as they check in, you know. Might be kind of bad for business. Besides, he seemed normal enough." She looked at Nick for a moment. It was nice to have someone else to worry with. "So what do you think we should do?"

"Nothing—"

"That's silly." Minnow scooped the ice cream and dropped it onto the cut pieces of pie. "The guy could be ready to take the two of you down and you're going to sit around and wait for him to do it?"

Nick lay an exasperated look on Minnow. "What I was going to say is we do nothing until we figure out what the guy's gig is. Maybe he really is just a guest here."

Minnow snorted. "Yeah, and maybe I'm a nun. When he leaves his room, Annie, you should go in there and look around—"

"I'm not going to go digging through his stuff. That's illegal and unethical and—"

"Couldn't you be making the bed and, oops, just happen to flip through his briefcase?"

Annie raised her eyebrows. "No."

"Yeah, okay. Then we need to set up surveillance on him, every minute of the day. We need to know where he goes, who he sees—the works."

Nick shook his head. "No way. There's only three of us, and it's a small town. Unless he's blind, he'd have to notice one of us showing up wherever he goes."

"Nick's right. We'll just draw attention to ourselves following him around," Annie said. "Since he's staying here, I'm sure we'll get some chances to learn something about him without being too obvious."

She picked up two plates of dessert. "Now, let's get back into the dining room before Father or Luella comes looking for us."

———

Hours later, after everyone had gone home, Annie wandered out into the yard. Nick had gone upstairs, and the house was quiet and dark. She used to cherish this time of night, her time alone when she prepped for the next morning's breakfast. But for some reason, being alone tonight felt oppressive.

The light from the nearly full moon bathed the yard in a silver glow. The air still held some of the heat from the afternoon sun, and a warm breeze touched her skin and blew wisps of hair around her face. Beneath her bare feet, the soft grass teased her with coolness. Ever since she'd come to Bedford, nights like this had made her feel as if she was one with the universe, part of a greater plan.

But tonight, all she felt was lonely.

Pregnancy made her more tired than usual, and she knew she should call it a night. But she couldn't face climbing into bed with Nick right now. Not when he'd brought up children and pretended that, someday, they'd have three of them. Years ago, she'd once told him she wanted three children. Had he remembered that? Or had he just plucked the number from the sky?

She picked up two orange life vests that had been discarded in the sand by her guests, shook them off, and hung them inside the storage shed. Then she got out the rake and began to clean up the beach, gathering pine needles, branches, leaves and other of nature's debris into a pile near the edge of the woods.

Three days with Nick and already she was a wreck. How would she make it to nine? Did she even want to try? The longer this went on, the more she was beginning to think it wasn't such a great idea. Maybe something urgent should come up, like the military needed him back, pronto. That would work—the military did stuff like that. People would accept it without question.

Yeah, that was probably the answer. The more she thought about it, the more she realized the answer to her whole dilemma about Nick was to get him out of here—and soon.

She stood back and surveyed her work, then wandered across the beach to the water's edge, her feet sinking into the wet sand, cool water lapping at her ankles. Holding her shorts high so they didn't get wet, she waded over to the pier and hoisted herself up to sit on the end, feet dangling in the dark water.

A pebble splashed near her feet and she jerked her head up and around to find the source. Nick stood at the end of the dock, grinning. Her stomach tumbled over itself.

"Hey," he said. "Whatcha doing?"

Thinking of you. She shrugged.

"Mind if I join you?" Without waiting for an answer, he dropped down beside her, his muscled thigh coming to rest against hers. Which was quite enough, thank you, to set her heart pounding.

She shifted her leg slightly to break the contact. "I thought you went to bed."

"Too restless to sleep. You worried about Mr. Lewis?"

Not as worried as she was about her feelings for Nick, but she wasn't going to say that. "Yeah."

"We'll get him figured out. And if he's up to no good, I'll pound him for you." He flexed a bicep.

She laughed. "Thanks. I feel so much better." The whole problem was, while all this might make her feel better on the outside, inside she was turning to mush. Of all the dumb ideas she'd ever had, this charade had to be the dumbest. She should just tell him, right now, that he didn't have to stay the whole nine days, that she would fly to Las Vegas—or wherever—for a quickie divorce.

Nick swung his feet back and forth in the water, the movement making his quad rub against hers. She shifted away again and drew a breath. *Right now. Get him out of here before you throw your arms around him.* She stared across the lake at the dark wall of pines and hardwoods that lined the distant shore. *Say it, you gutless chicken.*

She opened her mouth and the words came out all on their own. "Nick, I had a kind of epiphany at dinner, a realization—"

"I think we did pretty well, considering Father Thespesius's questions," Nick said.

"Well, yeah, but my point is, I'm worried we won't be able to keep this up for another six days—"

"Sure we will."

"No, what I mean is, it's going to get harder. Look at the monkey wrench Mr. Lewis has already thrown into the works."

"Annie, when I've got a mountain to climb I don't keep my eyes on the summit the whole time—otherwise it's too overwhelming. I set goals for where I want to be at the end of each day." He patted her knee. "We'll attack this beast one day at a time."

He sounded like he was beginning to enjoy the whole situation. Annie let out a sigh. He wasn't getting it, and she sure wasn't going to tell him that the real reason for her concern was the effect he was having on her every time she came near him.

It was now or never. She had to move this man out of her life. "Nick, look, you've been here three days already." Her words picked up speed as they rolled out of her. "If you suddenly got an emergency call from the military and had to leave, no one would question it. Everyone's met you now, they know you're real. Hell, you and I could say we're leaving for a little getaway. Then you go back to California, and I stay away a few more days ... and then I come back here without you. No one the wiser."

Nick didn't say anything for a long moment. Then he shook his head. "Annie, I don't have a problem staying—not anymore."

She could feel his eyes on her and turned to meet his gaze. Obviously he didn't understand. "I'm trying to say I'll get the quickie divorce. Now—tomorrow—as soon as we can."

"What about the museum opening?" His voice held more than a touch of bemusement.

She waved a hand as if it was no big deal. "Don't worry about it. If the military wants you back, you'll just have to miss it. Everyone will understand. Besides, I'd already decided last week—before you ever showed up—to start hinting that we were having marital problems. That way, when I finally announced our divorce, it wouldn't come as a surprise. Your leaving now would feed right into that."

Nick slanted his head and looked at her through narrowed eyes. It took all her self-restraint not to run her hand across his cheek, to touch the rough day's growth on his jaw, to—

"Damn!" he said, his eyes on the yard behind her. "Here comes Mr. Lewis."

Before she could turn to look, Nick's arm was around her shoulders, and his mouth came down on hers. Hard. Sensations shot through her, pleasure that made her heart thud, her skin shiver. She grabbed the edge of the dock to prevent herself from succumbing to the moment, to keep the rational side of her brain in control.

This was, after all, just a ploy to keep Mr. Lewis from coming over and asking questions.

He held her jaw and kept her from moving away from him. His tongue slid between her lips and she sank beneath its erotic assault, meeting it with her own because, she rationalized, *of course, we have to make sure this looks believable, and this is how one would kiss one's husband after months apart. After all, it's sure how I would kiss my husband.*

His lips moved over hers, insistent, and she let herself follow him, let her hand move to grasp his shirt and pull him closer. His mouth was on her throat, her jaw, teasing her ear, and she leaned into him, feeling his warmth, wanting more of him.

Control, control, her brain warned, and she swirled her foot in the water, as if the cold around her toes would douse the fire building inside her.

Nick's hand came up to cradle her breast, braless because of the heat. He caressed her through her knit shirt, *combed cotton for extra softness, the catalog had said.* Yes, they were right about that. She was going to lose her mind over all that softness. He slid his hand beneath her shirt and she pressed into his palm, his touch rough and arousing and almost more than she could bear. Reality started shouting at her. *Maybe this was going a bit too far for Mr. Lewis.* She shoved the thought away. No, it wasn't. *Want to bet?* Yeah, okay, maybe a bit.

She wrenched her mouth from Nick's and pushed back to stare at him. "What about Mr. Lewis?"

"What about him?" Nick asked in a thick voice. He pulled her toward him, his eyes heavy-lidded and hot. Her stomach flopped.

"I think we're doing more than he needs to see." She glanced over her shoulder. Mr. Lewis had apparently fled the scene—probably mortified over their open display of affection. Disappointment coursed through her and then evil took over her mind. That's all she could attribute it to, evil is what caused a sudden lie to burst from her mouth.

"Oh!" she said on a gasp. "Kiss me again—here he comes!"

When finally they came up for air, Annie's lips throbbed, her chin felt rubbed raw, and she knew she had to put an end to this right now or she'd never be able to forget Nick even if he did leave tomorrow.

They both glanced back at the house at exactly the same moment. "He's gone," Annie said on a breath.

"Yeah. Nice job." Nick sat up straight.

She could hardly breathe, and he said *nice job*? If he only knew.

This had reached the point of being awful. Talk about desperate. Here Nick was doing this to help her and she was pretending Mr. Lewis was nearby just so Nick would kiss her. This was pitiful—no, *she* was pitiful.

Oh, but the man could kiss. What she wouldn't give to wake up to that kiss every morning for the rest of her life.

Melissa. Right, Melissa was going to get that kiss, Melissa was engaged to that kiss. Annie had no right to even covet that kiss—it was, after all, only on loan for nine days. She had to stick to her latest plan—get Nick out of here. She had been so shortsighted to ask—beg—force—him to stay. Sure, she might be convincing the town that they were happily married, but she was also convincing herself that she'd never gotten over this guy. *He had to go.*

Annie forced herself back to the topic. "There are just too many close calls. What if Mr. Lewis had overhead any of our initial conversation that first day? As Minnow would say, it would have blown our cover. Nick, I'm letting you out of our agreement. Tomorrow, we find the first flight to wherever we have to go to get that divorce, and after that you just head back to California."

14

THE HELL HE WAS GOING TO LEAVE. NICK WATCHED Annie as she logically laid out their next plan of action. Was the woman immune to him? Two minutes ago he'd have sworn she was as attracted to him as he was to her.

When she'd first said he was free to leave, all he'd wanted to do was find a way to shut her up. Mr. Lewis had been a handy excuse—even though it had been a lie. Lewis hadn't been anywhere in sight. Lucky for him, though, the man eventually showed up, so Annie would never have to know Nick concocted the whole thing just so he could kiss her.

And had it helped? Apparently not. She still seemed determined to get rid of him. Well, he wasn't going anywhere. Melissa was in France. And he was here with Annie for the next week if he wanted it. *And he wanted it.*

His thoughts skidded to a halt. What the hell was he thinking? He was engaged to someone else. And Annie was offering him the very thing he'd come here seeking—her signature on the divorce papers. Why would he turn her down? His lawyer had called that morning with the news that he and Annie could get a quick divorce in a couple of different places. All the pieces were falling into place. So why wasn't he jumping at her offer?

"So we'll fly out tomorrow?"

He jerked his head up. Why the sudden rush? "There's nowhere to go," he lied. "I haven't heard back from my lawyer about where we can get a quick divorce."

"How hard can this be to figure out? I can probably find it on the Internet in ten minutes."

Nick shrugged. "I have more trust in my lawyer. Besides, I can't leave Bedford yet—I made a commitment to judge the Women's Club flower contest tomorrow night, and I'm a man of my word."

"For God's sake, they can find another judge."

"They asked *me*."

"That's only because I told them you're a gardening whiz."

"And now you're going to tell them you exaggerated just a bit?"

"Nick, the flower-judging is only one part of the problem. If we're having trouble fooling Mr. Lewis, how on earth will we pull off you faking expertise about flower arrangements?"

He shook his head. "I'm not going to bow out. Don't worry—I won't blow it."

"Okay, fine. Call your lawyer tomorrow, and tell him we need a place to get a divorce so we can get out of here the next day."

"What about the museum opening?" he asked.

"It's not that big a deal."

"That was the whole reason you insisted I stay nine days."

She waved a dismissive hand. "Look, I said I'd sign the divorce papers. What more do you want?"

What more did he want? He stared at the moon reflecting on the dark, quiet water, and thought about Melissa, about how the action and connectedness of Los Angeles suited her. Just as this place—its stillness broken only by the rustling of the leaves in the birch trees and crickets chirping their song into the night—suited Annie.

I think I want you.

Realization slipped through him slowly, like a soft breeze sifting off an inland lake. He didn't love Melissa. The thought cleared his mind, made him see the past year with fresh eyes. *Had he ever really loved her?* She was a beautiful woman, fun, easy to be with. But love? He faced the question honestly, and the answer came swiftly. *No.* And then, just as swiftly came the acknowledgement of something he'd kept buried for a long time—he didn't want to spend the rest of his life with her.

He looked at Annie through narrowed eyes. "You can agree to sign the papers tonight. But I'm not going anywhere for a while." *At least, not until I find out how much of that kiss was real and how much was playacting.*

———

Her stomach had turned to jelly. That's what was wrong. Nick was going to stay, and, soon, her whole body would be jelly. She wouldn't be able to walk without collapsing into a shivering, quivering heap on the ground. She'd have to lie there and say to people, *Don't mind me, I'll be fine in another six days.*

Did he not realize the effect he had on her? "You really don't have to stay," she said weakly.

"A deal is a deal. I'm in."

Her mind let out a whimper. If she kept protesting, he was going to get really suspicious. How could she not have realized when she proposed this whole charade that the more time she spent with Nick, the more likely her old feelings might resurface?

A fat lot of good that knowledge did her now.

Fine, he could stay—mostly because she had obviously lost any say in the matter. But, she would do her best to avoid him, keep him out of her sight, remain focused on the goal of making it through this without letting Nick know how much she cared about him.

If only they weren't sharing a room.

If only they weren't sharing a bed.

———

Staying away from Nick was proving to be next to impossible. This morning, she'd walked into the bathroom and there he was, soaking in an oatmeal bath for his poison ivy. He'd grinned and said, "Throw me a towel, will you?" She'd whipped one his way before backing out in mortification. After last night's kiss, he probably thought she had come in on purpose.

She sighed and shook her head.

Once Nick finished his bath, he'd discovered she and Luella were going to flip all the mattresses—a job that had been scheduled for the day he arrived and gotten postponed in all the chaos. He insisted on helping—and that Luella should do something less strenuous.

So, she and Nick had spent the morning together, flipping mattresses. He did most of the heavy lifting because he kept saying she should take it easy because of the baby, while she mostly stood around and watched him—and his muscles. Throughout the entire ordeal the most intelligent sentence that came out of her mouth was, "You can double the life of a mattress if you turn it regularly."

She could have asked if he was nervous about judging the flower arrangements at the festival tonight, could have expressed interests in his trips and his writing ... hell, she could have told him the history of Bedford. But no, she babbled ridiculous things about mattresses.

It didn't help that she'd decorated the inn so romantically that every room they entered further weakened her resolve to keep her distance from Nick. It didn't help that her brain couldn't seem to let go of their interlude on the pier last night. But regardless of all that, somehow she had to stay focused on the fact that his life was headed in a direction that didn't include her.

To her immense relief, he'd finally gone for a run and she'd come into town to have Minnow trim the ends off her hair. She sat in the vinyl beautician's chair facing the mirror, her head like a trophy on top of the black plastic cape covering the rest of her body.

Minnow stood behind the chair, frowning at Annie in the mirror. "That's it?" She held up the ends of Annie's sandy-blond hair. "One inch off the length? Come on, live a little, take a risk."

Annie looked at Minnow's fuchsia locks and winced. "Maybe another time."

"You don't have time to wait for another time. The moment is now. How long you been wearing your hair just straight like this?"

"Not that long."

"That would mean ... since high school?"

Annie shrugged. "So?"

"I rest my case. You've gone out of style and don't even know it." She began to comb though Annie's wet hair.

"Long hair never goes out of style."

"For teenage girls, it doesn't. You left *teenage* behind ten years ago. And now you've let yourself fall into that old familiar rut."

"You mean the rut where you don't change your look because you look absolutely fine as you are?"

"No. I mean the rut where you don't care whether you look hot to your husband or not."

Annie snorted out a laugh. "Yeah, that's high on my priority list—*looking hot for my husband.*" Good thing she and Minnow were the only people in the shop right now.

"He's from California. He *loves* that West Coast look. Why don't you give it to him?"

Annie stared at Minnow's rapt expression in the mirror. "Are you talking about Nick? He grew up in Chicago."

"He's a California boy now."

Annie talked to the mirror. "For this month, maybe. Who knows where he'll be next. Anyway, who cares what he likes?"

Minnow swung the chair around so Annie was facing her. "You should. He's your husband."

Annie opened her mouth and then shut it without saying a word. She tried again. "Minnow. It's not for real, remember? He's leaving in five days. We're getting divorced. He has a fiancé. Any of this sounding familiar?" She waved a hand between them. "Hello? Not to mention, you know as well as I do that Nick couldn't care less what I look like."

"Don't make assumptions. I've seen the way he looks at

you. Now, consider what you'd look like if we cut you to shoulder length." She used her hands to demonstrate where the hair would end. "What do you think?"

Annie had to admit it changed her look entirely, but it wasn't her hair that concerned her at the moment. "What do you mean *the way he looks at me?*"

Minnow smiled like Mona Lisa and picked up the shears from the counter. "You ready?"

"No! I've got to be able to get it in a ponytail. I need to be able to get my hair out of my face when I'm in the kitchen. But what did you mean—"

"Okay. We'll take three inches off and add layers. Long, sleek layers. And we'll do some highlighting. Strawberry-blond. Sun-kissed. You'll look great."

"Minnow! What does he look at me like?"

She grinned. "Oh. Right. He looks at you like ... like he can't quite believe you're real—"

"Oh, great, he's repulsed."

"No, no. In a good way. It's like he thinks you're really special and he only now just realized it and he can't believe he never figured it out before."

"Really?" Annie's stomach flipped, and a slow, mellow joy rolled through her. Then reality pounced on her like a cat with its claws unsheathed. "Yeah, but he's engaged to someone else."

Minnow waved her scissors cavalierly. "The only thing I know for certain is that, right now, at this very moment, you two are married. When he looks at you, there's something there. And when you look at the guy, you get goo-goo eyed. Seems to me that if the guy you want is the guy you already have, then you should do whatever it takes to keep him."

Annie stared at her dumbfounded. "Am I that obvious?"

"To me, you are."

"Oh, God. I probably am to him, too. Last night Nick and I were sitting on the dock when Mr. Lewis came outside. So Nick kissed me to keep the guy from coming over and talking to us."

She could feel her cheeks begin to burn. "Then I lied that Mr. Lewis was still nearby so that Nick would have to kiss me again. And he did. Only, he kissed me because he was playing a role. And I kissed him *because I meant it.*"

Minnow swung the chair round again. "Layers. I'm cutting in some very cool layers. We're doing some highlighting, and you are going to go for it."

"I can't do this."

"Yes, you can."

"There's more to catching a guy than getting a new haircut."

"Yeah, well, we'll cover the rest while I'm cutting. Are you with me?" She held the scissors poised at Annie's head. "What was it you told me once your grandma said to you and your cousins—*go get the bachelor next door?*"

Annie snorted out a laugh. "Not exactly. She said, *Don't search so far and wide you miss out on the bachelor next door.*"

"Yeah? So let me edit that fine advice a bit. What she should have said was, *Don't search so far and wide you miss out on the bachelor husband in your own bedroom.*"

She waved the scissors again. "Now, are you with me?"

Annie hesitated, then drew a deep breath. "Just keep it long enough for a ponytail."

Seconds later, she saw the first pieces of her hair fall to the floor. She closed her eyes briefly and hoped this sudden change didn't come across to Nick as an obvious come-hither ploy. "The hair is just the first step," Minnow said, interrupting her thoughts. "You have to show the man you're interested. You have to prove to him that *you're* the woman he wants—not that bimbo, Melissa."

"And you're going to teach me these little skills?"

"Me and my team of experts." Minnow picked up a stack of fashion and women's magazines that were piled on the counter. "Just in time for the festival tonight."

Annie groaned. "I knew there was a catch."

"Now, while I'm turning your hair into a thing of exquisite beauty, you can take a few little quizzes I've gathered." Minnow held the magazines up one at a time, setting them back on the counter as she moved through a list of self-improvement topics. "I thought we'd start out with a little self-analysis. For example, *Just How Sexy Are You?* Once we've got that nailed down, we'll move on to *Do You Have What it Takes to Catch the Man of Your Dreams?* And then, just to make sure he's worth all the effort you're about to put forward, our final quiz will be *Is He a Player or a Keeper?*"

Annie let loose a chortle. "So once we're finished here, when I get home, I can expect Nick will drop to one knee and ask me to marry him—or should I say, stay married to him?"

Minnow picked up the top magazine and flipped it open to a dog-eared page. "Cynicism will get you nowhere. Now, are you ready?"

Annie sobered. What did she have to lose? Nick was the man she'd always wanted. She gave a nod.

Minnow grinned. "Be sure to answer as honestly as possible or we won't know exactly what you need to work on." She set the open magazine on the counter and straightened her back like a prim schoolteacher. "Now, let's get started, shall we? Question one. Just how sexy are you? If you were a dessert, you'd probably be (a) apple pie—sweet and all-American, (b) chocolate soufflé—decadent and irresistible, (c) cream puff—firm on the outside, but soft inside, (d) lemon torte—smooth and a little tarty."

Annie choked back a laugh.

"So, which will it be?"

"This is ridiculous."

"You want the guy or not? That's the real question. Are you willing to give it a try?"

Annie sighed. "I've always wanted him. Thing is, he's never wanted me. And I hate to sound like a broken record, but he's engaged to someone else."

"Humor me here. Pick a dessert."

"Only if as you agree my participation doesn't mean I'm going to do anything with the information. If Nick, on his own, decides to end his relationship—"

"Because he's fallen madly, passionately in love with you—"

"For whatever reason—then maybe, just maybe, I might stick a toe into the water. But otherwise, shit Minnow, think how you would feel if some woman started coming on to the guy you were engaged to. I have to respect the choice he's made."

"Fine. Respect it. You just don't have to like it. And if, along the way, you happen to become what he's looking for, well, it's what's-her-name's loss. Now, pick a dessert."

An hour later, her hair wrapped in tin foil, Annie was deep into an article titled, *Unleashing the Real Woman Inside You.* So far, after three quizzes and two articles, she'd yet to discover any brilliant revelation that would make Nick suddenly decide he preferred her over Melissa.

In fact, thus far, the only conclusion she'd been able to come to was that she was a combination apple pie and dry martini, and she appealed to guys who liked to play chess and dance the meringue.

Awesome.

15

———

THE DOOR TO THE SALON CREAKED OPEN, AND VIVIAN waltzed into the room with her chin high, glancing around as if she was royalty expecting a reception. "Oh, dear, where is everyone? I was hoping to sneak in and get my nails done before the festival tonight."

"At lunch." Minnow strolled to the front desk and checked the appointment book. "Jenny could squeeze you in at one."

"Thank goodness. Look at these cuticles." Vivian held up her hands before stopping to pat Annie on the shoulder. "I hope your stomach isn't aflutter in nervous anticipation, dear, being on the court. We'll be announcing the festival's Pansy royalty winners before three o'clock."

Annie gave Vivian a wan smile.

"I'll be back in half an hour. Now, girls, I do have you both down to help pass out hors d'oeuvres tonight. So don't be late. Oh, and Annie! I met a guest of yours, Mr. Lewis, at the village hall. We had the nicest conversation. He was so interested in our little town that I invited him to the festival. He seemed a little worried that he wouldn't have the right clothes to wear, so if you see him, can you reassure him that anything clean and pressed will be fine?" Not waiting for a reply, she swept out the door with flourish.

Annie turned a stricken face to Minnow.

"Let's not overreact," Minnow said.

"Not overreact? These are the words of wisdom from the woman who used the code word yesterday?"

"Yeah, but he was asking about *you* yesterday, not the town. Maybe he's just a curious sort of guy, you know?"

"No." Annie pulled a hand out from beneath the black cape and began to gesture. "Maybe it's a front. Maybe he's trying to throw people off his tail by asking other kinds of questions."

"You're starting to sound like me."

"Well?"

Minnow frowned. "Okay, so I was thinking the same thing—I just didn't want to freak you out. This guy is up to no good. I'm sure of it."

"So what do we do?"

"I don't know—yet. But look at it this way. If he's at the festival, we'll be able to keep an eye on him without too much trouble. We can see who he's talking to—and then all we have to do is find out what he's talking about. There's three of us and only one of him. We just need to make sure one of us always has him in our sights tonight."

Annie nodded. "I'll tell Nick."

"Which brings me to the next most important subject— Pansy royalty." Minnow started to laugh. "You didn't tell me you and Nick were nominated."

"I didn't tell Nick, either."

"Oh, God, you'd better hope you lose."

"I can't believe this even happened. Nominations have

been closed for ages. Then suddenly they decided since Nick was back, we should be on the court?"

"Not to mention, prince and princess."

"Please. The Women's Club wouldn't do that to me."

Minnow shook her head, still laughing. "Don't hold your breath. I just wish I could be there when Nick finds out."

———

An hour later, Annie arrived home, swinging her hair across the back of her neck like one of those women in shampoo commercials. She caught her reflection in the hall mirror and stopped to marvel at the way her hair shimmered in beautiful, strawberry-blond-streaked layers. Minnow had been right. It was amazing what a difference a change in hairstyle made. If only the quizzes and articles had been as helpful.

She lifted the back of her hair with her fingers and let it slip and slide back into place. Who would have guessed she could have hair like this? Though she hadn't done it for Nick—well, not really—she wondered what he would think of her new look. Or whether he would even notice at all.

Hoping to casually run into him, she checked the parlor and dining room to see if he was around, then swung into the kitchen. No luck. Huh. Probably upstairs. Well, she wasn't going to go charging up there; she didn't want to be totally obvious. She had plenty to do to keep herself busy until he came down, including baking more cookies and finishing the cleaning.

But ... if she made cookies right now, she'd have to pull her hair back and then she'd look the same as she always did. And with her luck, that would be the moment Nick would show up.

She pulled herself up short. Just what was she doing, anyway? Was she really buying into Minnow's makeover plan? Did she really want Nick if the only way he liked her was because of her hair? Her mind wavered on the reply. Whatever happened to *beauty begins inside?* Was it all just lip service?

With a sigh, she pulled out a dusting cloth and began to dust her way through the house. She really had to quit obsessing about this and get back to keeping herself busy so she didn't have time to think about Nick. This afternoon with Minnow had clearly only made things worse.

She methodically worked her way through the parlor, adjusting a picture frame here, moving a knick-knack there, doing a more thorough dusting job than usual just to keep herself occupied.

The sound of a lawn mower engine roared past the parlor windows. Only one person could be mowing the lawn—and that was Nick. She forced herself to keep dusting. *He was doing yardwork without even being asked.* She painstakingly dusted the intricately carved wooden legs and claw feet of the marble-topped antique end table.

The sound of the mower rose and fell as it moved back and forth across the lawn in front of the house. She dusted the top edge of a row of pictures hanging on the wall, and then the bottom edges and the sides. *What could be the harm in one little peek?*

The smell of fresh-mown grass drifted in through the open windows. She wiped off the window ledge with great precision, poking her dust cloth into every little nook and cranny. And then, as though her hand were possessed of a mind of its own, it reached over the sofa and used one finger to pull the lace curtain to the side just a bit.

Shirtless. The man was shirtless.

Sweat glistened across his tanned shoulders and on the black hair curling on his broad chest. She drew a shaky breath. What a vision.

He glanced up at the window. And waved.

She jumped back, letting the curtain fall shut, heart pounding, cheeks burning with mortification.

Shaking her head, she dropped into the big wingback chair facing the hearth. What was she doing? She knew better than to go after Nick, knew that he was already spoken for. Yet she'd just spent two hours trying to figure out how to get him to like her.

She was trying to get an engaged man to fall for her.

Unbelievable. The more she changed, the more she stayed the same. This reminded her of the way she used to be. Wanting the wrong guy and refusing to accept that he was all wrong for her. Suddenly she felt like crying. Nick had come to Bedford to get a divorce. He'd stayed to help her out. There was nothing more to it.

And she was, once again, ready to play the fool for love —or lust or infatuation—or whatever it was she was feeling right now.

She squeezed the bridge of her nose with two fingers to hold back her tears. Time to put her hair up into a ponytail. Time to get back to the original plan. Four days down, five to go.

How on earth would she make it the next five days?

The front door opened and footsteps sounded in the hall. Damn it all, she didn't want to see Nick right now. Didn't want to face him like a beet-faced teenager caught stalking her latest crush—a teenager who'd gone out and had her hair cut and streaked to get his attention.

Thank God, this chair had such a high back. She jerked her legs up underneath herself and pulled her elbows in tight so she was hidden from the hall.

The footsteps paused at the entrance to the parlor, and she pressed herself lower in the chair as if it would make her invisible. *Go away, go away, go away.*

"Yes, yes, I realize that," Mr. Lewis said from somewhere behind her.

She relaxed and let out the breath she'd been holding. Wasn't Nick at all, just Mr. Lewis. On his phone.

"I don't want to appear unduly interested in their affairs," he said after a pause.

Annie couldn't help marveling over how crisp he spoke.

"I haven't yet had a chance to speak with the housekeeper, but in my experience, you learn more when people are unaware of your motives."

Goose pimples rose on her arms, and she turned her head so she could better hear.

"I'm still attempting to pull all the pieces together, but to the best of my knowledge—"

He broke off, and Annie had to keep herself from leaping to her feet and demanding he finish his sentence.

"It appears there's more to it than we thought," he said finally. "But I could be wrong. Just want to be sure I've got everything before I leave." After a pause, he said, "I'll email the photos as soon as I write up the overview. The full report should be ready for presentation in a couple of days."

She couldn't make out his next sentence because he had begun to walk toward the kitchen. Why had she ever told the man he could have as many cookies as he wanted?

A report with photos? What the hell was he up to? Was this about her and Nick? Was he on to them or not?

She waited until she heard him head upstairs, then jumped to her feet and dashed out the door to find Nick. Glancing frantically side to side, she finally spotted him cutting the grass along the edge of the woods at the far end of the yard. Chester pranced along behind him like he was Nick's devoted attendant.

In classic race-walker form, she hurried across the lawn, afraid to run in case Mr. Lewis looked out a window and spotted her. The breeze blew her newly shorn locks in her face and she shoved the hair out of her eyes, thankful she'd made Minnow leave it long enough to put into a ponytail—even if she hadn't done it yet.

As she neared, Nick shut off the mower and waited, one hand casually resting on the mower handle. Correction. Make that one strong hand, connected to a muscled bare arm connected to a broad bare chest. Annie steeled her resistance at this close-up of him. Chester bounded out to greet her and she reached down to pat his head and take a moment to rein in her thoughts.

She straightened and looked at Nick again, with every intention of telling him what she'd overheard. But her subconscious, that part of her mind that refused to ignore how little Nick was wearing, rammed itself forward again. Look at those abs, it whispered. *Washboard.*

Against her better judgment, she looked. *Legs ... check out the definition in those calves. This guy has better legs than pro soccer players.*

And with him wearing those tiny running shorts, how could she not notice his muscled thighs and that tight ass and that—

She gulped.

"What's the matter?" he asked.

She whipped her eyes up to his face and felt heat race up her cheeks. "Uh, how's the poison ivy?"

"You came out here to ask me that?"

No, but she wasn't about to admit the real reason she was staring at his lower extremities. A silly grin crossed her face. She knew it was silly because she couldn't control the quivering of her lips.

"Are you all right?"

"Actually, no."

"Nice hair."

He noticed? The temperature of her cheeks rose to combustion level. "Oh. Minnow convinced me to try something new."

He nodded. "Looks nice."

She nodded back.

He nodded again and his mouth slid into a grin. "So you came out here because ...?"

She gave her head a shake. "Right, yeah. I just overheard Lewis on his cell phone. He's putting together a report, sending pictures—and I'll be shocked if it doesn't involve you and me." She quickly related what she'd heard. "Not only that, but Vivian said he was down at the village hall asking questions about Bedford, and she invited him to the festival tonight. Minnow and I thought we should do some surveillance on him there."

Nick nodded. "What the hell is his gig? I'm thinking he's probably not a B & B reviewer, based on what you heard anyway."

"Cross that off the list. Any ideas?"

"Developer, maybe. Or, Minnow's theory, the IRS."

"*Or something else.* What if he's up to something we haven't even thought of? What then, Nick?"

He nodded. "I know. The bigger problem is that every possibility we've come up with has the potential to wreak havoc on your life if it comes out that you and I aren't what we say we are."

He wiped the beads of sweat off his forehead with the palm of his hand, and she tried to stay focused on the conversation and not on how the muscles flexed in his tanned arm.

"It goes back to what I said before," Nick continued. "Our best hope is that he makes a mistake. Lucky for us he's staying here. And even luckier, Vivian invited him to the festival. He'll never suspect we're keeping an eye on him. But when the guy finally trips up, we'll be there to catch him."

Annie put a hand to her chest. "I don't think I can take this kind of stress. It's like living in one of Minnow's spy thrillers. Except everything won't be tied up nice and neat on the last page, with everyone living happily ever after"

"The more I think about it, the more I bet he's a developer. It fits that he'd be asking questions at the village hall. And it would tie in with you because you have such a great piece of property."

"What I heard of his phone call didn't sound as if he was after land."

Nick glanced at the thick forest behind him. "I don't know. I'd be surprised if you didn't have developers after your land. Come on, I want to show you something."

"What about Mr. Lewis?"

"Nothing we can do about him right now. Come on."

He untied his T-shirt from the handle of the lawn mower and pulled it over his head, then started toward an overgrown footpath leading into the woods. Chester raced ahead into the underbrush.

Nick stopped and turned toward Annie. "Will he run away if we take him along with us?"

"No. Just yell *Chester McLester* and he'll come right back."

"*Chester McLester*? Why doesn't this surprise me?"

Hearing his words, the dog bounded to Nick's side and sat down as if waiting for his next command.

Nick lifted one foot and eyed the poison ivy bumps on his lower calf. "This little piece of information would have been helpful a couple of mornings ago."

Annie laughed. "Didn't Luella tell you? His previous owner trained him to answer to that. Kind of a weird guy."

"No kidding. Come on, let's go."

"Wait, Nick. I'm serious about Mr. Lewis. Shouldn't we stick around to see what he's up to?"

"How? Sit outside his door? Follow him on his walks? Steal his phone?"

"Maybe."

He laughed, the sound low and resonant, and she felt herself begin to melt.

"Come on, this won't take long." Nick retraced his steps and grabbed Annie's hand, lacing his fingers with hers.

16

———

Annie let herself be pulled along into the woods, almost shivering at the feel of his callused palm against her smooth one, her mind wishing he would slip those rough fingers through her new, silky-smooth hair and over her cheeks and lips and down her shoulders and—

"I hiked out here this morning," Nick was saying, "and I'm even more convinced. You're sitting on a gold mine."

The path narrowed, and he let go of her hand to move in front of her, leading the way. Annie swatted at the mosquitoes that were trying to feast on her face and arms. "Seems more like a mosquito mine to me," she muttered. "What are you talking about?"

"You'll see."

Ten minutes later, they came to a halt at the river. Nick looked at her, his enthusiasm evident. "What do you see?"

"Ah, a dead end?"

He snorted out a laugh. "Wrong answer. It's a beginning." He pointed at the shallow sandy bank that sloped into the gently flowing water. "What do you see there?"

"This is a trick question, isn't it? A riverbank."

"Annie! It's a launching spot—"

"Of course, that was my next guess. And we would be launching ...?" *He'd better not say canoes and inner tubes.*

"Canoes and tubes. I talked to the old guy who owns all that property where the river runs along his pasture. You put the canoes in here. And he's agreed to let you pull them out on his land."

Nick turned and gestured at the woods. "All you have to do is cut a narrow road in here to bring the boats in. And build a storage shed. With a little grooming, that path we took would be a perfect route for guests to follow as they start their wilderness adventure."

She tried not to gape at him. Had he completely forgotten their conversation the other day? Just when did he think she would fit all this extra work in? She didn't have time to build sheds and roads—let alone give canoe trips down the river. And she sure as hell didn't have money to pay someone else to do it.

"I—"

"Don't say *no* so fast."

"So fast? I already said *no* yesterday. And you promised to quit bugging me about it."

He winced. "I know. But then I realized you weren't making an informed decision. In order to do that you have to fully understand what you're turning down."

"I do."

"No. You don't. I've been hiking through the woods, following the river, thinking this thing over. *In detail.* Here's the beauty of it. This part of the river is pretty calm. So *you* won't have to go along on the adventures. Maybe you'd give some basic instructions before they set off. But that's it. A couple of hours later, depending on how long the adventurers want to be out, you pick them up at the end point."

He opened his arms wide as if to embrace the wilderness. "Bailey House Bed & Breakfast. Not just a place to sleep, but a place to awaken your adventurous spirit. Annie, it'll fill your rooms, summer, winter, spring, and fall." He grinned. "What do you think?"

A small thrill ran through her. She had to admit it sounded intriguing, especially with his energy driving it, his passion for the plan. But ideas like this had to stand up in the cold light of reality. And the truth was, there was no way she could do it on her own. Luella couldn't help with something like this, and the thought of having any more to manage on her own was enough to kill any enthusiasm she might have. She shook her head in discouragement and started back toward the house.

"No?" Nick caught up with her. "Annie, it's perfect."

"There're all sorts of reasons it won't work."

"Name one."

One? She could name several. "I don't own any canoes."

"An easy fix."

"There's no road in—and no storage shed."

"Another easy fix."

"It'll cost money—a decent amount of it, too."

"You have to spend money to make money."

"I can't lift canoes by myself."

"The customers lift the canoes."

"I'm having a baby."

"You mean to tell me that once you have that kid you're never leaving the house again?"

"Ohh!" She threw her hands in the air.

"You have some of the weakest excuses I've ever heard."

She drew in a long, slow breath. *Fine. Just fine.* She

stopped and turned to face him. He drew up short and narrowed his eyes as if trying to figure out what she was going to say next.

"Okay, Mr. Answer Man. I can't run a canoe business ..." She let out a sigh. "I can't do it because ... because ... I've never been in a canoe before."

A grin slid across his face and his eyes sparkled. And then he threw back his head and laughed. She watched him for about five seconds, then spun on her heel and began to march through the woods. Well, march as well as one could when much of the path was overgrown.

"Annie!" She could hear the laughter in his voice as he came up behind her. "There's nothing to it. Especially on a river like this one."

"Oh, please. This, the input from the adventure writer, the man who strives for ever-increasing adrenaline rushes. You probably consider roller coasters tame."

"Ah, some of them. But, Annie, you have to admit, this idea has potential."

He was right about that. Lots of potential for someone who had experience in the outdoors. But no potential for a woman who spent a childhood on military bases and an adulthood in cities. These woods were as close to nature as she'd gotten in all her life. She whacked a fat mosquito on her arm.

"Let me show you—I'll take you canoeing," he said. "Humor me. Give me one little canoe trip to show you what *could be* ... before I drop out of your life forever."

Drop out of your life forever. Well, didn't that about say it all? "I don't think so."

That was all she needed—to be alone with Nick in a little boat for hours, herself overcome with lust and him merely trying to teach her the finer points of boating.

"Why not? Come on, a little canoe trip. We'll put in right here on your property and the minute you say *stop,* we'll stop."

She glanced over her shoulder. "Where's the canoe coming from?"

"There has to be somewhere to rent one in town."

"Nope." Good. His idea was dead in the water. She smiled to herself about the bad pun.

They broke out of the woods into her yard, and Nick dropped into step beside her. "Then I'll buy one."

She stopped and stared at him. "Don't be silly. What'll I do with it when you leave?"

"It'll be the first of your fleet."

"I'm not going."

He eyed her perceptively, like he was seeing into her soul. She glanced away.

"Don't tell me you're afraid," he said quietly, but with a challenge underlining his words.

"I'm not afraid."

"Yes, you are. Then we're going for sure. You need a little excitement in your life."

Frankly, between Nick and Mr. Lewis, she could do with a little less excitement.

"Come on, Annie. How about tomorrow morning—say ten o'clock?"

"Nick—"

"Enough excuses. We're going. Just one canoe trip and I'll leave you alone."

She threw up her hands in resignation. "Oh, fine. Better make it ten-thirty. I'll have all my morning chores done by then."

Nick patted her on the arm. "Don't worry, it'll be fun. Once I finish cutting the grass, I'll find us a canoe."

She nodded and headed toward the house. Behind her, the lawn mower roared to life again, reminding her that she was a failure, an utter failure, at sticking to her convictions. All she had to do was say *no* and mean it. And she couldn't even do that. Why did Nick have to get so involved in everything here? Couldn't he just play his role for nine days and move on? He was going beyond messing up her life and moving well into messing up her head.

She bent to pull some weeds from one of the flower beds. Well, all right, if she was honest about this, he wasn't messing up her head so much as she was. It was *her* brain that had turned last night's kiss into something it wasn't, *her* brain that was going to make the next five days a living hell. She ripped a particularly stubborn weed out by its long, tenacious roots.

And seeing how it was *her* brain, surely she could control it. She could be near Nick and not be overcome by want, by need ... by insatiable attraction.

It might help if she concentrated on those flaws of his. Right, *flaws*. It might help even more if he were ugly ... or flabby. *Or not such a nice guy.*

No, none of that mattered. All she had to do was set her mind to controlling her brain—and not lose sight of the fact that he had a fiancé. Mind over matter. Forget the goal of staying away from Nick. That was next to impossible. She just had to remember: fiancé, Melissa, engaged to be married.

That really put a nail in it, made everything so simple and freeing. If she just kept reminding herself of those three facts, she'd should be able to go canoeing without a worry.

She tried it again. *Fiancé. Melissa. Engaged to be married.* Yes, this would work wonders.

Nick pushed the mower across the lawn as he watched Annie walk slowly away. Could she really be that afraid of a canoe trip? If that was the case, she'd led too sheltered a life. She'd taken steps in the right direction by going to school and buying this place. But she'd gotten complacent just when she should have found a new challenge.

Maybe she just didn't know how to take the next step. Maybe she just needed a hand finding it. Well, he could take care of that—finding challenges was his specialty. He grinned. That's what he would leave her to remember him by—a splash of excitement in her dull, small-town life, and just maybe, a path to a better future for the inn.

His thoughts turned to Melissa, and for the umpteenth time he mentally reexamined the revelation he'd had last night. The thoughts came quickly. Even in broad daylight he couldn't deny the truth. He didn't love her. *He couldn't marry her*. And he had to tell her soon. Every day closer they got to the date, the more pain this would cause her.

He glanced at his watch. Paris was seven hours ahead. It was always impossible to reach Melissa in the evening when she was on location. First thing in the morning was his best bed. Which meant he would have to make the call at one or two a.m. His gut twisted at the thought of breaking Melissa's heart. He may not love her, but that didn't make it easy to think about hurting her.

A silver Lincoln pulled into the driveway, and he watched Annie wave at the driver. Moments later, the door popped open and out stepped Vivian wearing a wild floral-print dress and big straw hat covered with matching flowers. No mistake about it—Flower Festival day had arrived.

Vivian stopped for a brief exchange with Annie before

the two turned to stare across the wide expanse of grass at him. Hopefully, Vivian wouldn't decide to come out and say hello.

No such luck.

The women marched toward him, one hand on top of her hat to keep it from blowing off in the steady breeze, the other holding a rolled sheet of paper. Annie almost had to run to keep up with her. He shut off the mower and waited, allowing himself to admire Annie's long legs as she strode across the lawn in Vivian's wake.

"Nick! I have the most wonderful news for you," Vivian said in a breathless voice when she reached him. She rubbed his forearm, then lifted her hand to look at her palm, wet with his sweat. Revulsion whipped across her face, then disappeared beneath a weak grin as she patted her hand gently on the side of her dress.

"At any rate," she said, as though she had been interrupted midsentence, "I've come to personally let you know that you and Annie have been elected Pansy Prince and Princess for this year's Flower Festival. Congratulations! Isn't it wonderful?"

Pansy Prince and Princess? Nick cleared his throat and raised an eyebrow at Annie, expecting any minute she would laugh and shout, "Gotcha!"

"This is a real honor," Annie said hurriedly.

It wasn't a joke? "I'm sure it is. Just what does being Pansy royalty mean?"

"You ride in a convertible in the parade." Vivian gave a gleeful laugh. "And of course, the two of you dance the first dance at this evening's celebration."

"Of course." He nailed Annie's eyes with his own, and she had the good sense to look contrite.

"All the past Pansy royalty come out on the floor for that dance—it's a lovely show of support for our fundraiser."

"I'm sure it is." He shoved a hand through his hair. "This is quite an honor, I'm sure—and a surprise. To tell you the truth, Vivian, I didn't even know we were nominated." Maybe he should write his next article about the strange culture in small towns.

Vivian looked at Annie in surprise. "Didn't Annie tell you?"

"I didn't want to get his hopes up," Annie said. "You know, in case we lost."

"That wife of mine, what a sweetheart," Nick said to Vivian. "Always looking out for my best interests."

Vivian touched Annie on the arm and reached out with her other hand to do the same to Nick, then appeared to think better of it and patted the air near his sweaty bicep. "That's what love is all about. So ... your robes are being pressed as we speak. I polished the crowns myself just yesterday. You need to be at the Women's Club at six-fifteen to dress. And the parade starts promptly at six-forty-five."

Crowns and robes? Nick slanted a look at Annie.

"Oh, and Nick, the prince always makes a toast. Just a few words. Nothing too spectacular. Something about the fundraiser and the flowers. Don't forget to mention that the museum will be the recipient of the money raised tonight."

"No problem. Thanks for delivering the news, Vi."

She gave him a disapproving frown. "*Vivian,*" she said in a stiff voice before setting off for her car, one hand on top of her hat again.

Nick waited until she was in her car before he turned to Annie. She looked stricken. "Nick, I'm sorry—I—never thought we'd win."

He let her sentence hang in the air so she would squirm a little. Her eyes widened. "Do you hate me?"

"Oh, no," he said. "Here I was, thinking you didn't have any excitement in your life—"

"I have plenty, thank you."

He smiled. *No, sweetheart, you don't.* But if he had anything to say about it, she would soon.

———

Nick adjusted the gold crown on his head and held up the purple velvet cape with its large yellow collar. How perfect, pansy colors. He hooked it around his neck and climbed into the convertible to sit beside Annie on the back of the rear seat. As evening had fallen, the temperature had dropped down into the mid-seventies—not low enough to make a heavy velvet cape comfortable, but a welcome improvement over the heat of the afternoon. He looked at Annie, regal in her own purple cape. He might look the fool, but she looked magnificent.

The only saving grace about this whole thing was that he got to ride in a white 1972 Cadillac El Dorado—a big boat of a car, but what a beauty. He could almost overlook all the pansies decorating the car just for the fact that he was riding in it.

The police car at the head of the parade set off its siren. The scream was promptly joined by other sirens from other police cars and the honking of the town fire engines—a noise combination that almost knocked him over.

Annie grinned at him and he grinned back, amazed to find he was looking forward to the night ahead. With a slight jerk, the car began to move. Nick attempted the royal hand wave that Vivian had tried to teach them twenty minutes ago: *elbow, elbow, wrist, wrist, wipe a tear, blow a kiss.* Now he really did feel like an idiot.

From the comer of his eye he could see Annie watching him. He blew her a kiss and she burst out laughing.

"I don't think the man is supposed to wipe a tear and blow a kiss," she said. "That's my job."

They turned onto Main Street, both sides of which were lined with people who had come out to watch a parade that consisted of three police cars, three fire trucks, six tractors, one marching band, one float covered with pansies, two convertibles—the one they were on and another carrying the mayor—and a bunch of kids throwing candy. This was one easy group to please.

He waved and smiled and waved some more. "Do you think real royalty does arm-strengthening exercises so they don't get tennis elbow?"

Annie smiled regally at him but didn't answer, just went right into the method: elbow, elbow, wrist, wrist, wipe a tear, blow a kiss.

"Superb, my lady," he said with a British accent. "Surely you are of royal blood."

"You may kiss my hand."

Nick brought the back of her hand to his lips, and nearby parade watchers clapped and whistled. He grinned and began to kiss his way up her bare arm.

"Stop!" With a laugh, she pulled her hand away from him. "Get back to work!"

"I rather liked the coffee break," he said. He began to wave again, his gaze sweeping absently over the spectators, not really focusing on anyone until he spotted Vivian, deep in conversation with—oh, shit—Mr. Lewis.

17

NICK ELBOWED ANNIE. "CHECK IT OUT. TEN O'CLOCK."

As if she could hear him, Vivian turned slightly and, still talking, gestured directly at Nick and Annie.

"Are they talking about us?" Annie asked from between clenched teeth and smiling lips.

Nick broadened his smile and waved directly at Vivian and Mr. Lewis. "Maybe he's just making small talk."

"He's getting a bit too cozy around town for me."

"Uh-huh. Let's hope he shows up at the festival so we have a chance to find out what this guy's all about."

The parade ended half an hour later and everyone went into the community center for the festival. Vivian led Nick away to judge the flower arrangements, while Annie reported to the kitchen for appetizer duty. A short while later, tray of mini quiches in hand, she made her way through the large crowded hall, stopping to offer hors d'oeuvres to nearly everyone she passed.

She spotted Mr. Lewis wandering among the flower arrangements. At least he wasn't talking to anyone ... yet. Where was Minnow? With this crowd, and Nick tied up judging flowers, there was no way she'd be able to keep an eye on Lewis by herself. She needed reinforcements.

Maybe she should wander over and offer him an appetizer. Maybe he'd choke on it and have to leave the party. Hmm, now there was a promising thought.

She scanned the gathering again, finally spying Minnow near the front door. Relief washed through her. She pushed her way gently across the room, apologizing profusely to each person she jostled, but determined not to waste a moment. Grabbing Minnow by the elbow, she dragged her off to a comer for a strategy meeting.

"Where have you been?" Annie shifted the tray of appetizers to her other hand.

"Emergency. Some kid tried to dye her own hair and it turned orange. Why? What's going on?" Minnow popped one of the mini quiches into her mouth and nodded at Annie. "Nice hair."

"That's what Nick said—"

"He noticed? Aha! He's hooked. All we need to do is reel him in."

Annie rolled her eyes. "It's hard not to notice when someone's hair is substantially shorter and blonder than it was two hours earlier. Especially when it's no longer in a ponytail."

"Maybe. Still, you look great." She shook her head proudly. "You must have a great hairdresser."

"I do. Thanks. Now, listen, we saw—"

"Nice dress, too. Ooh-la-la. I didn't even know you owned a black sheath. What did Nick have to say about that?"

Annie huffed. "He said, Baby, I want to tear that thing off and make passionate love to you all night long. Now, Minnow, be quiet a minute so I can tell—"

Minnow choked on her appetizer. "Oh, my God! He did?"

"Get real. He said, as he was putting on the sport coat Luella borrowed from her grandson, *I can't believe people get this dressed up to buy flower arrangements.*"

"Oh." Minnow took another mini quiche. "Well, if you ask me—if he noticed your hair, he noticed your dress. He's just trying to play it cool, that's all."

"Whatever! Can we drop that subject for a minute? I think we've got a real problem with Mr. Lewis. And if we don't take care of it, we won't have to worry about whether Nick thinks I look hot or not."

Minnow shopped chewing and swallowed. "What's he done now?"

"He was chatting up a storm with Vivian during the parade. Like old friends. He's up to something and tonight we'd better get a clue about what it is."

"Is he here yet?"

Annie tilted her head to the right. Her crown started to slip and she reached up to push it back into place. "Near the bar. See him? Now he's talking to an alderman."

"You know, he's just suspicious. It's one thing to vacation somewhere and go to a local festival. It's another to start asking questions all over town." Minnow narrowed her eyes. "I'm going to talk to him."

"Be careful. If he figures out we're onto him he might take off."

"You don't have to worry about *this* undercover agent. Small talk is my secret weapon. I'll start out with the weather and end up with what he does for a living."

Annie recalled Minnow's undercover act at dinner the night they'd discovered Mr. Lewis was a guest at the B & B. "If you think you can pull it off," she said dubiously. She spotted Vivian heading toward them, waving a hand above her head. "Oh-oh. The slave driver's seen us. Vivian's been going crazy waiting for you so she can give out the last work assignment. I'm getting out of here. If you need me, I'll be mingling near our prey."

Holding her tray out in front like a cowcatcher on a locomotive, she moved back into the party, greeting people and passing out hors d'oeuvres as she worked her way toward Mr. Lewis. The man was not going to have free rein here tonight—not if she could help it. She watched him stroll between the tables of flower arrangements, hands clasped behind his back, pausing every now and then as if taken by the aesthetic beauty of a specific arrangement.

Clearly a ploy. Well, he wasn't fooling her. Time to take matters into her own hands.

She stepped to his side, stomach slightly queasy with nerves. "Appetizer?"

"Thank you." He accepted the napkin she offered, then took one of the tiny quiches from her tray.

"Are you enjoying your stay in Bedford?" She tried to sound natural and not nosy.

"Very much. I love small towns."

"So you're from a big town then?"

"Milwaukee."

Aha. "Biggest in the state," she said in a chipper voice. "How'd you find your way to our little B & B?"

He frowned, and she cringed inside, afraid that she was being too obvious. "I'm asking because we want to be sure to continue advertising wherever it works," she said in a rush.

"You're on the Wisconsin Bed and Breakfast Association Web site." He smiled.

"Of course. Well, we're glad to have you. And it's nice

that you've come to the festival. We don't get many out-of-towners."

"Vivian invited me this morning. She's been a fount of information about your town history. I understand she's on the board for your new museum."

Annie laughed lightly, as though the two were sharing a private joke. "Yes, she is. She's served on just about every board in town at one time or another. Lived here her whole life." She swallowed and pushed herself forward. "I take it you're doing some sort of research?"

"In a sense. Yes, I suppose you could say I am."

Annie's heart hammered so loudly in her ears she was afraid she wouldn't be able to hear his answer. She tightened her grip on the tray and forced her expression to remain calm. "I love research. What are you looking into?"

He smiled apologetically. "I really am not at liberty to discuss it. Proprietary. I'm sorry."

Disappointment rolled through her. "I understand. My husband has the same situation ... with his job."

She glanced at Nick, deep in thought as he contemplated the beauty of the particular flower arrangement he was judging. Wistfulness stabbed at her, a longing for him to love her, for their marriage to be real.

"I understand he's with the military."

Her heart seemed to slow. "Yes. Yes, he is."

"It must be hard for the two of you, with him gone so much of the time."

Oh my God, the tables had turned. Mr. Lewis was quizzing *her* now. If she wasn't careful, she'd end up helping him destroy her life.

"It is, but we manage. Love is a powerful cement." She took a step back and smiled brightly. "I'd better get back to work. Have to get a fresh tray of appetizers before Vivian catches me loitering!"

———

Clipboard in hand, Nick paused in front of a large flower arrangement and pondered its lines. He glanced at question three on the score sheet again. *Is there a pleasing ratio of large to small flowers?*

Hardly.

Some were big, some were medium, some were small. There didn't seem to be any rhyme or reason to the arrangement. But then, what did he know?

It was easy, they'd told him. All he had to do was give it a score—one through five, with five being the best. He scowled. This arrangement didn't really seem like a five or four, maybe not even a three. But a two? That seemed harsh; he didn't want to hurt someone's feelings.

What was wrong with him?

He scratched a two in the space and glanced wistfully back at question one: *Are the flowers fresh, with no signs of dried edges?* If only all the questions were that easy.

And then there had been question two: *Do the colors complement one another?* That had been pretty easy, too.

But there were six questions total, and he was finding each more difficult than the last.

Not to mention it didn't help that several of the women who just *happened* to stop and say hello were singing the praises of one or another centerpiece—generally their own. He looked at question four: *How well does the grouping of flowers draw the eye into the arrangement?*

How should he know? He glanced around, hoping to spot at least one of the other judges looking just as puzzled as he was, but they were all intently scribbling on their score sheets, or staring, rapt, at whatever arrangement happened to be in front of them.

A small group of people strolled by, sipping wine as they discussed which arrangements each was bidding on in the silent auction. The *hideous* arrangement he was judging had already been bid up to forty-three dollars. Maybe the bidders knew something he didn't. He erased the two that he'd scored the last question and replaced it with a three.

Now where was he? Oh, yeah. *How well does the grouping of flowers draw the eye into the arrangement?*

About the only thing that would draw his eye into this arrangement was a bottle of beer stuck in the middle. And maybe even that wouldn't do it.

Speaking of liquor, maybe a drink would help his judging skills. And speaking of judging skills, where was Annie, his princess? Maybe she could lend him a hand with judging. He searched the crowd, finally spotting her near the bar, her sparkling crown off kilter, a tray of hors d'oeuvres in one hand and a glass of soda in the other.

He turned the current score sheet face down on his clipboard for privacy, and headed toward her. Vivian slid into his path. "Oh, Nick, what a surprise," she said with a slow smile. "How is the judging going? So many lovely arrangements, aren't there?"

He nodded.

She took his arm. "My own entry is a tasteful arrangement of yellows, golds and oranges, with some purple-blues thrown in for heightened contrast. Have you had a chance to see it yet?"

"No, but I'll look for it." He gave her his most charming smile. Vivian had just presented him with the perfect opportunity for information gathering. "Was that Mr. Lewis

I saw you talking to at the parade? He's a guest at the B & B."

"Oh, yes, very nice man. I combined mums with daffodils and daisies—all varying shades of yellow."

"Hmm." Nick nodded as though interested. "I imagine he's enjoying his stay?"

"Who?"

"Mr. Lewis, the man you were talking to at the parade."

"Oh. Yes, I imagine he is. I invited him to the festival and it's so nice to see he was able to make it. He's very impressed with Bedford, you know. At any rate, my entry has a gold vase—"

"Did he say anything about Annie?"

"Just what an attractive couple the two of you make. It's on table four—"

"What is?"

"*My arrangement.* Nick, are we going to talk about Mr. Lewis or my entry?"

"Your entry, of course. I've just been wondering whether or not Mr. Lewis is happy with the accommodations. Our aim is to please, you know."

She waved a dismissive hand. "You needn't worry that he is unhappy with the B & B—he didn't so much as say a word about it. He was actually asking about Bedford—tourist things. The only thing he asked about you and Annie was how long you two lived here, how long you've owned the B & B."

He wanted to know how long they'd lived here? Why did the guy care? Something was definitely fishy under the dock. "That's it?"

Vivian nodded.

He tried to move past her, and she stepped to counter his escape. "It's a low gold vase. Number eighteen."

He nodded.

"Bidding's already up to sixty-seven dollars, so it's doing quite well."

"You must be proud." He stepped to the left and she countered again, sliding her hand into the crook of his arm. She began to pull him toward table four.

"Ah, Vi, I was just going to—"

"Vivian." She smiled up at him. "The thing of it is, what with all your expertise in horticulture, I was wondering if you might be able to stop by my house some afternoon. Give me some advice about my ... hydrangeas. They just aren't blooming well this year."

They stopped in front of the table where her arrangement was displayed. She rubbed a hand along his forearm. "And I don't know exactly what to do to help them."

"Have you tried fertilizer?" he asked.

"Yes. But I've begun to think they need your magic touch. Annie seems to have blossomed since you arrived—I mean the flowers in her beds have. And, well, speaking of beds ..." She smiled coyly.

No way. Was Vivian coming on to him? This woman wanted to win the contest—and nothing was going to stand in her way.

Looking for help, he glanced over at Annie. She was engaged in an animated conversation with a small group of people he didn't know. He willed her to turn around and was disappointed when his desperate attempt at telepathy failed.

"So what do you think?" Vivian was saying.

Reluctantly, he focused his attention on her again.

"Ah, have you tried beer?" he asked.

"But—I don't have a problem with slugs."

Oh, was that what it was for? "I use it as a multipurpose cure-all with my plants," he lied. "Just sprinkle a bit over the leaves. You'd be amazed at the difference it makes. Kind of like with people—it relaxes them, helps them overcome their daily stressors."

Vivian had a look of awestruck horror on her face.

"In fact," he continued, "that's exactly what I was planning to do when I ran into you—get a beer." He squeezed past her, talking continuously so she couldn't get a word in. "As for your arrangement, there are so many lovely arrangements. Why, I haven't seen so many stunning warts of ark ... ah, works of art ... since the last—oh, there's Annie. I'm sure you won't mind—if you will excuse me, please."

Annie had finally turned in his direction—better late than never—and the grin that lit up her face seemed like a beacon calling him home. She raised her glass in a welcoming toast and he was half tempted to take her in his arms and kiss her the moment he reached her side.

Instead, he whispered into her ear, "Saw you talking to our boy."

Her smile faded, and she set her empty tray on the bar. "He's doing some sort of research but that's all I could get. It's up to you—I don't think I should try to talk with him again. He'll get suspicious."

"I got some info from Vivian—what he was talking about at the parade. Mostly asking about Bedford."

"Mostly?"

"He also asked how long we've lived here and owned the B & B."

Annie closed her eyes for a long moment.

Nick reached a hand up to gently massage the back of her neck. "Don't panic. It's just small talk. He's probably researching property to develop."

"Just as long as he's not researching people ... and marriages." Annie took a swallow of soda. "Feels like a never-ending game of twenty questions."

"Yeah. I hope we're all wrong about the whole thing. Because if any one of our theories is right, pulling this off could take a miracle."

"What'll take a miracle?"

Nick jerked at the sound of Father Thespesius's voice from behind them. *At the rate things were going, it would take a miracle for him and Annie to survive tonight.*

Annie threw him a panicked look before they both turned to say hello.

"What's this about a miracle?" the priest said, shaking Nick's hand. "You know, those of us in the service of saving souls are always on the lookout for such things."

Nick's brain raced for an answer. "I, ah, Annie was just wishing I could stay in Bedford longer, and I said that it would take a miracle for the military to give me more leave right now."

He put his arm around her shoulders. She rubbed his back affectionately and he pressed a kiss to her forehead. With any luck, the priest would fall for the whole thing.

Father Thespesius shook his head. "I'd sure like to see you stick around, too."

Nick nodded. "Wish I could. But duty calls. Would you like a glass of wine, Father?"

"Don't mind if I do."

Nick waved down the bartender and ordered a beer for himself and a wine for the priest. "Then I'd better get back to judging. Annie, sweetie, would you like to follow along as I judge? I think I could use a second opinion."

She reached up to pat him on the chest. "Vivian would kill me. I'm assigned to pass out appetizers, and she rules with an iron fist. If you get too desperate, come and find me."

Nick took the drinks from the bartender and passed the wine to the priest.

"I'll walk with you," Father Thespesius said after taking a sip. "I may not have your floral expertise, but I know a little something about flowers."

18

NICK FORCED A SMILE. SPENDING MORE TIME WITH Father Thespesius was the least smart thing he could do right now. The priest asked too many questions, and raised too many concerns about the state of Nick and Annie's marriage. Still, he couldn't very well refuse, not after he'd just been asking Annie to help him out.

"Okay, thanks," Nick finally said. "Let's get to work." He took a big swallow of beer.

By the time an hour had passed, the two men were on their third drink and the judging was getting easier by the minute. Why had he been so worried about having Father Thespesius help him out? The guy was great. And he hadn't mentioned Annie once, which really took the pressure off.

Nick peered at the next arrangement. "Check out this one. What do you think it's about?" Father Thespesius read the title. "Lady in Lavender. Hmm." He tapped a finger against his lips. "Perhaps *Elephant in Lavender* would be more appropriate."

Nick snorted, then started to laugh. "Or Whale in Lavender."

"How about Dinosaur in Lavender?" Father Thespesius said between guffaws.

"Dinosaur with Twins in Lavender," Nick choked out as he pointed to some pink flowers on one side of the arrangement.

By that point, they were laughing so hard tears were streaming from their eyes, and Nick had to lean on the table for support.

"I hope the woman who did this one isn't watching us," he said between gasps.

"She's not. This one's mine."

Nick sobered instantly. "You did this? Seriously?"

The priest nodded, blue eyes twinkling.

"Because I think it's actually quite good." Nick tried to hold in his laughter, really tried, but it burst out of him like air from a balloon. At the same moment a great guffaw exploded from Father Thespesius. "Father, at least you'll get a five for effort. And definitely, a five for creativity." Nick marked a row of scores on the sheet. "We're done, let's go turn these pages in—"

"And have a glass of wine to celebrate."

Nick clapped him on the back as they walked toward the bar. "A man after my own heart. You know, for a priest, you're an all-right guy."

"I take that as a compliment."

"Yeah. I didn't think I'd like it in Bedford. Thought I'd hate it, in fact. But even Minnow isn't really that bad once you get to know her." As he said the words, he realized he was actually beginning to like Minnow. "And Annie—she's changed, too—"

"You like her this way?"

Nick nodded. "This little town's been good for her." He looked across the room and his eyes settled on Annie as she flitted her way along the far side of the community center while passing out appetizers. "What a change in six years. I should have known she'd turn out special."

"Six years?"

Nick looked up. Shit. What was that old phrase? Loose lips sink ships? "Months. I mean months. I know she's been happy here—especially the past six months." *Not a bad save.* "It's a great town. Good people. The kind of place you want to stay—" He broke off and gave his head a shake to clear his thoughts.

"The kind of place you can settle down in?" The priest smiled.

Nick felt the room sway just a bit. *Right.* "No. I—I can't."

An expression of dismay settled on Father Thespesius's face. Nick could see genuine sadness in his eyes.

"My job is pretty important ... to our country." He felt a flush of guilt for lying to a priest. "Father—all I can say is, everything isn't exactly as it seems."

The priest sighed. "I was afraid of that. Try to remember that every marriage has its ups and downs. Is there anything I can do to help?"

Shit, now Father Thespesius thought they had marital problems. He glanced over at Annie again. Actually, maybe he was on the right path. It might be good for people to start thinking they were having marital problems. It fit with Annie's plans, would probably make it easier for her when she finally announced they had gotten divorced.

The priest cleared his throat. "I think I'll pass on the wine and take a walk-through to see the bids." He took Nick by the elbow for moment and said, "Just remember, those things hardest won are often the most appreciated."

Nick watched him walk away. He had a sneaking suspicion Father Thespesius had already figured out that there was more to his and Annie's marriage than met the eye. Even so, he felt certain the priest wouldn't bring it up unless Nick or Annie raised the issue. He brought his gaze to rest on Annie as she chatted and laughed with friends.

Five more days and he wouldn't be looking at her again—probably not for the rest of his life. Something stirred within him, a memory of what it felt like when Annie left town a week after their wedding. A hollow feeling. *Loss.*

He wasn't leaving for five days and he was missing Annie already.

A shrink would have a field day with this. Nick had money, the job he'd always dreamed of, and a gorgeous fiancée—who he was about to dump. Yet, in the midst of all that good fortune, he was attracted to, and missing, a woman he hadn't left yet.

Maybe this was just human nature.

Maybe.

And maybe this thing with Annie was something else. Fate.

Minnow sidled up to Annie and nudged her in the side. "He's gone."

"Who?"

"Mr. Lewis. I tailed him all the way back to your house."

"You did? Did he see you?"

"Maybe. But he had no reason to think I was doing anything other than taking a walk."

"Probably went home to file a report with mission control. He told me he's doing research—proprietary research."

Minnow's eyes widened. "Ooh. I'm dying to know what this guy's up to. We should search his room."

Annie rolled her eyes. "No way. That's all I'd need. An arrest for digging in the guy's luggage."

"Annie!"

She spun round to find Vivian at her elbow, the purple velvet capes across her outstretched arms.

"It's time for the toast. Where's Nick?" Vivian pushed up on tiptoes and tried to peer over the crowd.

"He was judging the flowers." Annie swung her cape over her shoulders and secured it at her throat.

"The band is ready to get started. Oh, there he is! Nick!" Vivian took Annie's arm and began to pull her through the crowd.

Annie tossed a look of long-suffering mock exasperation at Minnow. "Duty calls. Talk to you later."

Minnow waved her away.

As soon as they reached Nick, Vivian began firing statements at him in machine-gun staccato. "We're ready to begin. Here's your cape. Get dressed. The band's waiting. Is your toast prepared?"

He blinked. "I, ah, yeah. I memorized it." He hooked the cloak at his neck.

Annie grinned. This would be good. She knew he hadn't prepared even a sentence.

"Come along, then. We've got a schedule to keep." Vivian led them across the hardwood dance floor to one of the standing microphones in front of the band. An assistant handed them each a glass of champagne, then Vivian tapped on the microphone and blew into it, sending a *pfft-pfft* sound through the room.

"Hello, hello. Quiet down, please. Welcome, everyone, to our thirty-third annual Flower Festival. Once again, we've had a wonderful success and I'm sure we'll raise a great deal of money for our new museum. The flower arrangement silent auction ends at ten, so be sure to bid high and bid often. And don't miss that particularly stunning arrangement, number eighteen on table four. In a gold vase."

She smiled over the crowd. "Now, I'm proud to introduce our Pansy Prince and Princess, Nick and Annie Fleming. Nick, will you do us the honor of a toast?"

Nick stepped to the microphone. "Thank you, Vivian, and thank you to everyone who voted for us. I, feel a little awkward up here. Well, awkward and honored. I've only been in town for four days and already I'm the Pansy Prince."

He swished his cape, and a chuckle ran through the audience. Nick looked at the floor a moment, then raised his gaze again.

"I have to say, all of you sure know how to make someone feel welcome. I've been all over the world, and this is the first time in my life I really feel like I've come home."

He reached out and took Annie's hand, drawing her next to him at the mic. The intimacy of that small gesture made her throat tighten with emotion.

Nick lifted his glass high. "So let's do a little drinking and a little dancing and a lot of bidding, and raise some big money for the museum tonight."

A roar went up, and the band swung into a rousing rendition of *Hail, Hail the Gang's All Here*. Nick's thumb caressed the back of her hand, and Annie looked up into his dark eyes. "I thought you didn't prepare," she said.

"I didn't. That just came out."

She had to hold herself back from reaching up and taking his face between her hands and kissing him, from begging him to stay and give them a chance.

From the corner of her eye, she spotted Vivian striding forward again, her words drowned out by the band until she had reached Nick's side. "No time for lingering. Royalty!" She clapped her hands together twice. "Quickly. The line is already forming."

"What line?" Nick asked.

Annie gave him a tenuous smile. "You know how you and I are doing the first dance of the evening? Well, beforehand, there's a grand march."

Nick snapped to attention so fast his crown almost flew off. "A what?"

"Yes." Vivian nodded. "With all the past Pansy royalty."

Annie reached up to straighten his crown and brush her fingers through the black waves of his hair. "It'll be over soon," she said in her most soothing voice.

"It better be. I feel like I'm in high school again. Isn't everyone a little old for this kind of stuff?"

"Hurry, the music is about to begin." Vivian pushed them past a long row of previous royalty to the head of the line. "Twice around the dance floor, then stop in front of the band. Annie, put your arm through Nick's. Don't forget to smile."

The band rolled into a song with an upbeat tempo. Nick leaned toward Annie as they began to lead the group around the perimeter of the dance floor. "Sweetheart, I think you're really going to owe me when these nine days are over," he said through his smile.

"More than you bargained for, huh?"

"I pictured a week and a half of swimming and sunning. A vacation in Wisconsin's Northwoods."

Annie laughed. "Real life is so much more stimulating. Why vacation when you can be part of all this?"

"Yeah ... this is right up there with climbing the Matterhorn."

She turned toward him, ready to shoot back a witty retort, but the smoldering expression in his eyes stalled her response. Her breath caught.

"By the way, you look incredible tonight," he said. "Royalty becomes you."

Annie stared up at him, at a total loss for words. The only thought in her head was that she hoped her lack of response made her look mysterious instead of idiotic. Could Minnow be right? Could Nick be interested, after all? And what if he was? Was it real or was it just a lust thing, an interlude before he went back to Melissa?

After all, this was the man who, years ago, had told her he never wanted to get married. For him to have gotten engaged, meant Melissa had to be something special. Would he really throw her over for Annie? The coffee shop waitress turned bed and breakfast owner-maid?

Or was she about to find herself at the losing end of love, just as she had so many other times? As tempting as Nick was, she had to keep a grip on her emotions. Unless he declared his undying love on bended knee, her heart had to stay encased in bubble wrap. This time, she wasn't getting caught short.

"What's on your mind, beautiful?"

She started. *Beautiful?* Oh, she didn't need sweet nothings like that. Not now. "Just thinking about Mr. Lewis.

Minnow said he was leaving. So she followed him to make sure. I just wish we knew ...”

“Stop worrying—she’ll let us know. Code word and all. You’ve got a good life, Annie, and good friends. I really can’t believe that whatever he’s after will destroy that. Even if it is all about you and me.”

“I hope you’re right.”

“You know what you need? You need to leave this place and your worries behind for a few hours.”

She laughed. “I’m not so sure a few hours would be long enough.”

“It’s a start.”

“Any brilliant ideas?”

“Yeah. Tomorrow’s canoe trip. Let’s make it more than just a quick lesson. We can pack a lunch, leave our phones behind, and really escape.”

She tilted her head. It sounded almost decadent. Hours alone with Nick in a little canoe. No phone calls. No worrying about Mr. Lewis. Just peace and quiet as far as the eye could see.

What was she saying about that bubble wrap? “Sounds tempting.”

“All you have to do is say *yes*. Let me take you someplace that can change your life.”

If he only knew. She just looked at him.

”Trust me,” he said.

She drew a slow breath and let her eyes roam over the party. What did she have to lose—well, except her mind after a few hours in close proximity to Nick? Oh hell. “Lunch on the river. Okay. I’m in.”

They came to a halt at the stage and Vivian pushed them onto the dance floor. “First dance, now. Just you two. Go.”

The band slid into the soft soothing melody of "Moon River," and Annie let herself sink into Nick's arms, up against his strong chest, her cheek to his. The music filled her, the words to the song reverberating through her mind, speaking to both of their lives.

Nick nuzzled her neck and kissed her by the ear so softly it sent a tremor through her. She opened her eyes and looked up at him.

"You're something, you know that?" His eyes darkened, and she felt her body respond.

This wasn't what was supposed to happen. She was supposed to be keeping distance between them. "I am?"

"Uh-huh." His head dipped, and he brushed her lips gently with his own.

"Wh-what are you doing?" she asked. This had to stop. Her bubble wrap was popping all over the place.

"I'm kissing my wife."

"Why?"

"So everyone in town will know how much I'll miss her when I'm gone. We've got a job to do, Annie McCarthy," he said in a low voice.

His mouth came down on hers again, his lips lingering a moment before he brought one hand up to hold her head close to his chest, so close she could hear the beat of his heart. She would remember this moment the rest of her life. And she would not forget again that *they had a job to do.*

Then the music changed and the moment shattered, and they pulled apart. And Nick grinned at her, an easy grin celebrating that they had just pulled off the biggest scam in history. And she smiled back at him in just the same way because, after all, she had to keep him from ever knowing how hard she had fallen for him.

———

Two-thirty in the morning and he was a free man. It just hadn't come about the way he expected it. Nick sat on back porch steps and stared at his phone, stunned. He'd worried over the right words to use with Melissa, how to break off their engagement in the least painful way, if such a thing was even possible. He'd been prepared for her to cry, to get angry, maybe even get hysterical. What he hadn't been prepared for was resignation.

Melissa had sounded resigned. Like she'd gotten bad news she had already known was coming. Her voice had quivered just once, when she asked if he'd met someone else. He'd been quick to answer *no*.

And then she said, "I really tried to like the outdoors. Nick. For you. But the only time I'll be sleeping in a tent again is if it's set up on a king-size bed in a hotel room. This is probably for the best." Then she'd wished him well and they'd ended the call.

Wow. He didn't love her. And she didn't love him. What the hell kind of marriage would that have been?

He bent forward to rest his elbows on his knees. The moon, full and round, cast a silvery fairylike glow on the yard, and he felt as if he had somehow gone to some surreal place.

Why hadn't he figured this out before? Long fingernails and mountain climbing did not a pair make. He supposed he should be happy he hadn't devastated her, supposed he should be devastated that she hadn't loved him after all, but all he could feel was relief that he hadn't married the wrong woman.

19

———

Annie ran a hand along the gunwale of the sleek silver canoe glinting in a ray of sunshine at the river's edge. "I still can't believe you actually bought a canoe. Isn't that a little extravagant for a half-day excursion?"

Nick set two paddles into the boat. He handed her a bright yellow life jacket and slipped into an identical one as he spoke. "The fact that you can't rent one around here bodes well for your business."

She gave a snort. As if she was really going to start offering canoe trips. She glanced down the narrow path they had just followed to the river. "How'd you get it in here?"

"Paid two high school kids from the hardware store." He set Annie's red cooler in the canoe, then shoved the canoe partway into the water. "Okay. Get in from the center," he said, still holding on. "Take the seat in the middle. Keep your weight low."

Annie didn't move. "What time is Luella getting us again?" she asked, stalling.

Nick laughed. "Downriver at one-thirty. We'll just pop

the canoe on top of my car and drive home. Come on, get in."

"I'm going, I'm going." She tossed her sweatshirt into the bottom of the canoe. After another hesitation, she climbed in after it, her movement making the canoe tilt to one side. Her heart flopped and she tried to counterbalance the rock by leaning the other way, succeeding

only in dropping onto the seat with an ungraceful plop. Sacagawea she wasn't.

Sheepish, she glanced back at Nick and was relieved to see he didn't seem to have noticed her clumsiness.

"We're off." Nick pushed the canoe into the water and deftly jumped aboard, taking several quick strokes of the paddle on one side to straighten them out and head the boat downstream. "Now for a quick lesson."

Twenty minutes later, Annie felt like a pro. Well, maybe not a pro, but certainly levels above novice. Nick was a natural teacher, with a real knack for instilling confidence. Too bad he wouldn't be around longer—he would have been the perfect person to run canoe trips for her B & B guests.

She gave herself a mental slap upside the head. Now she was buying into his idea? She focused on the peacefulness of their surroundings, on the blue crane standing along the shore that turned its head to watch them slip past. Overhead, high in the trees that lined both sides of the river, birds called and twittered to one another, unfazed by the canoe that glided through the water like a knife cutting soft butter, hardly a sound or ripple to mark its passing.

"I feel like I've gone back in time," Annie said in a hushed voice. "To the days of Lewis and Clark. What a country this must have been back then."

"Yeah. Makes you appreciate what we have."

Annie nodded. They paddled for an hour, speaking little, moving from calm waters to more exciting spots where the river flowed fast enough to make her adrenaline kick in, and then back to calm again. Before she even realized it, serenity had sneaked into her, a calmness she hadn't felt in a long time. Suddenly, Mr. Lewis and what he was up to no longer seemed so ominous. And, at least for the moment, the pieces of her life seemed to have fallen into their proper places.

"I'm starting to see why you became an adventure writer. There's something really soothing about being out here, alone with the natural world." She glanced over her shoulder at him.

"Way too many people try to escape their stress, soothe their spirits with liquor and drugs. After my years in L. A., I finally discovered this was a much better kick."

"And no hangover."

He laughed. "I'll warn you, though, it can get addictive. Fun, relaxing, exciting, all at once. Kicks endorphin release into high gear, the body's *feel good* chemicals."

"Does it ever get old? When you're so far from home, in foreign jungles and on other country's mountains? Does it ever feel like *work* to you?"

Her questions hung unanswered for a long moment.

"Sure," he finally said. "But it's my job—jobs are supposed to feel like work. I'm luckier than most people—my work is fun. Most of the time."

His answer felt brusque, curt, and Annie began to think she'd irritated him, though she had no idea why. She struggled with how to bring the conversation back to the light-and-easy place where it had been.

"Hey, Nick ... I didn't mean to pry. Forget I asked." She gazed up into the canopy of trees, the sunlight-dappled green leaves dancing against the blue sky high above them.

"No, no—I didn't feel like you were prying. Just made me kind of think about things from a different perspective. When I left L.A. after our wedding, I gave up my apartment. Just went from one adventure to another for years. Whenever I've had a few weeks between assignments, which wasn't too often, I stayed with friends—or my folks—or in hotels."

"Nothing wrong with that."

"But it wasn't home. And that was okay, actually. I liked the freedom. That's what I'd been striving for—to be able to go where I wanted to go, do what I wanted to do."

Annie thought back over the past six years and smiled sadly to herself. He'd been looking for freedom, and she'd been looking for a place to settle down. They couldn't be more opposite.

"Will Melissa travel with you once you're married?"

"Uh—"

"Haven't you talked about it?"

"Sure. Oh, yeah. It's just—well—she's got modeling to do ... and well, Annie, there's not going to be a marriage."

"Oh." *Oh?* She stared straight ahead. "When did this happen?" she asked with feigned disinterest.

"This morning. Two o'clock. I called it off."

Nick called it off? Her heart pounded. She couldn't think of one single word to say other than *awesome!* and somehow that didn't feel exactly appropriate.

"Anyway, it's over. Guess I'm back to the life of a wandering adventurer."

Eyes still forward, she nodded, wanting to know more and afraid to ask. She had no right to push him for details. He'd tell her more when he was ready.

If only, *if only,* he was ready right now. An awkward silence settled over them.

"You having a good time?" he finally asked.

"Totally. This is great."

"Good. Now, think about all those people in Milwaukee and Chicago racing to work, day after day after day. Fighting the traffic, the parking, the crowds on the 'L', walking busy city blocks to the office. Breathing in diesel fumes and smoggy air. Working late hours and getting home after dark. Got that pictured?"

"Uh-huh."

"What do you think they would pay to get away to a place that takes away their stress by connecting them with nature? What would it be worth to them to go back to the simplicity of Lewis and Clark days, even if only for a weekend?"

"You should be in sales." His idea really did make perfect sense for her business. Well, almost perfect. Because there was no way she would be able to pull it off alone— especially since she didn't have any personal experience in outdoor adventures. Not to mention her baby on the way. But maybe ... it might be worth looking into hiring someone, a part-time person to be her adventure coordinator.

She glanced back at Nick to thank him for insisting she take this canoe trip, for giving her hands-on proof that his ideas just might work. His life jacket was in the bottom of the canoe and he was stripping off his T-shirt. At the sight of his broad, muscled chest, her words lodged in her throat.

She whipped her head forward. Focus. She needed to focus. What was that mantra she had told herself to remember? *Fiancée. Melissa. Engaged to be married.*

Well, that sure wasn't going to work anymore. Her skin prickled with sweat. She was in real trouble now.

"You want to drive?" Nick's voice jolted her out of her self-induced insanity.

"What? You mean like switch places with you?" She didn't dare look back. "Isn't that kind of dangerous?"

"Not if you're careful."

"I don't think so."

"Put your paddle into the canoe and crouch down. I'll just climb over you."

No way. She steeled herself against the sight of his naked chest, and turned, determined to put an end to the idea. "I don't think—"

Thank God, his lifejacket was back on. "Nick, let's not," she said.

He set his paddle in the canoe, and moved into a high crouch, holding the gunwale on either side. "Get low. Here I come."

Annie let out a sigh and bent over. "Is this low enough?"

"Great." Seconds later, he'd finished his part of the maneuver and was squatting in the canoe in front of her, his bare shoulders and strong arms a mere foot away. Thank God a lifejacket was covering his back.

"Just step backward over your seat," he said. "Hold onto the sides as you go back to my seat."

She made a face at his back. *Ten minutes ago she had found serenity and already she'd lost it.*

Holding tight to the canoe, she stepped backward as he'd instructed. This wasn't so hard. Another step or two and she'd be on the back seat and ready to drive. A newfound confidence filled her. As she moved her foot toward the rear, she stepped awkwardly on the handle of Nick's paddle. Shifting her weight, she tried to push the paddle out of the way with her foot, then gave a little hop to get off it. The canoe leaned sharply left.

Panic shot through her, and she hurled her weight to the right to counterbalance the roll. The canoe rocked with her. She could feel Nick move his weight to fight the roll, but since she was already doing the same thing, their combined weight more than the canoe could handle.

"Annie!"

Even before his shout, she knew it was too late. The right side of the canoe dug under the surface, spilling them out like dice in a craps game. She hit the surface with a splash, managing to grab a bite of air before her head went under.

She popped to the surface and spotted Nick a few feet away, treading water next to the upside down canoe. "Sorry," she said with a wince.

"You okay?" He swam to her.

She nodded, glad he'd made her wear a life jacket. "I'm really sorry."

"Don't worry about it. Happens to everyone."

He looked around. "Grab the paddles. I'll get our lunch." He began to swim away from her toward the cooler, bobbing away from them in the current like a red-and-white buoy on the sea.

She took hold of one paddle and swam around the canoe looking for the other. Nick shoved the cooler toward her.

"I can't find the other paddle," she said. "Could it be under the boat?"

"Maybe." He rolled the canoe over so that it was floating upright even though it was full of water. The gunwales were just a couple of inches above water level.

Stroking overhand, she worked her way around the boat again, meeting Nick on the other side. Still no paddle. "How could we lose a paddle?"

Nick looked downstream. "I didn't think the water was moving *that* fast. No big deal. We can get home with one."

He grasped the rope tied to the front of the canoe and began to swim toward shore. "Let's get out of the water and regroup."

They pulled the canoe up on the riverbank and flipped it over to empty out the water. In the shady coolness, goose bumps rose on Annie's arms and she shivered. Nick pointed to a bright area through the trees. "Looks like some open ground over there. You can warm up in the sun before we get going again."

After a few minutes of picking their way through the underbrush, they broke out into a sun-drenched meadow of tall grass and scattered wildflowers. Teal-blue dragonflies danced in the air.

"Wow. Is this still your land?" Nick gazed around in appreciation.

"I don't know exactly where we are right now, but I don't think so."

"You could cut a deal with the landowner. Have your canoe trips stop here so people can take a break, hike around, have lunch. Annie—"

"I know, I know, I'm sitting on a gold mine."

He grinned. "At least you're getting into the right frame of mind."

He began walking in a circle, stomping down the tall grass. "Help me make a place for us to sit down, will you?"

Annie followed his lead, pushing down the grass with her feet until they had made an area large enough for the two of them and then some.

"Good thing I tied my shirt in or I might have lost it." Nick set the cooler down, then lay his wet T-shirt and their life jackets across the top of the grass to dry.

Good thing. Because if he was going to spend the rest of their trip naked from the waist up, she was going to have to hike back to town.

"My sweatshirt must have sunk. I'm glad I wore a tank suit." Annie stripped out of her shorts and lay them beside his shirt.

She sat on the cooler and shivered again, this time from the sun's warmth instead of the cool water. Or was it from the nearness of Nick?

Oh, please. Why did she have to dwell on the why? Her mind had gone positively obsessive lately. She bent to untie her wet sneakers.

"Hey, leave your shoes on—let's go see what's around here. Explore a little. I promise we'll stay in the sun." Nick took her hand and led her through the tall grass.

She looked down nervously. "Don't you worry about what's in there? Like snakes or spiders or something ready to bite you?"

"Your feet are safe in shoes. Besides, to those little guys in the grass, we're giant monsters coming after them. Their first reaction will be to run away."

Annie gave him a dubious look, and he chuckled.

As they crossed the meadow, he stopped to examine various plants, then pointed out and named several types of butterflies that were flitting about. Annie marveled at the breadth of his knowledge.

"Take a look at all these milkweed plants. This is probably a haven for monarchs. Which is great because they're struggling these days." He stared at the patch of plants for a long moment. "We lived in a subdivision outside Chicago, lots of woods and fields all around. When I was ten I brought home a handful of milkweed plants with monarch caterpillars on them. Stuck them in the ground by our front porch and watched them every day. Wasn't long before each one had spun a chrysalis. You ever see one?"

"Probably in a book."

"Pale green, almost iridescent. It's so incredible, it makes you appreciate—respect—nature, what it has to offer us. I watched those things and waited. You can't imagine what it's like to see a monarch butterfly work its way out of its chrysalis. From this tiny green case comes a beautiful, fragile butterfly that, eventually, has the stamina to fly to Mexico in the fall." His eyes shone with the memory.

"How many did you have?"

"I don't know—ten, twelve, something like that. My grandma was visiting at one point and took one of my chrysalises home with her." His smile faded. "When she brought back the butterfly, it was dead, its wings permanently spread open inside a big round paperweight. Some lady she knew made these things. I thought I was going to be sick."

In his story, Annie saw the boy who would become a man who reveled in the natural world. She reached out to touch his arm. "I'm sure she meant well."

"Oh, yeah, she did. Biggest heart in the world. She knew how much those butterflies meant to me and wanted me to be able to keep one forever. She died a couple years later. I'd take ten more of those stupid paperweights just to see her again."

He shook his head. "Sorry. What am I doing getting maudlin when I'm supposed to be showing you how fun all this can be."

"I'm having fun." Her stomach grumbled as if to underscore her words. "Starving, but enjoying every minute of it."

"Luella's probably packed us a feast."

"Last one to the cooler is a rotten egg." She dashed across the field, laughing, knees high, no longer worried about critters deep in the grass.

They reached the clearing they had made, and Annie dropped to her knees beside the cooler and opened the lid. "Look at this! Luella packed a blanket, too."

She spread the large black-and-white-checkered cloth on the ground, then emptied the cooler of the rest of its contents—chicken sandwiches, a peach and a plum, a bag of cut carrots, string cheese, chocolate chip cookies, and bottled water. They didn't speak for several minutes as they wolfed down the sandwiches and carrots and string cheese.

Annie sighed. "I didn't realize how truly famished I was until I started eating. You want the peach or the plum?"

"Peach."

She tossed it to him. "To me, ripe peaches have always been the taste of summer."

Nick took a bite and gave a groan of joy. "Exactly." He swallowed. "Especially this one. It's so sweet." He held the peach out to her, juice running down the palm of his hand. "Try it."

Annie leaned forward to take a bite. The juice dribbled down her chin, and Nick wiped it away with his thumb, rough against her skin—callused from hard work and adventure.

A tremor ripped through her insides. He licked his thumb and looked at her through narrowed eyes. She could melt in those eyes. Uh-huh. She could melt in those eyes and slide all the way down that chest.

No fiancée. No Melissa. Not engaged to be married.

20

———

Nick leaned toward her again and she caught her breath. *I want this. I don't. I want this. I don't.* All she needed was a daisy with petals to pick and this idiocy would be complete. *I want this. I don't.*

All thoughts flew from her brain except the certain knowledge that he was going to kiss her and she was going to let him.

I want this.

She closed her eyes and waited. No kiss. She peeked through her lashes; his mouth was mere inches from hers.

"Mr. Lewis is coming down the river," he said in a loud whisper.

She laughed, and he captured her lips with his own, slid his mouth across hers with exquisite gentleness. She could taste the sweet peach juice that still remained on his lips, could smell the clean scent of soap on his skin. He pulled back and she reached for him, leaned into him, awash in the heady exhilaration of his kiss.

He took her face in his hands and kissed her harder,

holding her head so she couldn't escape, and she wished it could go on forever. And she thought that maybe it might, and she could die like this. *Happy.*

She could feel the warmth of the sun on his back and the fire beneath his skin. He pressed against her shoulder and rolled her down on the blanket underneath him, the hard length of him stretched out on top of her.

So this was Nick.

No one had ever felt like this before; *she* had never felt like this before. He trailed kisses over her eyes, her cheeks, her jaw, then took her mouth again while he slid a hand up her side and across the silky nylon of her tank suit to cup her breast with only that very thin layer of material separating his hand from her skin. Heat shot through her.

She pressed up into him and ran her hands over his shoulders and down his bare back, trying to draw him closer, to feel all of him, as if she couldn't quite believe this was Nick and they were doing this.

She knew she should be thinking about the fact that he'd be leaving in a few days, that there was no way he'd leap from one relationship into another. She knew she should put a stop to this whole thing right now. But she couldn't do it. Theirs may not have been a true marriage, but it was a marriage. This was her husband. She had loved him when she married him, and she would love him after he was gone. And she would have this one time with him to remember in years to come.

"I was lying," he murmured. "Mr. Lewis wasn't anywhere in sight."

"I'm shocked," she said in mock consternation. She slipped her hands into the thick, wavy hair at the nape of his neck, and drew his head down so that she could kiss him again, so that she could drown in the lean, hard warmth of him. He eased his hand across her breasts and down the silky, slippery nylon tank suit, arousing her, touching her, sliding along her soft curves, pressing lower, harder, caressing as though the suit wasn't even there. She gasped and he teased her until she was breathless with need. His hand slid beneath the back of her suit to press her tight against him.

And then he stopped and pushed onto his knees. Breath ragged, he stared down at her. "Maybe this isn't such a good idea."

She met his stare for a very long moment. *Now? He was going to have second thoughts now?* She'd already been down this path and this was not the time she was going to start second-guessing things.

"Sure it is." She tried to act nonchalant, held herself back grabbing his shoulders and pulling him down.

"You're sure? What about the baby?"

"It's not a problem. Believe me. I've read all the pregnancy books."

His mouth curved in a soft smile. With tantalizing slowness, he slid the straps off her shoulders and kissed the line of her collarbone, hands pulling the suit lower as his kisses covered her throat and breasts, his fingers arousing her to exquisite joy as the barrier of nylon was slipped off and tossed to the side. She let herself revel in the moment, in his touch, in touching him, in wanting him, in finally knowing the hard planes of his body and the feel of his weight pressing against her.

After six years, she finally had her wedding night.

He looked down at her and pulled loose the tie of his waistband, lowering himself onto her again.

And then he loved her, beneath the heat of the afternoon sun, with the cicadas in the background buzzing like a choir. Afterward, he wrapped her in his arms and she drifted into that lovely state between sleep and awake, where she could pretend that all this was real, that this was a typical day in her life instead of just an afternoon fantasy.

When she finally opened her eyes, she saw him up on one elbow, watching her. He brushed the loose hair back from her face and kissed the tip of her nose. Need surged through her again, fierce and urgent.

"Wore you out, did I?" He grinned.

"I never knew canoeing could be so much fun." She ran a slow hand across the black hair on his chest, across his belly and over his hip, marveling at his body's instant response to her touch.

"If you liked that, wait till I take you whitewater rafting."

"Hmm. How about a sneak preview? And after that, I'd love to see what it's like to climb a mountain, and if you're really feeling educational, I've never been cross-country skiing, either."

His hand stroked across her breasts, fingers toying with her, tracing her curves. 'This might take more lessons than I can give in one day. Perhaps you'll need tutoring on a regular basis."

She was aching for him already. "Whatever it takes," she said on a gasp.

He bent to her, his mouth following the path of his fingers. She sank into his luscious darkness again, let herself begin to spiral out of control. She could spend the rest of the day doing this.

And then he froze and lifted his head.

She dragged her eyes open. "What?"

"I think I heard something. Shouting."

She pushed up on her elbows. "Who would be nuts enough to be out here?"

He raised an eyebrow.

"Besides us, I mean."

He cocked his head to listen for a moment and Annie closed her eyes as if not seeing would improve her hearing. Suddenly Nick's mouth was on hers again and his body was pressing her down, and she sank into that delicious place she had just visited and longed to go to again. Her wariness dissolved beneath the onslaught that was Nick.

Only when they came up for air did she hear the shout —this time loud, close, and definitely understandable.

"*Ann-ie! Ni-ick!*" came rolling over the meadow accompanied by the sound of a small boat motor.

She sat bolt upright. "Someone's coming!"

They scrambled for their clothes. Annie grabbed her swimsuit and wiggled into it while lying on her back, still hidden she hoped, in the tall grass.

"There! The canoe!" a voice shouted.

"Nick! Annie!" The first voice was joined by another.

"It's the police chief!" she muttered. "Hurry up!" Sitting up, she tugged the twisted straps of her swimsuit over her shoulders.

The crackle of a walkie-talkie and the murmur of voices carried across the meadow. She looked at Nick and shook her head. "What is this, Grand Central Station?"

He snaked a hand up to grab her shorts and his T-shirt still drying on top of the tall grass. If she wasn't so afraid of being caught, she might have laughed at the sight of the two of them frantically dressing like high school kids caught making out in the back seat of a car.

He pulled on his shirt. "Ready?"

"Hold on a second," she said as she wriggled into her shorts. "How do you want to do this? Just pop up out of the grass?"

"Got a better idea?"

She shook her head.

"So we tipped over. Came up here to dry off and have lunch."

"Got it." She took a breath to calm the pounding of her heart. "Okay, I'm ready."

A crash sounded in the nearby underbrush, accompanied by loud, deep barking. Before they could move, a huge black-faced German shepherd leapt into their midst, wagging his tail and panting, big drops of water dripping from his tongue.

Annie recoiled, then quickly recovered as she recognized the police chief's dog. "Thor!"

He danced toward her.

"I think we've been discovered." Nick stood and reached a hand down to pull her up beside him, waving with his other hand at the two police officers who were running toward them through the long grass.

"Somehow, something is just not right here," Annie said.

"And what was your first indication?"

"Annie! Thank goodness! Nick!" the chief shouted. "Well, don't that beat all! We were expecting the worst and here you are safe and sound."

He looked from one to the other. "You all right?"

Annie nodded, hoping her face didn't have telltale guilt written all over it.

"Just ... having a picnic," Nick offered.

"Tipped over," Annie said.

"Came up here to dry off and have lunch."

The other officer announced into his walkie-talkie that had found the missing persons alive and well, and that they would be bringing them in soon.

"We weren't missing. We took a canoe trip," Annie said. "Luella knew where we were."

"Luella's who called us," the chief said. "Said she was supposed to pick you up at one-thirty just past where the river runs by old man Henkel's pasture and you didn't show. Called both your phones and got no answer." He shifted his gaze from Annie to Nick, as though expecting an explanation.

"We left our phones at home," Annie said, at the same moment Nick said, "Guess we lost track of time."

"How late are we?" Anne asked.

"Hour and a half." The chief shook his head. "She waited about thirty minutes for you to show up. Then your sweatshirt came floating down the river wrapped around a canoe paddle and she went into a panic. Thought there'd been an accident."

"What? Oh no! I mean, we did, we tipped over. I caused it." Her words tumbled out. "Everything got wet and we came up here to dry off—and have lunch. But it wasn't an emergency. Poor Luella. She must have been beside herself."

The chief chuckled. "*Hysterical* would be more the word. She's got half the town stomping through the woods looking for you two. I was thinking maybe you just got waylaid somewhere." He nodded thoughtfully. "Figured you were probably all right and would make it back in time, but better safe than sorry."

Nick picked up the cooler. "Guess we'd better get back and start apologizing."

"I got a little trolling motor on a rowboat out here. We'll tow you down to Henkel's place since you only got one paddle. Come on, Thor." The chief slapped his thigh and set off through the tall grass toward the river, the dog and the other officer right behind him.

Nick let them get several steps ahead, then leaned toward Annie and whispered, "I think he knows we really did get *waylaid.*"

"No way. Why would you think that?"

"Your swimsuit's inside out."

She glanced down and felt her cheeks begin to burn. Maybe the chief hadn't noticed. After tank suits were pretty much the same inside and out.

Nick put his arm around her shoulders as they cut across the field toward the canoe. "Don't worry, sweetie. No one's going to care. We're married, remember?"

"Still ..."

"Nah. If anything, they're jealous. Wish they were making love with *their* wives in a meadow."

He pressed a kiss to her lips and pulled her head against his chest for a moment.

He'd called her *his wife.* She could feel the sun's warmth in his shirt, could hear the beat of his heart. And all she wanted to do was wrap her arms around his neck and ask him to take her again here in the grass.

And then what? Reality plunged a dagger of misgiving into her joy. Her impetuous choice—to have a moment to remember Nick by—now ensured she would *never* get over him. This was a man who just ended his engagement, who said he was going back to the life of wandering adventurer. This was not a man ready to jump into any kind of relationship. And he sure as hell wasn't ready for a commitment.

She'd wanted one time with him—and she'd gotten it. She had a memory of Nick to carry with her long after he left Bedford. But she'd gotten herself a memory when, the truth was, what she really wanted was the man. She wanted him to really be her husband, to father her children, to have root beers at the diner with, and haircuts at Minnow's.

What a fool. She should have stuck to her guns when she told Nick to leave a few days ago. She should have been up front and told him she had feelings for him—and then waited to see what his response was. But she hadn't. And now, here she was, stuck in some bizarre *almost married* state, hanging onto the fact that he'd called her *his wife*, and hoping that maybe he actually was beginning to think of her that way.

———

They arrived home an hour later. The instant the police car pulled up in front of the house, a crush of people spilled out the front door to envelop them with good wishes and hugs and slaps on the back. Not to mention a few joking comments about *afternoon delight*. Chester was beside himself in all the excitement, leaping and barking, and running in wild circles around the tall pine tree on the front lawn.

Luella pushed her way through the crowd and down the steps until she stood in front of them, hands on her hips, her expression a mixture of anger and relief. Her look reminded Nick of one he had seen many a time on his parents' faces when he was in high school.

"I tell you, this old heart won't survive if I have to go through that again."

"I'm really sorry," Nick said. "We tipped over and pulled up on shore to dry off. I—we—lost track of time."

Luella's eyes glistened. "Today, you two took twenty years off my life. *Twenty*. And at my age, I can't afford to lose a one."

Nick swept her into his arms and kissed her wrinkled cheek. She swatted him away and motioned toward the front porch. "What's everybody doing standing out here? Let's go in and break out the Pinot Grigio!"

To a roar of laughter and scattered clapping, everyone headed inside. Nick hung back and watched them go, watched Annie in her element, surrounded by this family she had found in Bedford. He still couldn't get over how different she was from six years ago. The same Annie, and yet not her at all.

The memory of her filled his mind, hot beneath him, her soft body illuminated in the afternoon sun, her cheeks flushed, her lips swollen from kissing him.

Damn.

He thought of making love to her in a bed, amid the down pillows and the cool cotton sheets and the night breeze stirring the lace curtains at the windows. And he thought about the new shower he'd put in and how it had different massage levels—pulses they called them—and wondered if taking her in the shower under the hard pulse would be better than under the one called Spring Rain.

He looked up at the house, at the people filtering in through the door to celebrate Annie's survival. These people had learned in two years what it had taken him six to find out—this was one special woman. And she was his.

Wait. Hold it. Stop it right there. Where had that come from?

He'd just ended one relationship—he didn't need to

dive right into another one. He'd come here to get a divorce and ended up staying nine days. Five down, four to go. That was it. Whatever this attraction, this lust, this need for Annie was about ... the fact was, she lived in a small town in Wisconsin.

She was happy here.

And life in a small town would drive him insane.

21

He gave himself a mental shake. Just because he'd ended his relationship with Melissa didn't mean he was going to stay with Annie. He couldn't. This was the life she wanted. But it sure as hell wasn't right for him.

Running from his thoughts, he took the steps two at a time and went into the house. Father Thespesius handed him an empty wineglass imprinted on the side with the name of some vineyard in California, then proceeded to fill it with Pinot Grigio.

"What Father, not red?" Nick grinned.

"Not a bottle of the stuff in this house. Luella says it gives her the migraines." He raised his glass. "Now, my boy, let's toast to your safe return."

"You know we never were in trouble, don't you?"

"Now I do. But by the time we learned that, I think all the votive candles had already been lit."

"Really?" An unfamiliar warmth slid through Nick. He hardly knew these people and they had been lighting candles in the church and praying for him?

"I wouldn't have let anything happen to Annie," he said.

"I know that." A wistful look crossed the priest's face. "Wish you could stick around. I think Annie's really going to be at a loss when you leave."

Suddenly, Minnow appeared in front of them. "Father T, I hope you're giving it to him proper!" She threw her arms open wide and wrapped them around Nick's middle. He looked down at her fuchsia hair and grinned, glad for the interruption.

"You scared the shit out of us." She pulled back to look up at Nick.

"Minnow, I can't believe I'm saying this, but thanks for caring." He gestured at the crowded room. "Sure doesn't take much for people around here to have a party."

"Any excuse pretty much does it," Father Thespesius said.

Minnow nodded. "Once the searchers heard you were found, everybody came over here. Just happy you're okay."

One of Annie's neighbors interrupted to shake his hand, and was quickly followed by others. Over and again, he heard how happy they were to learn he and Annie were all right, how glad they were that nothing serious had happened to *their Annie* and, *By the way, did I ever tell you what happened to me on the river when I was a kid?*

By the time he even had a moment to look for Annie, more than an hour had passed. He spotted her in the hall with Vivian, her back against the closet door as though she had tried to escape and only made it that far. Vivian's mouth was moving at warp speed, and though Annie had an interested expression on her face, he could tell by the glazed look in her eyes that she'd been talked at long enough.

He took a step toward the two women, then stopped

when a familiar voice asked, "Did you have to call on any of your survival training while you were out there?"

He pasted a casual smile on his face, then turned and centered his gaze on Mr. Lewis. "Not really. We weren't ever in any trouble. Just had to get the canoe emptied out. Then ate our lunch."

"I have a nephew in one of those elite Army units. Probably not the same one as you're in, but he's always gone on some sort of survival expedition. Do you have anything to do with those fellows?"

Just what did this guy want? Nick made a show of grimacing, as though he was torn about answering the question. "You know, I'm just not free to talk about what I do. Sorry. I can't even tell Annie the details."

Lewis chuckled. "That's what my nephew always says. I'll bet you two know each other—Andrew Benson. Sound familiar at all?"

Nick had the irrational urge to punch Lewis in the face. If he wasn't investigating them, then he was just nosy. Either way, he was irritating. On the other hand, maybe he was some guy staying at the B & B who was trying to make small talk.

Who could tell? The whole thing, including keeping up this charade, was getting old.

Annie leaned against the wall for support and her eyes caught his, pleading for help as Vivian blathered on.

"Excuse me, Mr. Lewis, but it looks like a rescue is in order."

The man followed the direction of Nick's gaze, then let out a laugh. "Ah, yes, Vivian. I know exactly what you mean."

Nick made his way to Annie's side. "Mind if I borrow

my wife a minute?" He put an arm around her shoulder and pulled her down the hall. "Had enough?" he whispered.

"She could talk a leg off a mule."

"Are you hungry? Let's get out of here and grab a burger. A greasy one with the works—"

"Fried onions—not raw."

"You learn fast."

"Onion rings."

He grinned. "And a chocolate malt. Large. Anywhere around here we can get such a thing? Besides the diner?"

"High fat, high carbs—just the thing at an old drive-in outside town."

"You game?"

"Sure—I'm eating for two!"

Nick grabbed her by the hand and sidled out the back door. Like kids escaping from a too-long church service, they raced down the driveway and jumped into his car, chortling gleefully over their escape.

———

"I'm not sure we're acting very appreciative, running away from our own survival party." Annie leaned back against the headrest and looked at Nick. Her heart seemed to stop. A day's growth of beard darkened his jaw. A touch of sunburn colored his cheekbones and forehead. God, he was handsome. Maybe not to some people. But to her, the sight of him literally took her breath away. And now, with the afternoon's memory still fresh in her mind, the smell of him still on her skin, she had to stop herself from reaching out and touching him, had to shove her feelings away before they burst to the surface like a bubble in the sea and she bared her soul to this man.

He backed out of the driveway, grinning at her. "Okay, so where do I go?"

"I forget you don't live here. Take a right and head out of town." It dawned on her that this would be the same route he'd take when he finally left Bedford, and *her,* for good.

Right now, with Nick in the seat next to her as if he were her date, or her boyfriend ... *or her husband ...* suddenly she couldn't hold back her desire for more, couldn't contain the hope that maybe today had been something more than just a playful diversion for him.

Her mind churned with all the questions she wanted to ask and knew she couldn't. Nick had wanted to stop this afternoon, had given her the opportunity to say *no,* and she'd been the one to insist they continue. She had no right to pressure him now, to ask why he'd ended his engagement, to question whether or not he had feelings for her.

'Take a left at the next road and then it's down at the next crossroads. Harbough's Drive-In," she said.

Nick followed her directions, and she watched his hands turn the wheel, strong hands that had held her, caressed her just hours ago. She sat up straighter and rammed the memory away, relieved when the drive-in came into view, the lot half-full of cars, trays hooked to their windows. The smell of burgers and fries wafted into the car.

"This is perfect. Just like the old days," Nick said.

As soon as they pulled into a parking space, a teenage carhop perkily dressed in a red-and-white uniform hurried toward them holding a pad of paper and a pencil. Nick rested an elbow on his open window and started speaking the moment she reached him. "Two cheeseburgers with the works. Fried onions. Two orders of onion rings. Two chocolate malts. Extra thick—with spoons. As quick as you can. We're starving."

As soon as the girl left, he turned to Annie. "It's a good thing we got out of the house. I can't tell you how many people were asking questions about the military."

"They all know it's top secret so they can't expect you to say much."

"Yeah, except I'm feeling bad about it. These are friends now … it's not easy to keep lying to them."

"Welcome to my nightmare. I had finally decided to set up our *divorce* by dropping hints that our marriage was in trouble. Then you showed up and put a monkey wrench in that idea."

"We seem to be plagued by bad timing."

She nodded, wondering if he was referring to something more than just his untimely arrival in Bedford—and too afraid to ask. When he didn't elaborate, she decided to move to a safer topic. "I have to admit you were right about canoeing," she said. "It's great. No motor, no electronics, just your own power."

"Sort of gives you a sense of control over your life, doesn't it?"

"Something that's been missing for me these past few days."

He nodded. "Just four more to go and you can go back to your original plan. Give it a month and then start mentioning things aren't going so well in Camelot. Maybe we should have a couple of public disagreements instead of getting along so well. It might help the cause."

His words made her stomach tighten, and she held up a hand. "Faking marital bliss is hard enough. I don't think I can fake marital discord, too."

"Good point."

The carhop returned to hang a tray on their open window and deliver their food, but Annie found her hunger had evaporated with Nick's comment that they only had to continue the charade for four more days. She didn't want to believe this afternoon had been just a quick roll in the hay to him, a meaningless romp. But he was a guy. And guys were so much more capable of separating the act from their emotions.

They probably should talk about it. She probably should broach the subject. But she didn't want to seem needy. Or clinging. Or desperate. She unwrapped her burger and stared at it, then shoved an onion ring in her mouth.

Too often in the past she'd stuck her heart right out front, thinking that once she and her new love discussed how they felt about each other everything would be wonderful. And time and again, she discovered that having *the relationship talk* ended with her getting her heart back in pieces.

"This malt is incredible," Nick said. "So many places think a shake is the same thing as a malt."

She smiled. "Not here. They're old school."

He grinned at her around a bite of burger. Shit, she was just no good at this relationship thing. Was too quick to want to figure out where they were going instead of patiently stopping to see the sights along the way. The therapist she'd seen had been great in helping her identify this character flaw. Still, it was one thing to recognize her faults, and another completely to be able to solve them.

The problem was, this thing with Nick didn't fit in a standard relationship box. It wasn't as if they had months and years to discover charming idiosyncrasies about each other, months and years to fall into like and lust and love, before having to figure out whether or not they wanted to stay together.

They had four days.

And then Nick was going away to—somewhere in the world, and nowhere he'd be easy to reach—and there'd be no hope for the two of them whatsoever.

She chomped on her hamburger, glad to have the food to concentrate on. At least it kept her from feeling as if they had to talk every minute—and it kept her mouth full so she couldn't speak even if she wanted to.

Either she could talk to him right now about what had happened between them. Or she could talk to him tomorrow, or the next day, or the one after that. And then she would be out of days.

Or, she take a different approach this time and say nothing at all.

As a preventative measure, she shoved a huge onion ring in her mouth on top of the bite of burger, forcing herself to think this through before blurting out words of love, passion, adoration, *stupidity*.

"Annie, about this afternoon ..."

"Hmphghaah." *Nice touch.* She knew her cheeks were bulging. She could hardly close her lips to chew all the food she'd jammed into her mouth.

Here it came, *the* conversation, the one she'd been waiting for. He was bringing it up—and the only way she'd be able to participate right now was if she spit all the food out of her mouth. And she sure wasn't going down that path.

"We've known each other a long time, you know, as friends. And we've been through a lot together. This afternoon ... I don't know what it means."

Oh, grand. She was about to get the guy version of what

today was all about. Here came the news that he'd had fun, but he hoped she didn't think this meant they were in love with each other or anything, that he'd just gotten out of one relationship, that sometimes people just get carried away, and if everyone is adult about it no one gets hurt. Well, two could play this game. She took a drink of her malt in an effort to wash down her food and felt the lump slide all the way to her stomach.

"Oh, yeah. No big deal," she said cavalierly, already beginning to feel the pain. She hoped her old therapist had an opening for the day after Nick left.

He sat back into his seat, and an unidentifiable emotion washed over his face. Probably relief. "Really?" he asked.

"I mean, these things happen," she said, nodding. "You just ended your engagement. We got carried away—"

"Yeah, we did. I—we—probably shouldn't have done that."

"It was the moment. The canoeing, the sunshine, the—"

"Relief from the stress caused by Mr. Lewis," he added.

"Exactly. Don't think that I have any expectations or anything."

"So you're okay with this?"

"Oh, yeah. Believe me, it was no big deal." Burgers and onion rings roiled in her stomach as if to protest the lie.

"It wasn't?"

"Oh, I mean, it was fun. Don't get me wrong. But we're adults. We both know it didn't mean anything."

His eyes narrowed, and he didn't say anything for a minute. "Right. As long as you're okay that we ... gave in to the moment. Hell, Annie. I just got unengaged. What am I doing making love to another woman already?"

Another woman? Another woman? Is that what she was to him? *Just another woman?* The despair she'd been holding back rushed forward like water through a collapsed dam. "That I can't answer for you," she said as though it didn't really matter what the reason was anyway.

He exhaled. "You used to be able to help me out in these dilemmas."

"Oh no. No more late night coffee shop counseling. All I ever did was pour you more coffee and listen to your escapades ... and your dreams."

"You did more than that."

"Okay, I told you to go home and sleep it off, too."

He laughed. "Besides that. You used to say something. You were always preaching the same damn thing, something about belonging. I heard it so many times you'd think it would be imprinted on my brain."

A small laugh escaped her as her old words returned, words and a belief that eventually led her to Bedford. "When you find the place where you belong, you'll want to stay."

"That was it?"

She nodded.

"I seem to remember it being more profound."

"It is. It's not just about a place, it's about people and jobs and friends and life." Sadness seeped through her. Not only was he still searching, he might spend his whole life searching. Not everyone settled down, not everyone found what she'd found here.

The realization hit her hard—she had two choices. She could wait and hope that he decided he wanted her ... someday. Or she could move on and put him out of her mind. Making love did not necessarily make a future. Though she'd known that already, apparently she needed a little reminder.

For the sake of her self-respect and her sanity, she knew there was only one answer.

Nick had to go back to his adventure life. And she had to go back to her little life in Bedford, have her baby, and raise him or her the best she knew how. If she was lucky someday, after a while—maybe months, maybe years—she'd meet a guy to help her purge Nick Fleming from her mind.

22

Annie propped the phone between her chin and shoulder as she scrolled through the October reservations on the computer. Even without checking, she knew she had an opening. "Yes, we have room for you," she said with a smile in her voice. "Would you like make a reservation?"

She glanced up at the sound of footfalls coming down the stairs and exchanged a friendly nod with Mr. Lewis. As the front door closed behind him, her mind registered that he was carrying a briefcase. *A briefcase.*

He hadn't once carried a briefcase in the days he'd been at the inn. A thought exploded in her brain: *the report.* Was he on his way to meet someone, to present the final report, the one that would expose her and Nick? What should she do? Should she stop him? Could she, even if she wanted to?

Was she believing in conspiracy theories? Maybe even losing it?

"Hello? Hello?" The sound of the caller's voice over the phone line overrode her frenzied thoughts.

"Yes, yes, I'm sorry," she hastily answered. "Lost you there for a minute. We're having some ... phone issues ...

and, oh, here's the repair man now! I'll put you down for the room, but would you mind calling back in an hour with your credit card number?"

The woman agreed, and Annie hung up, looking frantically in either direction as though the action would give her some sort of insight. Damn. Where had Nick said he was going this morning? Running? Running errands? Why hadn't she paid attention?

Stupid question. She hadn't paid attention because she was forcing herself not to notice him anymore, so she could get through the next few days ... until he left.

Which didn't matter at the moment anyway. If Nick was nowhere to be found and Minnow was at work, then this was up to her. What should she do?

It was probably nothing. Probably—

No! She couldn't risk it. The only thing to do was follow Lewis to see if he was meeting someone. Maybe she could run into him downtown and invite him for a cup of coffee. Maybe he'd take the report out to read. Maybe she could spill coffee on it, and he'd have to reprint it and she could get a look at it. *Maybe she should calm down.*

She tore into the kitchen to grab her cell phone, then raced out the front door, skidding to a halt on the porch. Lewis wasn't even a full block away yet. Thank God, he wasn't type A or he would have been long gone. She drew several breaths to calm herself, then paced the length of the porch and back, waiting for him to get far enough ahead so he wouldn't notice her on his tail.

After a couple minutes, she scampered down the porch stairs and crossed the street. Adrenaline pumping, eyes locked on Mr. Lewis's back, she slid along the inside of a leafy hedge bordering the sidewalk in front of one house, then cut through another neighbor's flower bed. Mud oozed up over her sandals and between her toes, and she glared at the ground in disgust. Who watered their flowers so early in the morning?

This spy life wasn't all Minnow made it out to be.

Suddenly Lewis stopped and appeared to be turning back. Annie spun to her left and pressed herself against the trunk of a big maple tree. After a long moment, she inched her head sideways to peer around the trunk.

Lewis was in motion again, heading away from her. She wiped the bottom of her sandals on the grass, then set off after him. A wave of power rolled through her. She was the cat; he was the mouse. It was almost like a dance—only he didn't know he was dancing. One, two, three. Look, move, hide. One, two, three. Look, move, hide.

She grinned as she stalked him, hopping from one front yard to the next, crouching behind bushes, trees, fences, whatever was available. She pressed her back into another tree and glanced around the trunk to get a line on Mr. Lewis.

This wasn't so hard after all. In fact, it was sort of fun.

"Annie, what on earth are you doing?"

She snapped her head around, right into a low-hanging branch. Rubbing her forehead with one hand, she forced a smile at the elderly woman standing in the doorway of a nearby house. "Good morning—afternoon—Ruth. Just going downtown."

A tan chihuahua shot out from between the older woman's legs and charged at Annie, barking like a mad dog. Annie scooped up the squirming animal and hurried over to Ruth to hand him over before the obnoxious noise caused Mr. Lewis to turn around.

"Heard your husband's back," the woman said. "You're not hiding from him, are you?"

For God's sake, this was how rumors got started. Annie shook her head.

"Because I remember what my Carl was like, rest his soul, when he would come back after being gone just a couple of weeks on business. These men and their needs, you know. Don't blame you one bit for hiding." Ruth's smile was filled with sisterly understanding.

Annie struggled to speak. "Oh, no, nothing like that. Just got a little tired. My legs did, I mean, so I thought I'd take a rest." She pointed at the tree she had been leaning against as though that would make everything clear. "Really nice to see you again."

She took off at a run before the woman could ask any more questions, but Ruth's voice floated after her. "Come over any time you need to get away, dear ..."

Shit, by the time Nick finally left Bedford, the whole town was going to think she'd lost her mind. She raced to the comer and looked both ways. Where did he go? How could Lewis have disappeared? Ruth hadn't held her up that long.

She spotted him almost two blocks away and slowed her pace to an amble, pausing now and then to gaze into a store window as though she were just window shopping. Lewis stopped at the new museum and tried the door. Ha! He should've checked with her first—the grand opening wasn't for a few more days.

The day before Nick was leaving.

The thought dampened her mood further. She watched as Lewis cupped his hands around his eyes and leaned against the glass to peer through the front picture window. After a moment, he turned and crossed the street.

She followed him at a block's distance, ducking into shop doorways so he didn't see her if he happened to look back. He stopped at the corner near a blue postal service mailbox, and she stopped too, waiting to see what direction he went.

Suddenly set his briefcase on the ground, flipped open the top, and pulled out an oversized white envelope with the red and blue markings of Priority Mail.

Realization blew open all her assumptions, and she caught her breath. Mr. Lewis wasn't meeting with a person today—he was rendezvousing with the United States Postal Service. She watched, horrified, as he dropped the envelope through the mail slot, spun on his heel like a man quite pleased with himself, and started back along the route he'd just come.

Any closer and he would recognize her. Holding her breath, she launched herself into a thick arborvitae hedge, landing with an *oomph!* on the grass on the other side. Spider webs clung to her face and she wiped them off with the frantic motions of someone with arachnophobia, which she didn't have—at least not until this moment.

She spat flat pine needles out of her mouth. "Minnow, you're wrong," she muttered. "This spy business sucks." She rubbed her grass-stained knees and peeked through the evergreen branches, waiting until Mr. Lewis passed by. He was whistling, for God's sake, acting like a man who had just won the lottery. Or maybe just a man who'd completed a difficult assignment.

Despair coursed through her. She pulled out her phone and called Minnow. "Oh baby," she whispered when Minnow picked up.

"It is? God! What? What? When? Why—"

"You sound like the rules for proper newspaper reporting," Annie said.

"I'm dying here! What's going on?" Minnow

demanded. "Wait! Just come to the shop. I'll have a couple of minutes between customers."

"It's Lewis," Annie said.

"As in Mr.?"

"Uh-huh."

"Get over here!"

Annie speed dialed Nick and left a message telling him she had news to report and he should come to Minnow's salon as soon as possible. By the time she reached the salon, one of her knees was bleeding from her dive through the arborvitae, and her mind was churning with theories.

If the envelope Mr. Lewis mailed contained his report, and it sure seemed like it might—and if that report was about her and Nick, she needed to know. Her livelihood, her life, depended on it. They were out of time. If she had to begin some start some sort of damage control, she had to know *now*.

She walked into the salon and nodded at the receptionist. "Minnow's expecting me."

She spotted Minnow at the farthest station squirting liquid from a plastic bottle onto about a hundred tiny perm rods wrapped with gray hair—all on one head. Minnow looked up and waved.

One of the other stylists was sweeping dark brown hair from the floor around her chair. "Hey, Annie. Met your husband at the Flower Festival. You ever get tired of him, just let me know," she said.

In a pig's eye. That woman came on to every guy in town. Annie gave her a tolerant smile, then turned to Minnow. "Got a minute?"

"Meet you in my office."

As Minnow wrapped a plastic bag around her client's hair and secured it with a clothespin, Annie opened a door along the back wall and stepped into the laundry room. The washer vibrated, the dryer hummed, and the room temperature could best be described as *sauna*. She swiped a clean washcloth from a basket, ran it under the faucet in the laundry tub, and dabbed at the blood on her knee.

The door opened and Minnow popped into the room. "Whew. Toasty in here."

"At least it's private."

She took in Annie's skinned knee and disheveled appearance. "What happened? Did you and Lewis get in a fight?"

Annie rolled her eyes. "I dove through a hedge. All in a day's work for a spy."

A grin lit Minnow's face. "I'm impressed. What's going on?"

"I followed Mr. Lewis—"

"Tailed him."

"Whatever. He left the house with a briefcase—which he's never done before. So I thought he might be meeting with someone."

"And did he?"

"He mailed a Priority Mail envelope," Annie said breathlessly.

"So?"

"*The report.*"

Minnow pulled a face. "Yeah ... but why wouldn't he just email it?"

"How should I know? Maybe he did. Maybe this is a backup copy. Maybe there's something he had to sign and return."

"Did you try to get it?"

"How? Tackle him and rip it from his hands? I was too far away. And anyway, if it's a report about me, nothing I could have said would have stopped him. So now it's in that blue post box on the comer of Main and Washington, waiting to be picked up and sent on its way—"

"To a destination that could bring about the destruction of your life in Bedford."

"A bit melodramatic, but probably true."

Minnow shook her head. "Desperate times call for desperate measures. Go stick your hand down the slot. Sometimes there's a big pile of mail in there. The envelope will be at the top—all you have to do is grab it."

"Right. And sometimes there's a cop nearby who'll arrest you for mail tampering or postal theft or whatever they call it."

"Okay, okay. On the other hand, we need to know what's in that envelope. It could be your undoing."

"On the *other* hand, so would committing a felony. And that undoing would happen first."

"But on the other hand—"

"Let's not waste any more hands on this. I'm not going to do it. This whole mess started with a simple lie. Now you want me to start stealing. Who knows what would come after that. Assault and battery?"

Minnow snorted out a laugh. "Did you tell Nick?"

"I can't reach him. Probably doesn't want to talk to me, anyway." She couldn't keep the dejection out of her voice.

She lifted the washcloth off her knee. "You got a bandage?"

Minnow pulled a first-aid kit from an upper cupboard and handed it to her, then began to fold the clean towels and stack them on the dryer. "Yesterday, after the big rescue, I could have sworn you looked like a well-loved woman. And he looked like a man who was smitten."

"It's all an act. At least on his part."

"Oh, come on. I saw the guy yesterday, how he was watching you at the party. You did it, didn't you?"

Annie pursed her lips and applied a flesh-colored bandage to her knee.

"Coy won't deter me," Minnow said. "Where?"

"In some meadow after the canoe tipped." She looked at her friend and grinned. "Oh, and did I mention he ended his engagement to Melissa?"

Minnow clapped her hands and let out a squeal. "I told you so! I knew you two belonged together."

"Don't get so excited. It was just a thing of the moment. A case of *love the one you're with.*"

"Nice try, Annie. It's me, remember? I know how long you've liked this guy." Minnow shoved aside the pile of folded white towels and hoisted herself up to sit on the dryer.

"Yeah, well, I fell for him six years ago, and now I've only made it worse. I wish I hadn't convinced him to stay because it's like I'm doing Chinese water torture to myself."

"No way he's not feeling anything. No way. I can see he's attracted to you."

Annie contemplated Minnow's words. "Yeah, but *attracted* doesn't necessarily equate to *wanting to stay here.* Last night we kind of came to an agreement that we shouldn't have done what we did."

"He needs a push. The new *Cosmo* has an article about—"

"You're reading too many magazines again." She sighed. "I don't have time to spend being lovesick—and I don't have time to try to fix it. Forget about Nick for a few minutes and concentrate on the bigger problem. What do I do about Mr. Lewis? Do I have any options? Or do I just sit tight and wait?"

The door opened a crack, and the woman with the headful of perm rods peeked into the room. The scent of perm solution wafted in with her. "Minnow, the timer's going off," she said.

"Right! Let's get those rods out." She jumped down off the dryer. "Annie, let me think about all this a little. Maybe I can come up with something from one of the *research books* I've read."

Just what they needed, advice from spy thriller novelists. "All ideas will be considered," she said as she followed Minnow into the salon.

"Say hi to that husband of yours," the other stylist called as Annie headed for the door. "Tell him to stop by for a complimentary *welcome to Bedford* cut."

Annie eyed a bottle of green kiwi-melon shampoo on the rack and considered opening the top and lobbing it at the woman like a grenade. Restraining herself, she shoved through the door and strode down the sidewalk in the direction of home, her emotions a jumble of anger, fear and —damn it all to hell, life wasn't fair—*love*.

23

NICK SAT AT THE BAR IN THE DEER FLY INN, A RUSTIC tavern in the next town up the road, just east of Bedford. The place was cool and dim, with wood paneled walls and beer signs everywhere. He wrapped his hands around his nearly empty mug of Miller High Life, and let his thoughts wander.

He'd needed to think and there was nowhere in Bedford he could do it—not without someone coming up to talk about Annie or ask about the military or just shoot the breeze. And if he tried to think at Annie's place, he'd have to see Annie.

And that was no good, either.

So he'd gone out for a drive and ended up in this little hole in the wall. Which, as far as he could tell, was just about perfect. He was anonymous here, just some guy passing through town.

Outside, the day practically glowed in the bright afternoon sunshine. But in here, the atmosphere was subdued, dark and quiet. The bar was nearly empty—just the bartender, a couple of guys playing pool, and him. He hadn't been in a tavern in the afternoon in a long time, and it felt odd. Almost as if he'd gone back to college. He half expected a bunch of old friends to tumble in the door and join him for a cold one.

He finished off his beer, wiped the foam from his upper lip and shoved his glass at the bartender for a refill.

The heavyset man pulled the tap back and filled Nick's glass. "You staying around here?"

Nick nodded. "Bedford."

"Nice little town."

"*Little* is the definitive word." He focused his attention on his glass, and the bartender moved away to wipe down the other end of the bar.

When you find the place where you belong, you'll want to stay.

Nick tipped up his glass and took a swallow of beer. This stuff was going down way too easy.

Thing was, Annie did feel like a place where he belonged. And if he was honest with himself, sometimes Bedford did, too.

But *sometimes* wasn't good enough. What if he made a mistake? What if he stayed in Bedford because of Annie and ended up hating it? Then he'd end up resenting Annie.

"Wanna talk about it?"

Nick glanced at the bartender. "What?"

"Whatever it is you're drinking to solve. Woman?"

"Sort of."

The bartender chuckled. "Give me the condensed version."

Nick shook his head. "Too complicated."

"All right, then here's my best decision-making advice, free of charge. List your options. Do pros and cons for each. Make a decision. Don't look back."

Nick nodded. "Thanks."

The bartender pulled a bag of beer nuts off the display behind the bar and tossed them at Nick. "On the house," he said, before ambling into the poolroom to chat with the boys back there.

Pros and cons. Okay. Plenty of pros for Annie. Fun and smart and pretty and caring and sexy in a down-to-earth sort of way. The only con, really, was the town she lived in. The closest thing to real excitement around here could well be the annual Flower Festival.

It really came down to two choices. Either go back to the life he'd led before, the constant stimulation of new people, new countries, new adventures. Or stay with Annie in Bedford, where he'd probably end up feeling trapped, like a dog tied to a post.

He was a man without a place where he belonged. *Exactly the same as he'd always been.*

Hell. He had a major proposal out for consideration with the TV networks—a proposal that could make him a household name. And if that one didn't go through, he had plenty of other ideas, all with the potential to make him a real player in the adventure travel industry.

The answer seeped slowly into him. He knew where he belonged. For him there really was only one choice—go back to the life he'd chosen six years ago.

The thought was so sobering, he reached for his beer.

And then his cell phone rang for the second time in the last hour. Though he'd ignored Annie's earlier call, this time he swiped the phone on without even looking at the screen. Instead of hearing Annie's voice, though, Minnow was whispering the code word and diving into a description of Annie's latest escapade with Mr. Lewis.

"She's on her way home, and I think she could use some support," Minnow said.

"On my way." He shoved the half-full glass of beer to the side, picked up his change from the bar leaving a few bucks for a tip, and stepped out into the stifling heat.

———

Lost in her thoughts, slouched on a bench outside the coffee shop, Annie didn't even notice Nick's SUV until he hung out the window and shouted, "Hey lady, want a ride?"

Her heart flopped in spite of her best intentions to feel nothing for him. "You missed the debriefing."

"I got here as fast as I could. What's up?"

She crossed the street and climbed into the vehicle, recounting the latest turn of events as she directed him to the blue mailbox at the corner of Main and Washington. They got out of the car and stared at it.

"That's the one, huh?"

"Minnow thinks I should stick my arm in the slot and try to get the envelope."

He snorted. "And go directly to jail."

"That's what I said."

Nick pulled back on the handle and peered into the dark opening.

"Nick!" She looked up and down both streets to make sure no one was paying attention to them.

"I'm just looking."

"See anything?"

'Tonsils. Adenoids."

She slapped his arm, and he let go of the handle. The door clanged shut with a sense of finality.

"So what do we do now?"

Nick screwed up his face. "I guess we ask him."

"*Ask him?* As in ... hey, Mr. Lewis, we're super nosy and were wondering if the report you've been compiling has anything to do with us? And if it does, would you mind sharing what you've got?"

"I'm thinking something more along the lines of ... hey, Lewis, I'm a top-secret military man. And *ve have vays to make you talk.*"

"Works for me."

He took hold of her arm. "I'm not kidding about this, Annie. I think it's time we asked the guy a few questions. Maybe not specifically about the report. But about what he does for a living."

"The not-knowing is killing me." She looked up into his eyes for support. Big mistake. Sex was in them—hot and steamy and long and lush. She could smell the faint odor of beer on his breath.

"Have you been drinking?"

An easy smile slid across his face. "Busted."

"What have you been up to today?"

"Thinking. Had some serious thinking to do." He slid his hand around her waist. Goose bumps prickled at the back of her neck, her heart quickened. Could Minnow be right? Might Nick feel something for her after all?

He touched his lips to hers in a chaste kiss, then deepened it, pressing her up against the mailbox, making her heady with want. "What are you doing?" she whispered.

"Kissing. On the corner," he murmured. "Vivian just came out of Minnow's hair salon.

Disappointment surged through her. She should have known this was just an act. Scene ten, take one. When was she going to learn?

Nick sat back in his chair and watched Annie on her hands and knees furiously scrubbing the kitchen floor. He shouldn't have kissed her this afternoon, but she'd looked so damn cute, that when he spotted Vivian it just seemed like the perfect excuse. "By the time Lewis finally gets back here, this place will be spotless," he commented.

"I can't just sit around and wait. I'll go insane. If he doesn't hurry up, Luella will be back from her meeting, and we won't be able to say anything. Now that we've decided to confront him, the least he could do is show up."

"*Confront* sounds a bit aggressive."

"How about *interrogate?*"

"Oh, yeah, that's so much better. There's an old saying, *you catch more flies with honey than with vinegar.*"

"All I can think is that, for the first time in my life, I have something worth keeping. And now I could lose it all. Not knowing what's going on is making me obsess—and I hate it."

She sat back on her haunches and looked at Nick. "Where could he be? We've been waiting almost two hours already. Throw me that towel on the table, will you?"

Nick tossed the towel at her. "At the risk of sounding like Minnow, why don't we put together a plan?"

"Such as?"

"How we're going to ask him what he's up to. If we charge at him firing questions, he'll probably get suspicious—"

"And clam up."

Nick nodded.

"Okay, spy boy, what do you propose?" Annie started to dry the floor with the towel.

He grinned. "How about good cop, bad cop?"

"Doesn't he sort of need to be a prisoner for that to work?"

"No. I've seen it on TV and—"

"Minnow is really rubbing off on you."

"Watch it. Seriously, we work the guy. You go after him tough for the info and I'll be the nice guy, his friend."

"How come I can't be his friend?"

"Because it's your B & B."

Annie stood and began to move the towel around the floor with her foot. "Fine. So he comes in the house and I say, *Beautiful day, isn't it? Want a chocolate chip cookie?*"

"That's too nice. You're supposed to be tough."

"I can't even be pleasant to the guy?"

"What you say is, *Hi, Mr. Lewis. Do you have a few minutes?* Then you invite him to sit down. But you stay standing—a psychological advantage."

A laugh burst out of her. "Tell the truth. You *have* been talking to Minnow, haven't you?"

Nick put on his best hurt face. "I can come up with good ideas on my own."

Annie bent to pick up the towel. "Okay, so he sits down—"

"As the good cop, I'll offer him the cookie—"

"How domestic."

He ignored her, ignored the sparkle in her eyes, the rosy flush of her cheeks, the upturned corners of her lips that were almost begging him to kiss them. "Then I say, *Annie's a little concerned about something—*"

"Only I'm concerned? Aren't we both? We're married, remember? If the husband is concerned, too, it gives it more credibility. Men always pay more attention to what other men think."

"They do?"

"Without a doubt." She said distractedly.

He could see fear in her eyes, worry in the set of her lips. He took a step toward her and reached out to cup her cheek, to reassure her that everything would be all right. Her eyes, full of question, locked with his, and his brain began to shout: *Keep away from her. If you stay here you'll be miserable for the rest of your life.*

He dipped his head—what did his brain know, anyway? —and put his mouth to hers. She kissed him back, deep and fiery and long. Her hands were grasping his shirt and pulling him close and he knew he was making a mistake— this was Annie and he was leaving in three days—but, shit, she was hard to stay away from.

The front door slammed, and they broke apart breathless and gasping and staring at each other as though shocked by what they'd just done.

"He's back!" Annie ran her hands over her face and drew a breath.

"Easy. There's no rush."

"Yes, there is." Annie started for the hall, and Nick grabbed her arm.

"Wait a minute. Let him go to his room, get settled. We don't want to scare him by being too in-his-face." *Plus, you look flushed and just kissed, and this isn't the best state for us to be seeing Mr. Lewis in.*

"Right. Right. You're right." She paced from the pantry to the stove and back again, nearly running into Minnow as she crept through the kitchen doorway dressed in her usual black, but now also wearing a black stocking cap and gloves, and carrying a black briefcase.

"Was that you in the foyer?" Annie asked in a disappointed voice.

"Nice to see you, too."

Nick stifled his own discouragement and dropped into a kitchen chair. "New fashion, Minnow?"

"These are my undercover clothes."

"Yeah, but it's not dark yet."

"They help me get the job done and that's all that matters." She popped open the briefcase and pulled out a white Priority Mail flat rate envelope. "May I present one envelope retrieved from the mail—"

"Oh, my God!" Annie blurted.

"Retrieved from the mailbox on the comer of Washington and Main. My first attempt at intelligence gathering is a resounding success." Minnow gazed at the envelope in her hands as if she were holding a newborn child.

"You stole the envelope?" Nick couldn't contain his disapproval.

"You stole the envelope?" Annie, on the other hand, sounded ecstatic.

"*Stole* is such a harsh word. I prefer *borrowed*." Minnow handed the envelope to Annie, who looked at it and grinned.

Nick couldn't believe what he was seeing. "Annie, you just took possession of stolen property—"

"Not quite," Minnow said. "I waited at the box until the mailman came to empty it, then I told him that Mr. Lewis at the B & B had asked me to see if I might be able to get back an envelope he had accidentally mailed this afternoon."

"And he believed you?" Nick shook his head.

"Well. It helped that it was Jason Drenconin and he's been asking me out for the past six months. Course, now I have to go dancing with him on Friday night."

"Jason Drenconin? You're going out with *Shake-It-Baby Drenconin?*" Annie began to laugh.

Minnow sniffed. "It was the only way I could get the envelope. And I told him the minute he shouts *shake it, baby, shake it,* I'm out of there."

There was a time, Nick thought, he would have found this conversation strange. Now it didn't bother him at all. And the realization that it didn't, bothered him even more.

Annie looked closely at the front of the envelope, then set it on the table by Nick. "Do you know the person it's addressed to?"

He shook his head. "Never heard of her. What I do know, though, is if we get caught with that envelope, we're in deep trouble."

All three stared at the envelope. Then Annie ran a finger under the address line. "What are those initials— WFRA? I think that's a radio station."

Minnow scrunched up her face. "I don't get it. He works in radio?"

"So what do we do now?" Annie looked at Nick.

"Open it," Minnow said. "We need to find out what he's up to."

"Are you out of your mind? Put it back," Nick said.

Annie fixed her eyes on the envelope, her struggle almost palpable. Nick could feel the pain of the choice she had to make, her need to know what was going on versus her need to do the right thing.

She exhaled sharply. "Get it out of here, Minnow. Get it back in that mailbox before I'm tempted any more than I am right now. I may be a liar but I can't be a thief too."

24

———

"Are you crazy?" Minnow asked. "All that effort and we're not going to find out what's inside?"

Annie shook her head. "Sorry."

"You mean I'm going out with Shake-It-Baby Drenconin for nothing?" Minnow looked between Annie and Nick.

"I'll make it up to you." Annie leaned against the dining room doorway. "Just get that thing out of here before—Hello! Mr. Lewis! How was your day?"

Nick jumped to his feet, snatched the envelope and shoved it at Minnow. "Get rid of it—"

"Beautiful day, isn't it?" Annie was saying.

As Lewis stepped into the room, panic flashed across Minnow's face, and she hugged the envelope to her chest. "See you guys later! I really need to get to the post office. I'm expecting a mailing. Hairdressing supplies. And I have to mail in these orders!"

She barked out an overly loud laugh. "Don't want to miss the last pickup." She raced out the back door before anyone could say another word.

The room was filled with shocked silence. Annie gave a careless shrug and smiled apologetically at Mr. Lewis. Though she looked calm, Nick knew that, inside, she was a wreck.

Mr. Lewis smiled. "I just wanted to let you know, I've finished my business in the area. Once I gather my things together, I'll be checking out."

"Now?" Annie squeaked. "Wouldn't you like to sit down and talk?"

He shook his head. "I've certainly enjoyed my stay, but I should really get going."

"How about one last cookie?" Nick asked, mentally cringing at how ridiculous the question was.

"I'll grab one on my way out," Lewis said as he left the room.

Nick turned to Annie. "That went rather well, don't you think?"

"Oh, yeah. Good cop, bad cop. Just like the movies."

"I've got a new idea," he said. "Once he's gone, we search his room for clues. Maybe there'll be papers in his garbage can, the first draft of his report."

"Now, you're really sounding like Minnow." Annie crossed the room to look out at the lake. "Probably a wild goose chase, but okay."

———

Nearly an hour later, Mr. Lewis came downstairs with his suitcase and briefcase. Stomach jumping, Annie finished the paperwork and thanked him for choosing Bailey House. It took every ounce of her inner strength not to let the man see how anxious she was for him to leave.

Nick came out of the kitchen with two chocolate chip

cookies in a plastic sandwich bag. "Here's that snack for the road," he said, walking Mr. Lewis to the door.

As soon as the man had stepped onto the porch, Annie pushed the door shut. She hesitated, one foot on the stair, waiting for the go-ahead from Nick who was spying through the lace curtains in the parlor.

"Is he gone?"

"Just ... pulling ... out. Let's go!"

Like excited children on an egg hunt, they took the stairs two at a time and raced down the hall to Mr. Lewis's room. Annie threw open the door, pausing in the doorway with Nick at her shoulder. Late afternoon sun poured brightened the cozy room.

"There'll be two garbage cans," she said. "I'll take the one at the desk, you take the bathroom."

She grabbed a discarded newspaper from the nightstand and emptied the garbage can on it. There wasn't much to be found—just an assortment of snack bags, banana peels, a crumpled sheet of paper, apple cores, tissues. Yeeck.

"Hey, hey! Annie, Nick!" Minnow shouted from the first floor.

"Upstairs!" Kneeling, Annie open the crumpled paper to find that the only thing it contained was doodles.

Minnow charged into the room and drew up short. "You're searching Lewis's room? Isn't that against the law?"

"Nothing like the pot calling the kettle black," Nick called from the bathroom.

"Hey, I re-mailed the envelope! No one's the wiser."

"Lewis checked out—it's not his room anymore." Annie rolled the trash in the newspaper and stuck the whole bundle in the waste can.

"You should have told me you were going to do this—I

would have come back sooner. This clandestine stuff is my specialty."

Nick stepped into the bedroom. "Bathroom's clean, Annie. Nothing in the garbage but garbage."

"You're sure about that?" Minnow tossed her fuchsia-tinted hair and put her hands on her hips.

"Yeah. But feel free to double-check."

Minnow went into the bathroom and shut the door. Moments later the shower started. Nick looked at Annie and raised his eyebrows.

"Don't even ask," she said, turning her attention to the dresser and the desk.

Nick got on his knees and drew aside the bed skirt to look under the bed. "Nothing but dust bunnies down here."

One by one, Annie opened the drawers—and found nothing unusual. Her discouragement grew. She pulled out the Bible and gave it a shake, hoping a note might be hidden in its pages, but all that fell out was a dried four-leaf clover someone had stuck in there to press.

So much for good luck.

While Nick stripped the blankets and sheets off the bed, Annie quickly flipped through the pages of the local tourism directory, searching for anything that might help them uncover Mr. Lewis's motives. A phone number scrawled in the margin caught her eye, and she gave strangled shout just as Nick tossed the bedding on the floor and said, "This guy didn't leave so much as a business card behind."

"Yes he did! Look at this—a phone number!"

"With a name?"

"No—but it's local. Looks kind of familiar. You have your phone?"

Minnow opened the bathroom door just enough to stick her head out in a cloud of steam. She was fully dressed. "You guys find something?"

"A phone number. Minnow, what are you doing in there?" Nick asked.

"I'll be right out." As she ducked back into the bathroom; Annie and Nick exchanged a look.

A moment later, the shower shut off. Minnow opened the bathroom door and waved one hand to clear away the steam rolling into the bedroom. "Whew, it's like a sauna in there." She flipped on the exhaust fan. "You were right. The bathroom's clean."

"What were you doing?"

"Oh, well, I read a book once—"

"I should have known."

Minnow frowned at him. "The victim had written the killer's name in the steam on the bathroom mirror. But the mirror unfogged before anyone found the body, so the name disappeared. Once the CIA agent turned on the shower and the mirror steamed up again, the writing became visible. They solved the case!"

Annie held in a smile at the expression of restrained disbelief on Nick's face. "You thought Lewis might have written some key information on the mirror?"

"Never know. Leave No Stone Unturned, that's my motto."

Nick snorted.

"Enough, you two! Let's go call this number and see if it means anything or not." Annie waved the scrap of paper in the air like a flag and led the way down to the front desk.

"I'm too nervous—you call." She handed Nick the phone, then read off the number to him as he punched it in.

"It's ringing." He grinned and clenched a determined victory fist at shoulder level.

Annie held her breath and prayed this was the break they were looking for.

"It's a recording—" Nick held up a hand for silence.

Annie and Minnow crowded closer. Suddenly Nick's smile faded and his jaw dropped. Annie's heart began to thud in fear. What had they just discovered?

"It's the museum." Nick set the phone back in its cradle. "The phone number for the new museum. Lewis was probably looking for something to do—"

"When he wasn't investigating me." Tears stung at the back of Annie's eyes and she reached up to squeeze them back with her fingers. "This morning when I followed him he even stopped there and looked in the window."

She went into the parlor and dropped down on the edge of the sofa. "I'm getting a worse and worse feeling about this. The guy wouldn't talk about what he was researching. And now it's like he went out of his way to make sure he didn't leave behind even a trace of what he was doing."

Minnow sat on the arm of the wingback chair and let herself fall sideways into the seat cushion. "Don't let your imagination run away with you. He's probably just a businessman who came to town for an entirely different reason. Building a new manufacturing plant or something."

"Nice, Minnow. You were the one who raised the suspicions in the first place. Are you telling me you're changing your mind now?"

"I don't know what to think."

Annie blew out a breath. "Then think about this. If he doesn't care about Nick and me, why was he asking questions about us? We're no more special than anyone else in Bedford."

Nick sat beside her and put an arm around her shoulders. "Who knows? Small talk. Maybe we were just his way of starting conversations. It would come across as pretty natural because he was staying with us."

"I suppose."

"Annie, this is getting nuts. There's nothing you can do about the guy. You really need to give it a rest."

He was right. Minnow's spy mania had made them all a little crazy. Her attraction to Nick and her pregnancy had made her hormones run rampant. And the fact that they were faking a marriage and lying to everyone in town had made them paranoid. She was probably seeing trouble where it didn't even exist.

Which meant she could either keep worrying about something she couldn't control and drive herself and Nick insane in the process. Or she could take a deep breath, relax, and wait to see what happened.

The second choice seemed infinitely better for her psyche. "You're right. Let's give it a rest."

Minnow raised her hand. "I move that Mr. Lewis was just a nice guy on a business trip."

"You're making a motion?" Nick shook his head.

"All in favor say *aye*."

"Aye," they chorused.

Annie forced a smile. She only wished she felt as confident about this as they were all pretending to be.

———

So far so good. Almost twenty-four hours had gone by and not a word out of Mr. Lewis.

Nick wiped the sweat from his face and bent over the storm window lying across two sawhorses in the garage. He pressed glazing compound into the groove along the glass, then drew a putty knife over the compound to form a neat triangular bead.

He shook his head. Lewis was probably just a salesman or something equally nonthreatening. And Annie, Minnow, and Nick were probably just three idiots with oversize imaginations who should be writing spy novels of their own.

Straightening, he stood back to survey his handiwork, immensely satisfied with himself. Five windows reglazed; all they needed was a coat of paint and they'd be ready for fall. Good thing he still had the fix-it book from the library so he could continue to pretend to be a master of home repair.

He thought again about Mr. Lewis, more convinced than ever that Minnow's imagination had blown this whole thing out of proportion—and he and Annie had bought into it way too easily. Now with just two days to go until the museum opening, he could see the brass ring. This whole escapade was almost over. Annie could go back to life as she knew it. And so could he—adventures all over the world, lots of new people and new places.

And no place to call home.

He wiped his hands on his shorts and headed across the yard toward the house, his mind chasing down the idea of a cold beer and a refreshing dip in the lake. It was so hot, he was half tempted to strip down naked and dive in right now. Wouldn't that be a hit with the guests?

Taking the stairs two at a time, he crossed the porch and went into the kitchen. Annie was emptying the dishwasher.

"Hey, got the windows all glazed," he said. "Only thing is, they can't be painted for a week—not until the glazing cures."

"Thanks. I'll do it before the snow flies."

He smiled. She had at least three months to finish the job. "Want to go for a swim?"

"Ahh, tempting, but I've got too much to do."

"You're making me feel guilty."

She laughed and waved him away.

He went upstairs to change into his swim trunks, his mind caught up in thoughts about Annie, about swimming, about life. Some night, when the B & B didn't have any guests, he might just take her skinny-dipping. The old Annie would never consider it, but the new Annie ...

What was he thinking? He was leaving in two days. He wasn't staying in Bedford and would probably never return. He wouldn't ever be taking Annie skinny-dipping. He gave the door to their bedroom an irritated shove and stepped inside.

Going to the window, he stared across the back lawn to the lake. And thought of Annie. And making love to her in the sand, rolling her beneath him in the shallow water. Shit, but he was obsessed. He felt like a teenage boy in the throes of uncontrollable hormones.

A faint chime sounded alerting him to a voice message on his phone. He turned toward the nightstand where he'd left his phone when he went out to fix Annie's windows. For some reason, he didn't feel like he had to have his phone on him all the time anymore. Life was slower here, less connected. *More peaceful.*

Sinking into the overstuffed chair by the window, he replayed his messages. Two, both from his agent, neither saying anything except that Nick should call—quickly.

He pressed his agent's speed dial number and waited through several rings until the guy answered.

"Jack, it's Nick. What's up?"

"It's about time!" the man boomed. Nick jerked the phone away from his ear and gave his head a shake.

"What's up?"

"I've got good news. What you've been waiting for."

Nick frowned.

"You there? Get ready—your proposal's been accepted! Not only do we have a television and book deal, but they'll fund half of it, too."

"They bought it?"

"Pack your bags—you're going to Outer Mongolia," his agent said gleefully.

His proposal had gone through. Nick couldn't believe it. He, a team of scientists and a TV crew would spend the next year chasing down the elusive Almastis, a race of yeti-like creatures in Outer Mongolia. And once that was done, he would have an exclusive contract to write a book about the experience. This was the big break he'd been working toward.

But what about Annie?

He glanced around the bedroom filled with everything that was her. The lotion she used that smelled like vanilla, the new dog bed in the corner that had never been used, the—

"Nick? You there? You still want this, don't you?"

Did he? "Absolutely."

"Good. Because you need to be in New York the day after tomorrow to sign the contract."

The museum opening was the day after tomorrow. "I can't be there that soon. Change the date."

"You don't have a choice. The head man is leaving for a month in Europe—he has exactly one available day and it's the day after tomorrow. You know how these guys are. Meeting's already set for first thing that morning."

"I've got a conflict."

"More important than this deal?"

Nick hesitated. "Why the rush? They've been sitting on this proposal for almost six months. Now suddenly we only have one day to get it done?"

"Nick, what's the matter? This is what you wanted. You gotta get when the gettin's good. Don't give them the chance to change their minds or find someone else more well known."

He couldn't bring himself to answer.

"Nick? Talk to me."

He drummed his fingers on the armrest of the chair.

What was the matter with him? This was exactly what he'd been working toward for almost six years now. His dreams were about to come true.

He drew a long, slow breath. He would have killed to do this project before he came to Bedford. He'd no doubt be thrilled about it again once he left.

He just had to stay focused on his goals, not let all this extraneous stuff confuse the issue. Annie would understand. It wasn't as though he and Annie were anything but an afternoon fling. She knew that. She'd understand.

Would she?

Sure. Hadn't she been the one to tell him he was free to leave a couple of days ago? Wasn't she the one who said she'd make up an excuse about the military needing him back right away? Hadn't she told him after making love that she didn't have any expectations? Obviously, she'd accepted their relationship for what it was.

"Thing is, I've got my car out here," he said, stalling.

"So you fly back to Wisconsin when we're done and

drive the rest of the way to California. Big deal. Come on, are you with me?"

Nick sighed. "Yeah. Yeah, I'm with you. I'll see you in two days."

25

HE SHUT OFF THE PHONE AND STARED AT THE WALL. Ecstatic. He should be ecstatic. So why wasn't he? He'd wanted this to go through in the worst way. Would have sold his soul for it two months ago.

When he'd put together the proposal, it hadn't bothered him that he wouldn't see Melissa for a year. But the thought of not seeing Annie for a year made his gut ache. A year? If he did this project, he would probably never see her again.

He closed his eyes and let his head drop back against the soft cushion of the chair. Mistake number one: making love to Annie. The memory of their afternoon in the meadow came back to him, the connection they'd found that day.

No, that hadn't been a mistake. That had been the first right thing he'd done in a long time.

He rubbed his face with his hands and contemplated his future. He had to tell Annie. She'd had a way of cutting through the gray and getting to the black and white. Together they'd figure out what he should do.

———

Annie shifted the basket of clean towels to her hip and tapped on the bedroom door, then entered without waiting for a reply. She dropped the basket on the floor by the bathroom and grinned at Nick slouched in the chair. "You forget where you put your swimming suit?"

He didn't return the smile. "I just got a call from my agent."

"Bad news?"

"Yeah. No! Great news. Remember that proposal I told you about the first day I was here?"

"The one about Big Foot?"

He nodded. "They're called Almasti ... or Almas. Anyway, my proposal's been accepted."

Her heart soared for him. "Nick, that's wonderful!"

"I'll be part of an expedition trying to track them down. See if we can find out if they're real. And if they are, well ... we'll have one hell of a documentary." He grinned. "About twenty years ago, a team of Russian and French scientists tried to do the same thing and failed."

"I thought those creatures were a myth."

He shook his head. "There's a lot of evidence that the Almas exist. Too much for them to be a myth."

"Where are they again?"

"Mongolia. I'll be there a year."

"Mongolia." *Halfway around the world.*

A lump of disappointment rose in her throat. She tried to swallow it down and smile at the same time. She'd known he had aspirations—what had she really thought he would do? Stay with her? In Bedford? Population 7,500? She knew better.

He clasped his hands together and leaned forward to

rest his forearms on his knees. "Annie—about what's happened—between us ..."

Her stomach lurched, and the fake smile on her face collapsed. "We've covered all this, remember? Don't worry about it. I don't expect you to stay or anything. We're both adults, we know what this stuff is all about."

She began to move around the bed, straightening and smoothing the bedspread as the words rolled out of her like a river. "This sort of thing happens and no one should get too carried away about it. Of course, we'll still be friends—we'll always be friends, right? But you and I are so different—so very different that—"

"Annie. Shut up."

Bent over the bed, arms outstretched, she froze and looked over at him. A tiny ray of hope bloomed. Maybe he didn't want to go.

"Annie, I care about you. A lot. But I'm not the kind of guy—" He shook his head. "You said it yourself—I'm always off chasing the next adventure. And this is a once-in-a-lifetime opportunity."

She was an idiot. She sat on the edge of the bed facing him and blinked hard to hold back the tears. She'd known when they started this thing that it wasn't real, that there was no future for the two of them. So she had no right to be disappointed now.

Problem was, she was way beyond disappointed. *Devastated* might be a better choice of words.

"Opportunities like that don't come along every day," she said chirpily. No way was he going to know she was dying inside.

He shoved a hand through his hair. "The thing is, they want me in New York for a meeting—day after tomorrow."

"The museum opening."

"I tried to change the date, but it was no-go." He looked down at his hands. "I agreed to be there. I leave tomorrow."

"No problem. I'll just say the military suddenly called you back." Her voice cracked and she hated herself for showing weakness. "Listen, thanks for helping me out by staying as long as you did. I think we really pulled it off." She started for the door, eager to get out of the room before Nick saw her break down in tears.

"Come with me."

His words, spoken quietly, stopped her in her tracks. Holding her breath, she turned slowly. *"To Mongolia?"*

He nodded.

"To traipse through the mountains?"

"Only for a year. After that, I'll show you the world, Annie. Places you've never seen, things you've never done."

"I tip canoes."

"We won't be in a canoe."

Leave Bedford? She looked around the room. "Leave this house? Leave what I've built here? Raise my baby on the road?"

"It'll be an adventure. Come with me and you won't have to worry about what's in Mr. Lewis's report."

Weariness rolled over her. He didn't get it. He would never get it.

"I'm not an adventure girl," she said flatly. "I'll *never* be an adventure girl. What I want is here, don't you see? And what I need is someone who wants the same thing, to share it with me. I don't care what's in Mr. Lewis's report. Not really."

A tear slipped from her eye and she whipped it away. "Oh, I do care, but there's nothing I can do about it, anyway. Adventure? Mongolia? Do you know how much of an adventure it was for me to actually buy this place? And then to be caught in a lie about being married? And then to have you show up? I already have more adventure than I can handle."

She threw her hands up in frustration. "All I've ever wanted was a place where I belonged, where people invited me to block parties and baby showers, where they stop to talk in the front yard. Where I bring them chicken soup when they're sick, and they mow my lawn when I'm gone. I've found that here."

She shook her head sadly. "You go, Nick, because you have to. Because I want you to. Because that's who you are. But this—" she spread her arms wide "—is who I am. I'm fresh lemonade. And you're Jack Daniel's on the rocks. And there's no way the one is ever going to become the other."

———

Nick rested his hands on the back porch railing and stared at the lake. Dusk had fallen, bringing a slight drop in temperature, but not enough to disperse the heat. He watched Annie down at the beach, raking the sand in preparation for another day. A couple of guests who had checked in earlier in the day stopped to talk to her, and she gestured as she answered their questions. Even from this distance he could tell she was smiling. Even from this distance he could tell that she had found the place she belonged. He envied her that.

Maybe he could belong here.

No, this was her place, not his. People had to find their own way—not piggyback on someone else's happiness.

It was possible, he supposed, that he might be one of those people who spent a lifetime searching. One of those guys who never married—or else married six times. One of those guys who had the greatest adventures all over the world, lovers in every port, and an empty apartment back home. The thought made his shoulders sag. What had Father Thespesius told him? Things hardest won are often the most appreciated.

Maybe those things never won were the same.

He didn't think he'd done this much introspection since Annie left him the week after their wedding.

Annie bent to pick something from the sand, then let loose with a sidearm swing. A stone skipped across the water—one, two, three skips before it sank. He smiled when she bent again and sent another stone bouncing atop the water.

Though she claimed to be a city girl, she'd taken to the country pretty easily. He loved the shine he'd seen in her eyes when he'd taken her canoeing. She'd shoved aside her fears and wasn't afraid to try.

A third time she picked a stone from the sand and sent it bouncing over the water. And a third time it dropped after three skips—embarrassing. The girl needed a stone-skipping lesson.

And a little convincing.

He trotted down the steps and across the lawn to where she stood facing the lake, hands on her hips, an expression of frustration on her face.

"Need some help?" he teased.

She laughed, and he felt himself slip into the joy of the sound. He couldn't imagine never hearing her laugh again.

"I've gotten as high as nine."

"Not bad. Once I got fourteen."

"Liar." Her eyes sparkled.

"Really. It was the perfect stone. Round, flat, smooth,

like it was polished. And the water was mirror-flat. It just kept skipping and skipping and skipping."

He walked across the beach, head down, bending every now and then to pick up a stone and rub it between his fingers before discarding it. Finally he spotted just the one he needed. He dug his fingers into the sand and triumphantly pulled it out.

"Now, watch the master." He bent at the waist and let the stone sail out with a sidearm pitch. He straightened just as it hit the water, skipped twice, and sank with a plop.

"Two? The master got two?"

"It must have hit a wave." He looked at the still lake and winced.

A laugh burst out of her. "Yeah, a ghost wave."

"Let me try again." He scooped up a stone and let it fly, not really caring whether he got a long series of skips or not. Then he looked at her. "Have you thought about what happens if Mr. Lewis does expose us? What will you do then?"

She turned toward the house, now a hulking gray shape in the rapidly falling night. "I don't know. I've tried to think about it and, honestly, can't come to an answer. It feels so unreal."

"Would you come with me then? If he blows your cover?"

Her eyes saddened and she shook her head. "It's not as simple as all that, Nick. You know that."

Yeah, he did.

He looked up at the sky and noted a line of dark clouds moving rapidly toward them on the horizon. Storm coming in. Kind of felt like his life. Nothing was simple anymore. Frustration filled him over his inability to make this work.

He pointed at the sky, and Annie's gaze followed the direction of his hand.

"The radio said we'd get thunderstorms tonight," she said.

They watched as the dark clouds devoured the dusky blue sky. In the distance, lightning flashed, and muted thunder rumbled toward them.

"It's going to be a good one." Annie tilted her face upward and closed her eyes. "Here comes the wind!"

The temperature dropped so quickly, Nick swore they lost ten degrees in a matter of minutes.

Annie squealed. "Here it comes. We've got to close the windows!"

They dashed for the house, reaching the porch just as lightning cracked overhead and large, fat drops began to splatter the ground.

Luella met them at the door. "I've closed up the first floor already."

"You check the second floor; and I'll get the third." Annie ran for the stairs.

Racing through the second floor, Nick slammed down the open windows against the rain pelting the glass. Within minutes, he was back downstairs, bypassing the dining room where Luella sat chatting with the new guests. He was in no mood for small talk—or questions about the military.

In fact, he was in the kind of mood you get when a vacation is just about to end—and you're ready to go home, but you don't really want to go. Shit, but he was becoming a head case.

He took a wineglass from a kitchen cupboard and filled it from the box of white wine chilling in the refrigerator. Before he left town, he really had to buy Luella some decent wine.

Annie rounded the corner and he raised his glass. "Thought I'd watch the storm. Want to join me?"

"Sure." She poured herself a glass of lemonade, then flicked off the kitchen light. "We'll be able to see better," she explained.

"I haven't been in a Midwest storm in years," he said. "But I remember they're about the best."

They stood in the doorway in the dark, not speaking, and watched the storm increase in ferocity. Lightning ripped open the sky, followed by blasts of thunder that shook the house. The few lights that glowed in the house flickered with every blast. Rain, blown almost sideways by the powerful wind, hammered against the windows and roof.

Nick shoved open the door and stepped out onto the porch, into the driving rain.

"Don't go out there. It's dangerous."

He walked down the steps to the yard and lifted his face to take the full brunt of the storm. The warm rain slashed his skin like needles.

"Nick! Get back in here! You'll get struck by lightning!"

He looked into the darkness. Lightning lit the sky, and he caught a glimpse of Annie in the doorway. She motioned him in.

And he motioned her out.

Therein lay the problem. He was alive out here, not just drifting through life, but feeling it, experiencing it. And for Annie, life was best when she was peeking out from behind the door. She'd come a long way since she was in L.A., but then, so had he. So instead of getting more alike, they had just stayed that much apart.

Here he was thinking, if only Annie could throw open the door and run into the rain. And there she was, probably thinking, if only Nick could learn to be happy watching instead of doing.

He had to give her credit—she'd pegged it correctly. They were as different as Jack Daniel's and lemonade. Question was, why could she accept it and he couldn't?

He shoved the wet, dripping hair out of his eyes and motioned her out again. *Come on, Annie, take a chance, a little risk. Come out on the porch at least. Meet me halfway.*

He could see her behind the screen door, watching him, but not moving.

Come on, Annie.

———

She watched him dance in the rain, arms outstretched, feet kicking water out of the puddles that were forming all over the lawn. Her lips turned upward. He was so unafraid. He went out and challenged life on his own terms. He was everything she wasn't. She leaned her head against the screen. Everyone knew you don't go out in thunderstorms.

He turned toward her and waved her out again.

"I suppose you talk on the telephone during storms, too," she shouted.

He threw back his head and laughed as the rain poured over him. "Sometimes I even take a shower."

She couldn't help but smile. What would it hurt to join him out there? Depending on your point of view, *safe* and *secure* could also be defined as *stifling* and *boring*. God, where had that thought come from? She wrapped her hand around the doorknob. Her heart started to beat a little faster. She hadn't gone out into a storm on purpose in her whole life.

She drew a breath for courage, gripped the doorknob

more tightly, and gave it a turn. In that instant, Nick began slogging through the grass toward the porch.

A sense of relief filled her that she didn't have to go out after all—a sense of relief wrapped in regret.

She released the knob and stepped back to get out of Nick's way. He shook his head like a dog, and water flew out in every direction, spattering her with droplets.

She laughed and flipped the light switch on again. "Better hang your clothes on the line in the basement before Luella catches you dripping all over the floor. I think there's some clean towels in the dryer."

He started for the basement door. "You missed it out there, Annie. It was something."

Was it? She'd been happy with her life until he'd shown up—was still happy with it. Just because his personal fulfillment included dancing in the rain and canoeing down rivers didn't mean hers did.

It had taken her a long time to get to being who she was now. If therapy had taught her anything, it was that she wouldn't find happiness by making herself over for a guy. She'd tried that too many times, and all it ever got her was heartache.

He was leaving tomorrow, for God's sake. If she had changed who she was just because he'd been here for nine days, who then, would she be after he was gone?

It was a damn good thing she hadn't gone out into the rain.

And it would be an even better thing when he was gone.

26

———

Nick picked up his empty duffel, gave it a shake, and concentrated on packing his stuff, as if the very action could ease his discontent. He went into the bathroom and removed his toothbrush from the holder, took his deodorant, after-shave and razor from the medicine cabinet. He slipped his towel from the rack and threw it in the hamper, then stepped from the room, pausing in the doorway to look back for anything he might have forgotten.

His gaze fell on the new showerhead he'd installed, the new shower curtain rod. Those would be Annie's only reminders that he'd even been here.

He heard the hall door open and turned just as Luella entered carrying a stack of folded clothes.

"Here's the last of your things. Still warm from the dryer." She set them on the bed and watched him a moment before clucking her tongue and shaking her head.

"I'm old enough now to say whatever I want. No one gets too mad when I do, because they figure I'm just an old woman, and old women, well, what are you going to do about them?"

Nick swallowed a grin. "Something on your mind?"

"Sure is. Nick Fleming, it's not right you're going off again. This is no kind of a marriage, with one person always away. And the two of you seeing each other only a few times a year."

He nodded. Wouldn't be his first choice for marriage, either.

"Annie's happy now. Happier than I've ever seen her. I don't want her to go back to the way she was before."

"What do you mean?"

"I know you two were having some problems ..."

"She told you about that?"

"No. But it wasn't hard to tell. You never came home to visit, didn't send letters or call. She didn't talk about you like she used to when she first bought the place. I figured the rose garden might be getting a few thorns, if you know what I mean."

"No relationship is perfect."

"No. But they take work. Forgive me for speaking out so, but it doesn't seem to me you're working at this very hard."

Nick's jaw dropped. If she only knew. "It's my job, Luella. I can't just not go back."

"But you could apply for a discharge or whatever it is that you do to get out of the military."

He was half tempted to tell her the truth so she would understand. But if he did that, he'd be leaving a bunch of pieces behind for Annie to pick up. And no way was he doing that to her.

"I appreciate your concern, Luella. Annie and I have talked about my leaving the service, but I'm just not ready yet."

"Hummph. Haven't talked enough, then. You just think

about what I've said." The old woman left the room, shaking her head.

Irritated, Nick picked up the pile of clothes and shoved everything into his duffel. His thoughts turned to his upcoming meeting in New York. By tomorrow this time, he would signing a contract for one of the most visible projects he'd ever been involved in. He'd be guaranteed more money than he'd ever made before, virtually assured of fame. People would kill to be offered an opportunity like this.

Just because Annie didn't want to come with him, didn't mean he shouldn't be happy with where his life was headed.

———

Annie pulled open the kitchen drawer and began to empty its contents onto the counter. What a mess. How did things get like this? Why did she save things thinking they might come in handy? What a packrat.

She felt a prickling of sweat on her skin. The air had grown heavy with humidity as the morning heat met the remains of last night's storm. She sorted rubber bands, paper clips, and twist-ties into piles. She needed to get better control over all this stuff she saved, over her life. She needed to restore order. Now.

She thought of Nick, upstairs packing, getting ready to walk out of her life as simply as he had walked in. She gripped the edge of the drawer for support. How had she allowed herself to fall in love with him?

Dragging the garbage can closer, she began tossing things away. It felt good to clean house, get rid of some of this junk, restore order, maintain some control. She worked quickly, finishing that drawer in several minutes and turning to the next.

"Ahh, it's a drawer-cleaning sort of day. Closets next?"

She started at the sound of Luella's voice. "Is there something wrong with putting things in proper order?"

Luella touched Annie's cheek. "No, dear. But he's upstairs packing, and you're down here sorting. Shouldn't the cleaning wait until your husband is gone?"

Annie turned back to the drawer so Luella wouldn't see the tears in her eyes. The old woman was entirely too astute. Whoever said the mind dulls with age was wrong, wrong, wrong about Luella. If this was a dulled mind, Annie was almost glad she hadn't known the woman when she was younger.

"He's your husband, Annie, and you don't know when you'll see him again. Go upstairs. He's leaving today."

Annie stared into the drawer and fought the urge to tell Luella the truth. She wanted Luella to understand. Yet, what would it accomplish to tell her that Nick was never coming back, that she would never see him again, that he was going off to chase Neanderthal men in Mongolia?

"Avoiding him doesn't change the fact that he's leaving," the old woman said softly. "Don't let yourself have any regrets once he's gone." She took Annie's arms from behind and gently pushed her toward the hall.

———

Nick smiled as Annie came through the doorway. "One thing about traveling light—when it's time to leave, there's not a lot to do. You come to help me?"

She shook her head. "Luella thought I should spend some time with you because you're leaving today."

"She lectured me on the state of our marriage."

"Sorry. It's only because she likes you."

"I know. But I get the feeling she thinks I'm a jerk because I won't leave the military and stay home with my wife."

"When I go back down, I'll reinforce that it's a joint decision, that we made it together. Do you want some breakfast before you take off?"

"Just coffee." He pulled the zipper shut on his duffel and hefted it off the bed. His eyes met hers and he saw regret there, and suddenly he wanted to kiss her and lay her down across the bed, to feel her with him again. "Hey, Annie."

"Yeah?"

Stupid, stupid adolescent infatuation. *Don't humiliate yourself by begging her to come.* "Thanks—for everything. I'm glad I stayed. Hope everything works out for you."

She nodded. "Thanks. Me too."

Half an hour later, they sat in the kitchen making small talk like strangers and sharing a cup of coffee before Nick left to drive to the airport in Milwaukee. He watched Annie pour cream into her decaf and stir it longer than necessary. "So you're sure it'll be okay I miss the museum opening?" he asked.

"No problem at all. Minnow's spreading the word that you received an urgent call from the military and had to leave."

"She's a good friend."

"I never would have thought you'd say that—not after the first night you met her."

"I didn't say she isn't annoying sometimes."

Annie smiled knowingly.

Luella brought the mail into the room and set it on the

table next to Annie. She waggled a finger at Nick. "You tell the general, or admiral, or whoever it is you report to, that you need time off to come home more often."

Home. He'd begun to think of it that way, too.

He thought of the divorce papers Annie signed last night, now tucked away in his computer bag, ready for filing at the courthouse. He'd come to Bedford for Annie's signature so he could be free. And he'd ended up getting her signature so that he could set her free. What a switch.

Luella took a step toward him. "I'm leaving for the market, so best I give you a hug now."

Nick stood and embraced the old woman. "Thanks for everything, Luella."

She pulled his head down to kiss his cheek exactly as she had the day he arrived. "You take care of yourself. I'll keep an eye on Annie, make sure she doesn't overdo it. And you give some thought to what I was telling you upstairs."

She pushed through the back screen door and it banged shut behind her. He really should fix that thing. The pit in his stomach grew.

Annie topped off her coffee and began to riffle through the mail. "Bills, bills, junk mail, and junk mail." She held up an official-looking gray linen envelope. "Look at all the trouble advertisers go to so their junk mail looks like legitimate mail. No company name—just a return address. How much you want to bet this is a credit card application?"

"Platinum, preapproved with a twenty-five-thousand dollar limit." Nick grinned, though he didn't feel very funny. He really should get going. Just stand up, say goodbye and get on his way.

All he was doing right now was prolonging the agony.

Annie slid her thumb under the flap and ripped the

envelope open. With great flourish, she removed the letter inside and shook it flat.

"Very nice," she said with a nod. "It's addressed directly to me. *Dear Ms. McCarthy. It is my pleasure to inform you—*"

She shrieked, the sound so shrill and loud he reacted with a jerk, splashing coffee across the table. He jumped to his feet and threw a dishtowel on the spill before it cascaded to the floor. "Shit Annie! What?"

"We got it! We got it!" She jumped to her feet and began to wave the paper in the air. "We got the grant!"

Nick snagged the letter from her hand and began to read aloud. "First, let me apologize for the length of time between your application and our response. It is my pleasure to inform you that the Wisconsin Foundation for Renovation and Antiquities has approved your application for a grant in the amount of $15,000 for your General Store Museum. Checks are cut quarterly, and yours should arrive in approximately six weeks. Our investigating representative, Mr. Edward Lewis—" Nick's jaw dropped open.

"Mr. Lewis?" Annie squeaked. "Was here for the museum?"

Nick felt a weight rise from his shoulders. "Wisconsin Foundation for Renovation and Antiquities? WFRA?"

"It wasn't a radio station!" A laugh exploded out of Annie. "How dumb can we be?"

Nick began to read again. "Our investigating representative, Mr. Edward Lewis, was extremely impressed with your endeavor. WFRA assessors are tasked with keeping a low profile so that their presence does not cause people to change behavior or try to influence the assessment. Once we received samples of your new museum literature we knew that—"

"He was undercover! Wait until Minnow hears this!"

"Makes sense," Nick said. "Easier to make sure it's all legit."

"All those times we thought he was talking to people about us, he was assessing the museum."

"And the board. Probably checking out each board member, not just you." Nick exhaled, relieved that Annie no longer had to worry. She was free to stay in Bedford as long as she liked. He grinned at her. "You know what this means, right? *We pulled it off.*"

He opened his arms and she did the same and they fell into each other's embrace, dear friends celebrating a shared victory. He spun her in a circle, then kissed her one last time so he would never forget what she tasted like.

"Come with me." He searched her eyes for some sign of hope and saw only the faint shimmer of unshed tears.

"Stay," she whispered.

They pulled apart. She patted his chest and he reached up to twine his fingers with hers.

"Take care of yourself," she said. "Don't get any more poison ivy. I'm pretty sure they don't sell calamine lotion in the mountains of Mongolia."

He tried to smile. "I'll send you a postcard."

Her mouth curved upward, but the smile didn't reach her eyes. "I'll hold you to it."

He kissed the knuckles of her hand.

"You'd better get going or you'll miss your plane."

He nodded, but didn't move. "Annie ... I'm sorry."

"For what? I think we're even now."

Maybe so, but his heart felt pretty much like it was ripping in two. He knelt to rub Chester's head with both hands. Unbelievable, but he was even going to miss this crazy dog. "See ya, mutt."

Standing, he walked out the screen door and out of Annie McCarthy's life. And the door banged shut behind him like an exclamation point on the end of a sentence.

———

She refused to cry. Annie emptied the dishwasher, baked a few sheets of cookies, took out the garbage. It was too quiet in the house to stay inside. She wandered down to the lake, to the pier, to dangle her feet in the water with her one true-blue companion, Chester, at her side. She waited, hoping Nick would change his mind and surprise her by sneaking across the yard to join her on the dock. She waited, even though she knew in her heart he wasn't coming back.

At least she still had her life—*her wonderful life.*

A knot lodged in her throat, growing so large it broke loose with a quiet wail. The pain of loss ripped through her and she wrapped her arms around her middle and bent forward, great heaving sobs racking through her. She had let Nick go. She had found her bachelor next door just like Grandma had said to—and she'd lost him.

Suddenly, somehow, her wonderful life seemed like a consolation prize, hollow and meaningless. How wonderful a life could it be, really, when so much of it was built on a lie? When the person you loved most wasn't there to share it with you?

Sobbing, she viciously kicked at the water, breaking its smooth surface and sending ripples out in every direction. That's what her first lie had been like, ripples, spreading out and out, changing perceptions, one lie breeding more so she could keep the truth hidden.

She loved this town, loved the people—and she'd been lying to them since the day she got here. And lying to herself. She'd convinced herself it was okay to lie in order to get this house, to live in this town, to have these people as her friends, *to belong here*. When, in her heart she knew, she had used them by lying to them.

It didn't matter that she hadn't meant to harm anyone. It didn't matter that the first lie forced her on the path that led to all the rest of the lies. Didn't matter that she had planned to put an end to the whole thing with one last lie—that she and Nick had gotten divorced. Didn't matter that it was truth and a lie all in one. In reality, it was really just one colossal lie.

Here she was worried that she might lose the friendship of the people of Bedford, when the truth was, the people of Bedford didn't even know her. Not the real her.

She wrapped an arm around her dog and buried her face in the back of his neck. "What's happened to me, Chester?"

He licked her face. The odor of dead fish wafted into her nostrils and she straightened. "Ugh. Nick was right—your breath is awful."

He licked the tears on her cheeks.

"Yeah, I know. You love me no matter what. Problem is, that's your job."

She kicked the water again and watched the spray fly onto the lake. She had really screwed up this time.

Realization dawned slowly, slid into her soul the way fingers of light seep across the dawn sky at sunrise. And then, suddenly, everything was clear. She didn't want this life anymore—not like this. The people of Bedford had trusted her, had believed she was the person she claimed to be. They deserved to know the truth.

And her baby deserved to be born into a life free of deceit.

Whatever the consequences, she had to clean up this mess, had to let people know the truth. She had taken charge of her life several years ago, changed herself from a wilting violet into a woman strong enough to own her own business.

She was strong enough to do this, too.

But how could she do it? Her mind flittered over her options ... A newspaper ad? A door-to-door literature drop? Tell Vivian? She smiled. Vivian would have the news all over town in no time. Unfortunately, with Vivian's skills at embellishment, the story might become completely different—possibly even worse—in the retelling.

She dropped her chin, thinking. Maybe she could tell a few people at the museum opening tomorrow.

No. She could tell them all.

A shiver raced through her. Nearly everyone in town that she would want to reach would be at the opening. It would be the perfect opportunity to clear the air. Once the speeches were done, the ribbon cut, and the applause finished, she would step up to the podium again, most likely for the last time ever in Bedford.

And she would tell the truth.

27

———

AN HOUR INTO THE MEETING WITH HIS AGENT, publisher, and the studio head on the fifty-fifth floor of an ostentatious glass-walled New York skyscraper, Nick realized he hadn't been listening to the conversation for the last twenty minutes. Though he'd been nodding his head, his thoughts were all on Annie. And on the museum opening at seven o'clock. And on Minnow, and whether or not Annie had told her that Mr. Lewis was a spy after all—in a sense.

He warmed at the memory of his first day in Bedford. How Annie had flung herself into his arms and kissed him. And then Minnow had shown up, fuchsia hair and all, and started them thinking about espionage and undercover operations.

He started to chuckle.

The other men broke off their discussion to look at him.

"Sorry," he said, swallowing his laughter.

The men returned to their negotiations, discussing the details of the expedition, the documentary, and the book Nick would write when the search for the Almasti was over.

Damn! He'd left that home improvement book in the garage, hidden behind a bag of birdseed. He'd planned to sneak it back to the library when Annie wasn't around and forgot all about it. He'd better call her later and tell her where it was—or she'd owe one big fine. Probably never let him live it down.

He really should call her, anyway. On the plane he'd come up with a great idea for the B & B. She could offer two-day/one night canoeing-camping trips on the river—a back-to-nature package that could be included with a week's booking at the B & B. Instead of tents, they could stay in tepees. That would bring in a few guests. How many people had ever camped in a tepee before? And once that was under way, maybe what they could do was offer—

His brain screeched to a halt. *They?*

He was going to Mongolia for the next year. There would be no canoe trips, no tepees, no hotel guests, no hiking, no camping ... *no Annie.*

He looked at the three men who were intently discussing his future—a future full of fame and money and adrenaline rushes.

And no Annie to love.

He loved her.

The epiphany made the hair on his arms stand up. He loved her, and he'd left her to do the museum opening alone. He'd left her to face all those people and lie one more time by saying her husband's meager nine-day military leave had been cut even shorter.

He loved her. Suddenly his great Almasti search, with all its potential for fame and wealth, no longer seemed so significant. He'd been all over the world, always thinking the next thrill, the next rush would be the thing that satisfied the odd, empty space in his spirit. But it never did.

The only time he'd ever really felt at peace, completely at home, was during the last week in Bedford ... with Annie.

When you find the place where you belong, you'll want to stay.

He wanted to stay with Annie. Wherever she was, that was where he belonged.

He glanced at his watch. Two-fifteen. That meant it was just past noon in Wisconsin. Bedford was a three-hour drive from the Milwaukee airport. If he could catch an early afternoon flight, he could be back in time for the ceremony tonight. Just in time to tell everyone in town how much he loved *his wife*.

He pushed his chair back from the big mahogany conference table and stood. The three men looked up at him in surprise. He cleared his throat. "Gentlemen. The deal is off."

"Nick?" Jack jumped to his feet.

"I don't want it."

"Are you talking to someone else about this?" the publisher asked. "We'll match their offer."

Nick looked directly at him, a fifty-something guy, graying around the temples, probably more than a few pounds over his high-school graduation weight. Comfortable-looking. "You got a wife and kids?"

The man's expression showed his surprise at the question. "One wife, three kids—seventeen, fifteen, twelve."

"Any regrets?"

Jack shook his head in warning. "Nick, we can talk about this stuff later."

The publisher held up one hand and gave Nick a wry smile. "No regrets. Though, life in my house is sometimes more adventure than I want after a day of work. Not that I would ever trade it."

"*Adventure.* What an interesting choice of words."

The man leaned back in his chair, a perceptive smile on his face. "You've gotten a better offer. And it's got nothing to do with this proposal, does it?"

Nick grinned. "Nope. Go ahead and find someone to take my place. I've got to get to the airport. I tipped a canoe in Wisconsin and I have to get back in time to right it."

He picked up his briefcase, pulled out his phone and strode from the room, already calling the airline to change his ticket.

———

The plane landed right on schedule. Nick pulled his bag from the overhead compartment, waited impatiently for the people ahead of him to clear the aisle, then charged to the parking garage to retrieve his car.

He pulled out of the parking ramp, well aware that the museum opening was in two-and-a-half hours, and it would take him three hours to get to Bedford—if he stayed at the speed limit. He opened the window, then turned the radio on. A song from his senior year in high school came over the airwaves, the words about falling in love. He threw back his head and laughed. He felt just like he had the summer after graduation. Totally free. Old enough to drive, old enough to make major decisions, old enough to fall in love, and waiting for it to come along and turn his world upside down.

Except it hadn't happened. Until now. Until Annie.

They'd lost six years while he'd tried to chase down the place where he belonged. He didn't want to lose another day. He turned the sound up and began to sing along as the soft, warm summer breeze slipped in through the window and wrapped him in hope.

He pictured Annie's face when he arrived. Pictured her shock, her smile, her laugh, her throwing herself into his arms just like she had when he'd arrived last week. Only this time the kisses would be real.

He set the cruise control for seventy-five and kicked back. An hour passed and another, the miles flying beneath the wheels of his car. The time passed so quickly, he didn't realize he was almost there until he spotted an official green and white road sign that said Bedford, five miles.

Anticipation made his stomach jump, and he sped up. Minutes later, he passed the gas station at the edge of town and waved to the owner as she cleaned the windshield on a customer's car. He tried to stop smiling.

It took a moment for his brain to register the police car parked on the side street. Even though he had slowed down when he entered the city limits, he was still going least twenty miles over the limit. In the rearview mirror he watched the squad car pull out behind him, red lights flashing.

"Shit. Shit. Shit." Nick hit the brakes and pulled over. This was good for at least a fifteen-minute delay. And he was already late. He bent to dig his wallet out of the laptop case on the seat beside him.

"You know how fast you were going?" a man asked from the driver's side window.

He turned. "Chief! What are you doing writing tickets?"

"Nick? Aw, some of the guys wanted to go to the museum opening so I said I'd take a shift. I thought you left town—military needed you back."

Nick shook his head. "Not anymore. I'm staying home." *Home.* It felt good to be here. "I wanted to surprise Annie but I'm running a little late."

The chief pushed his sleeve off his wrist and looked at his watch. "More than a little. You better hurry up—it started twenty minutes ago." He grinned. "Hey, I got an idea."

———

Annie watched the museum director cut the blue ribbon stretched across the stairs at the front of the building. A flush of fear ran through her. While everyone else was clapping and cheering, her heart pounded with anxiety. Her introductory speech was past; now she just had to contend with the truth.

She forced her feet to take the steps to the platform and walk to the podium. The air seemed to buzz around her; her head grew light. *No fainting allowed.* Not now. Later would be okay, but not now. She grasped the microphone with one hand to stop from trembling and cleared her throat.

"There are refreshments inside." Her voice sounded unnaturally loud and high. "Please come in, tour the new facility, and join us as we celebrate our grand opening."

The crowd whistled and clapped and began to move together toward the museum doors.

Damn, what a stupid choice of words. She should have told the truth before inviting everyone in. At this rate, no one would be left to hear her confession.

"Wait!" Her sudden pronouncement blasted from the PA system like a shout.

All eyes swung to the podium.

"Before you go ..." She swallowed hard. "There's one more announcement I need to make today. Actually, it's a confession."

Everyone quieted in anticipation, and she struggled to

ignore the churning of her stomach, to ignore the certain knowledge that by the time she finished this announcement, everyone would know she had spent the last two years lying to them. Her reputation would be in tatters. She would probably have to sell the inn and move out of town.

Tears threatened at the back of her eyes. She reminded herself sternly that she had no one to blame for this mess but herself. She alone had told the lies that got her here today. And she owed it to all these people to tell the truth.

"I, ah ... don't know quite where to begin. Nick and I—we—he didn't go back to the military. He actually isn't in the military at all. Never has been in the military. He's a writer. An outdoors writer. He travels around the world, goes on adventures and writes about them."

Confused faces looked back at her from the crowd.

"We don't much care what he does, Annie," someone shouted.

She smiled sadly and looked down at her hands a moment. This was harder than she'd thought it would be. "The thing is, Nick and I—we're not married—well, we are married, but ..."

Why hadn't she written down what she was going to say before she got up here? Now, not only would she be remembered as a liar, but also as a blabbering idiot.

The crowd shifted restlessly, anxious to get into the party and she knew if she didn't get this out fast, she would lose her opportunity.

"The truth is, until Nick showed up a week ago, I hadn't seen him since we got married six years ago. We didn't love each other then, and I thought we were divorced years ago. Somehow the paperwork fell through the cracks. It didn't go through, so we were still married—"

"Spit it out, Annie," someone called in a friendly voice. "What are you trying to say?"

The bottom line. Tell them the bottom line. She inhaled.

"I've been lying since the day I came to Bedford. I lied about being married so I could buy the B & B. I lied about meeting my husband on trips. The baby is—artificially inseminated. It's all a lie. I didn't mean for it to go on, but I didn't stop it. Then Nick showed up last week to tell me our divorce never went through."

She drew a deep breath in preparation for the next statement. "And I convinced him to stay a week and pretend to be my husband so you wouldn't learn the truth, so you wouldn't know I've been lying to you. He's gone now —back to his real life. I'm sorry. You don't know how sorry I am."

A police car headed down the street toward them, siren blaring. A murmur ran through the crowd as they turned in unison to watch the car pull to a stop in front of the museum. Annie sighed. Leave it to Vivian to add some last-minute hoopla to the grand-opening that she failed to mention.

The front passenger door opened and a man stepped out. Annie's eyes widened. Her stomach flopped. If she didn't know any better, she'd think it was—*Nick?*

The crowd exploded in a roar of applause and cheers, of people calling Nick's name and welcoming him back. Like a wave rolling off the shore, they stepped back to create a pathway. Nick shook hands and exchanged greetings as he moved through the crowd toward her. Annie closed her gaping mouth and stared.

What the hell was going on?

He took the steps to the podium two at a time and grinned at her.

"What are you doing here?" she asked. Her eyes darted toward the crowd that had obviously pressed forward so they wouldn't miss a word of the exchange.

"I forgot some stuff."

She hadn't noticed anything left behind. "Like what?"

"My toothbrush."

The crowd tittered again and moved closer.

"What?"

He nodded. "And my favorite socks—they're probably under the bed."

Had he lost his mind?

"My dog—I also forgot my dog."

"He's *my* dog."

Nick shook his head. "I distinctly recall you telling me he was *my* dog." He scanned the faces of the crowd until he spotted Luella. "Luella, didn't Annie always say Chester was my dog?"

The old woman nodded vigorously.

"You're not taking Chester to hike through Mongolia! Luella, didn't you hear anything I said three minutes ago?"

Luella beamed.

Oh, good. Everyone had gone nuts. Maybe she'd been committed to an asylum for the insane and didn't remember —because she was crazy herself.

"I forgot something else, too," Nick said softly. He took a step toward her. "I forgot that it took me a long time to forget you after you left six years ago. I forgot what it did to me to see you again after all these years." He paused. "I forgot how much I love you."

She gasped and tears sprang to her eyes. A lump formed in her throat so large she couldn't speak, couldn't swallow, couldn't breathe.

"I canceled out of the project," he said.

"You're not going?" she choked out.

He smiled and shook his head.

"But it's your dream—"

"My dream is bigger than that. I have a canoeing-adventure business to start ... tubing, rafting, hiking ... cross-country skiing in the winter ... That is, if you'll have me."

If she would have him? She shoved the back of her hand across her eyes. Did everything between them always have to have a complication? Now she had to tell him his dream wouldn't happen in Bedford. Would he still want her then? She glanced down.

"I won't be staying here. They know. I've told them the truth about us ... about my lies."

A murmur ran through the crowd.

"Then we'll go somewhere else," Nick said. "I don't care where I live—as long as it's with you."

She raised her eyes to his.

"Marry me, Annie. Or rather, stay married to me."

She pressed her lips together and fought back the tears stinging her eyes. "You've lost your mind, haven't you?"

He thought about it a moment. He'd spent years searching for the unusual, experiences to give him an adrenaline rush, to give his life a sense of meaning and excitement. And yet, the more of that he'd done, the less he felt like he was finding what he was searching for.

Until now. Here in this little town with this woman and her oddball friends and acquaintances, he felt more alive than he'd ever felt before. If this was losing his mind, then he would embrace it the rest of his life.

"Maybe I have," he said. "But they say there's only a very fine line separating insanity and genius."

"Come on, Annie. Say yes!" someone shouted.

Startled, she glanced at the crowd.

"The microphone's on." Nick searched for the *off button* but couldn't find it. "Looks like everyone's in on this conversation."

"I'm having a baby, Nick. *A baby that's not yours."*

He looked at her belly, ever so slightly rounded. "Yeah I know. Luckily our child will have two parents who love it very much. Now, what do you say?"

"Yes! She says yes!" Father Thespesius worked his way forward through the crowd.

"We forgive you, Annie," someone shouted. A myriad of other voices echoed the words.

Father Thespesius stepped up to the podium. "I think what these folks are saying is, we don't want you to leave."

His final words were almost drowned out by a chorus of cheers and whistles and shouted agreements. In the midst of the commotion, Annie heard a familiar voice shouting her name.

"Hey, Annie! Annie! Annie!"

She scanned the crowd, spotting Minnow with her arms raised above her head in victory. "It's a wonderful lie!" Minnow shouted.

Annie's eyes widened, letting loose the tears she'd been fighting to hold back.

"So will you ..." Nick began.

"Yes," she whispered. "Yes, yes, yes!"

She threw herself into his open arms and a roar went up.

"Everybody inside for the party!" Father Thespesius announced into the microphone. "We've got an opening and a marriage to celebrate!"

As everyone streamed into the museum, Nick slung an arm around Annie's shoulders and walked with her toward the entrance.

She cast a sly smile his way. "What do you say we cut out of here and go canoeing?"

He raised an eyebrow in surprise. "I didn't realize you enjoyed it that much."

"Oh, but I did." She grinned.

"Annie McCarthy, I do believe you're a fellow thrill-seeker." He bent to kiss her lightly on the lips. "If you thought canoeing was fun, wait till I take you whitewater rafting."

"I thought you'd never ask."

He laughed out loud and gathered her into his arms, knowing that from this day forward he would be embarking on the greatest adventure of his life.

———

If you enjoyed this book ... I would be forever grateful if you would post a review on the site where you bought it.

———

Please enjoy the following excerpt from **OVER EASY**, the first book in *The Continental Breakfast Club* series.

Excerpt from
OVER EASY
The Continental Breakfast Club, book one

Chapter One

Something really needed to change.

Unfortunately, as it was turning out, that something was my life.

I came to this unsettling conclusion one night when Megan, Bree, and I were lifting weights at Better Fit, the fitness club in Minneapolis where we had signed up for free, one-month trial memberships. Not because we wanted muscles (although they were a nice bonus), but because we wanted to meet men.

In theory, it was a great idea—there were lots of guys in the gym. But in reality, after twelve consecutive days of pumping iron after work, our plan had yet to deliver. Lots of muscles, yes. Interested men, not so much. All of the guys seemed to care way more about how many pounds they could power lift with their bulging, tattooed biceps —*guns*, they called them—than the three, *attractive* women in form-flattering spandex doing curls two feet away.

"Allie, this is not working," Bree puffed out from the bench press that night, arms trembling as she pushed the barbell up.

"Maybe you should use smaller weights." I reached for the bar to give her a hand.

"Not the exercise. The men."

She was lifting so much weight—for her anyway—I was

surprised she had enough oxygen left in her brain to think about anything other than preventing herself from getting crushed beneath that barbell. Then again, Bree had been fixated on finding a guy ever since her boyfriend dumped her, so maybe the thought was simply a reflex action. Like blinking when you go out into the sun. Or jerking your leg when the doctor taps your knee with a rubber hammer.

Bree lowered the bar to its holder, then sat up and eyed a sweaty, overbuilt guy grunting as he leg-pressed what appeared to be three thousand pounds. *Grunting*. Believe me when I say this, guys, grunting is not a turn-on. If you can't move the weight without making noise, cut the poundage. We really, really don't enjoy picturing you creating a hernia. Or worse.

Bree shoved her short brown hair behind her ears, grabbed her towel, and strode across the fitness center toward the juice bar, all the while muttering under her breath. Megan and I exchanged a look and dropped into step behind her, happily leaving the weight machines, cross-trainers, exercise bikes, treadmills—and their panting inhabitants—behind.

Clearly it was time to regroup. And not a moment too soon, as far as I was concerned. I was running out of time. I needed to find a guy impressive enough to bring to my parents' forty-fifth wedding anniversary celebration next month. Not because it was a milestone anniversary, but because my whole family would be in attendance, and having a "keeper" on my arm would be the perfect way to show all of them that, yes, I had reached adulthood.

This whole idea came to me a few months ago, after my parents didn't tell me that my grandmother was in the hospital—dying—until she had been discharged, alive and well. I only found out when my mom called and said, "Allie, honey, good news. Grandma made it."

"Made it where?" I asked.

"She didn't die."

"Was that a possibility?"

"Oh, honey, we didn't want to worry you, but she's been in the hospital since last week—her lung again. The doctor didn't think she'd make it. Father Joe even gave her the last rites."

For God's sake, I'm nearly twenty-eight. I'm enlightened and liberated (yeah, I understand that looking for a boyfriend kind of contradicts that), support myself (sure, Grandpa shoves a twenty-dollar bill in my hand every time he sees me but that's not my fault), live on my own (okay, with a roommate), pay my bills (mostly on time), am informed about world affairs (more Twitter than CNN.com, but I'm working on it), and even run my own business (although I really need to get more customers—and I'm working on that, too).

And, yet, my parents and siblings still treat me like *the baby*.

I never get told the bad news until it's past. My dad can't stop himself from reminding me to floss. And it goes without saying that I sit at the kids' table for Thanksgiving dinner.

It doesn't help that I come from a long line of overachievers. My oldest brother is a surgeon, my sister and other brother are lawyers, just like my parents—for once, could they try to be original?—and me, baby of the family, was supposed to be a veterinarian because I love animals. Except after graduating from college, I couldn't bear the thought of studying another day, let alone four more years.

So I moved into a lower flat with Bree and started a pet grooming business, *Flawless Paws*.

Now I groom dogs. Big ones, little ones, hairy ones, bald ones, smelly ones … My parents are mortified. "Allie Parker, *doggg groooomer*," is the way my mother says it, her voice sinking progressively lower with each syllable. Not that she has anything personally against dog groomers; it's a fine profession—for someone other than her daughter, that is.

Anyway, I was complaining about this to Megan and Bree when we were watching The Bachelorette and critiquing the prospective fiancés. "My family treats me like the baby," I groused during a commercial.

"But you are the baby," Megan said in her best *this-defendant-is-guilty* voice, because, yes, she's an attorney. And though she isn't nearly as know-it-all as my own family members who are lawyers, she does tend to think she knows best, which would be a bit irritating if she wasn't usually right.

"Hard to get around that when your nearest sibling is fourteen years older," Bree said.

"And married," Megan added.

That's when it hit me. The solution was so obvious, I couldn't believe I hadn't thought of it before. If there was anything that would make my family begin to respect me as an adult, it was stepping into that oh-so-grown-up institution, marriage. I shoved a fistful of popcorn in my mouth as I mentally searched for flaws in my thinking—and found none.

"What I need is a husband," I said.

"Hear, hear," Bree chimed in. "But I'll settle for a man."

This, of course, led to a discussion about where to find single men, which in turn led us to Better Fit and free, one-month memberships. It had seemed like such a perfect solution. The fitness center was full of men—and that was just what I needed.

So there we were, striding across the workout room like a team of race walkers in the national championship, about to embark on my favorite part of belonging to a fitness club —the juice bar. After we settled into tall chairs at the bar, Megan and Bree both ordered something new, a cucumber cooler, while I went for my usual chocolate milk, the perfect recovery drink.

The guy behind the counter was wearing a T-shirt made out of one of those moisture-wicking tech materials, the fitness center's slogan emblazoned across the front: *Better Fit makes everything Fit Better.* I couldn't argue with that; his biceps were bulging out of the arm openings and the shirt was so tight I could see the outlines of his sculpted six-pack abs.

"Time for Plan B." Bree picked up her glass. "Nearly two weeks and not one nibble among the three of us. Clearly, we aren't going to find men here. *And I need a man.*" Bree may be a self-assured, beloved high school math teacher, but she sure doesn't do *single* well.

I had to agree. "If I'm going to have a potential life partner to impress the family at the anniversary party I can't afford too many more days buffing up."

Megan shook her head, her curly dark hair bouncing. "Maybe we should give it a rest. Husbands are so ... ugh."

She had married at twenty-one, divorced at twenty-two, and wanted nothing more to do with the institution. But then, she was an attorney not a dog groomer, so try as she might there was no way she could totally relate to my concerns about being treated like a baby. Not that there's anything wrong with dog grooming. I'm just saying.

"You know how your arms feel stressed and shaky when you've lifted a really heavy weight too many times?" Megan said. "That's what marriage is like."

"Too young," Bree said.

"Wrong guy," I added.

"Are you with us or against us?" Bree gave Megan a pointed look, then took a big swallow of cucumber cooler and grimaced as it went down.

I'm never sure what's in the different drinks the juice bar sells—generally carrots and lemon and radishes and stuff—which explains why I stick to chocolate milk after exercising. Bree eyed my glass. I tightened my grip on it and gave her the stink eye. She'd made her choice; she needed to stick with it.

Megan heaved a sigh. "Online dating?" she said without conviction.

"Church groups?" I offered.

Bree snorted. "Who do either of you know that online dating or church groups has worked for?"

I opened my mouth.

"And don't tell me about Joey Neander because he really, really is the only person *ever* who met someone at a church social."

And Joey, as my Irish grandmother used to say, had a wee bit o' problem with the drink. So a teetotaling Baptist girlfriend was exactly what he deserved. "How about a young professionals group?" I asked.

"Gag," Megan said.

"Coffee shop?" Bree proposed.

"Oh, please." Megan took a big swallow of juice. Based on her expression, I didn't think she liked the cucumber cooler any better than Bree did.

"If you aren't part of the solution, you're part of the problem," Bree said.

"How could I possibly be part of the problem?" Megan asked. "It's not my fault there aren't any single guys left."

"Okay, Ms. Negative Force Be with You." Bree held up her index finger. "I challenge you to come up with an idea, just one, for how we can meet single men ages twenty-six to thirty-five."

"That's the only criteria? Twenty-six to thirty-five?"

"Intelligent," I interjected. "Not necessarily rocket scientists, but smart enough."

"Fun, but not party animals. And reasonably attractive," Bree added.

"With decent jobs. After all, these are our future husbands, we don't want bottom dwellers."

Megan ticked off the list on her fingers and asked, "Anything else?" as though once we had nailed down the requirements she'd be able to deliver the goods.

I rubbed the bridge of my nose, thinking. What sort of man would make my parents—*I mean, me*—happy? "I've narrowed it down," I said. "What I want is an S man. Single, straight, sober, solvent, stable, successful."

"And slung," Bree added.

"That's hung," I said.

"Whatever. He just better bring it."

Megan almost choked on her juice, then nodded thoughtfully.

Bree and I exchanged a grin. This was great. Once Megan put her mind to something, the rest of the world better get the hell out of her way. I took a chug of my chocolate milk and waited, confident that a solution was only moments away. But as the moments stretched into minutes, I began to despair. Could it be that even one of the world's preeminent problem-solvers was stumped by this one?

Then Megan gave a Mona Lisa smile, small but so full of promise you knew she had an awesome idea, one so good it might just make you burst. She pressed her hands onto the counter and leaned forward. "When I was in college and broke—"

She stopped so abruptly, I knew she was having second thoughts about sharing what she'd been about to say.

"Yes?" I urged her.

"I'm not proud of this."

"We've all done things in our youth that we regret." Bree waved an impatient hand. "Come on, spill it."

Megan blew out a breath between clenched teeth. "Okay. I used to put on nice clothes and sneak into continental breakfast at hotels."

"You mean like, donuts?" I asked.

"Donuts, bagels, cream cheese, waffles—"

"We're trying to get married," Bree said. "Not fat."

Megan ignored her. "At almost every table would be some guy, alone, dressed to kill, fueling up for a morning business meeting."

The meaning of her words hit me with such force I jerked upright on my stool. "And?" I asked, almost faint with the possibilities. Adrenalin surged through me and I felt renewed. How many hotels were there? How many continental breakfasts? How many men, glorious men, were at breakfast waiting to meet the women of their dreams over blueberry waffles and raisin bran?

"And, unlike the guys hanging out in hotel bars, the men at continental breakfast wear their wedding rings." Megan grinned at us, then finished off her juice and triumphantly plopped her empty glass on the table. "Instant, irrefutable identification of marital status."

Her words delivered the luscious fulfillment of a morning bun on an empty stomach.

"Omigod," Bree said on an exhale. "You are so worth every penny of that six-figure income they pay you."

"Did you ever get caught?" I asked.

Megan shook her head. "Look like you belong, act like you belong—"

"And you belong," Bree said breathlessly. "But how—"

"Side door. Just fumble in your purse like you can't find your key. And when someone leaves—"

"You're in." I couldn't believe the brilliance. "At the very least, we'll get a free breakfast."

"And at the very best, we'll meet eligible men," Bree said happily.

Megan tapped her fingers on the countertop. "As your attorney I feel compelled to warn you—be careful what you wish for, you might just get it."

"One can only hope." Bree laughed and gave her head a shake.

"Amen," I added. "Here's to finding the men of our dreams."

OVER EASY excerpt
Copyright © 2016 by Pamela Ford

ABOUT THE AUTHOR

PAMELA FORD is the award-winning author of contemporary and historical romance. She grew up watching old movies, blissfully sighing over the romance; and reading sci-fi and adventure novels, vicariously living the action. The combination probably explains why the books she writes are romantic, happily-ever-afters with plenty of plot—and often, lots of laughter.

After graduating from college with a degree in Advertising, Pam spent many years as a copywriter and freelance writer before inserting a plot twist in her career path and writing her first book.

Pam has won numerous awards including the Booksellers Best, the Laurel Wreath, and a gold medal IPPY in the Independent Book Publisher Awards. She is a National Readers' Choice Awards finalist, a Maggie Awards finalist, a Kindle Book Awards finalist, and a two-time Golden Heart Finalist.

More than a half million copies of her books have been sold worldwide.

Sign up for Pam's mailing list at: www.pamelaford.net
Contact: pamelafordbooks@gmail.com
Facebook.com/pamelafordbooks
Instagram.com/pamelafordbooks

9 781944 792114